# THE
# CURSED
# SEA

Also available by
LAUREN DESTEFANO

THE GLASS SPARE

# LAUREN DeSTEFANO

# THE
# CURSED
# SEA

BALZER + BRAY
*An Imprint of* HarperCollins*Publishers*

ISBN 978-0-06-249135-0

18 19 20 21 22  PC/LSCH  10 9 8 7 6 5 4 3 2 1

First Edition

# THE
# CURSED
# SEA

# ONE

THE DEAD PRINCESS OF ARROD returned to her kingdom at sunset.

The kingdom itself was none the wiser. Wil arrived un-ceremoniously, amid weary travelers and crates of fabric bolts and sewing notions.

Moments after disembarking and regaining her bearings, she could already see that the kingdom was different. Darker somehow. The winter clouds were gray as smoke, and the people moved about the capital in collective silence. Even the small children did not cry or laugh as they were harried this way and that by adults taking hasty strides.

The snow had yet to arrive here, but the late October air carried its ominous chill; winter came early in the North, and stayed late. Wil dug her gloved hands into the pockets of her coat and made her way through the Port Capital, mindful to avoid brushing against the shoulders of passersby. She did not want to add another face to her list of kills.

Even the smell was different. Moldy and musty, like old coats in an attic where nothing had stirred for years.

Around her, there were carriages offering rides to neighboring towns, but Wil left the cobbles behind and made her way into the woods. If she wanted to reach the castle without arousing suspicion, there was no way but to walk.

After a week at sea, now that she was on land the anxiety began to seize her. The king might make good on his promise to kill her if he saw her again. After the attack he'd waged on the Southern Isles, it was clear his ruthlessness had exceeded her expectations. But her mother was the one whom Wil was most afraid to face. She would have to tell her the truth of what had happened that night by the rapids. Would have to reveal the monstrous thing she had become.

And Gerdie—the thought that she would see him in just a few minutes hardly seemed real. What state was he in? What had their father done to him? She'd had nothing but time to think about it on her journey, but when she tried to conjure up an image of her brother, all she got was a shadow.

The winter sky was dark and starless by the time she arrived at the castle. Here, her breath came in shallow bursts and she stopped, working to compose herself. The last time she'd seen her home had been in September. A cool night that smelled of leaves and dirt, all the trees beginning to shed their fiery leaves. She hadn't looked back at the castle as she left it, because there had been no reason to think she wouldn't return.

Now weeks had passed, and snow coated all the fallen leaves. It seemed a lifetime ago since she'd set foot in her home. Since her father, clutching Owen's gleaming corpse, had promised to kill her if she ever returned.

She could see the guards standing outside the gate. There were thrice as many as before, all of them bearing electric lanterns that spread as far as the line of trees, where she at last paused to collect herself.

After the attack her father had commanded upon the South, of course there would be more security. But it wasn't the guards Wil found menacing, or their blades gleaming brightly at their hips. It was the castle she could just see over the top of the towering stone wall.

She forced herself to take a step, and then another, until the light of the lanterns revealed her and the guards raised their weapons in anticipation. Ferocity fast turned to amusement when they saw what they were dealing with. At her size and with her weapons hidden, she hardly seemed like any sort of threat, and just her luck, all these guards were strangers who wouldn't recognize their dead princess even if they could believe she'd come back.

"Wherever you're headed, girl, you've taken a wrong turn." One of the guards advanced on her, weapon still drawn. "This here is the Castle of the Royal House of Heidle."

Wil stiffened her posture. "I need to speak with the queen."

"The queen does not receive visitors," another guard said.

"She'll see me," Wil said. "I'm her daughter."

"The queen doesn't have any daughters," the guard said, and the words lanced through her. She was prepared to be a dead girl, but to not exist at all?

Wil's eyes were drawn to the light shining through Owen's bedroom window. It was such a familiar sight, and it flooded her with warmth and the notion that she was home. The feeling was darkened by the reminder that Owen could not be there, spending all hours of the night reading as he often had, his brow furrowed, his intelligent eyes burdened. He was gone.

"Listen," Wil said. "I—"

"Who's out there?" Baren's voice came from the darkness behind the gate. "Guards! Who are you talking to?"

Her brother approached the metal bars, and it was an effort for Wil not to gasp at what she saw. Baren, second in line for the throne after Owen, had never possessed softness in his features. He had their mother's blue eyes, but none of their kindness. Still, when Wil had seen him last, he had at least looked like the young man he was. Now, despite his royal dress, he looked no better off than the starving denizens in the slums of the Port Capital.

His eyes were sunken and dark. His straight blond hair had grown scraggly and taken over the frame of his face. His cheeks were gaunt. His back was hunched as though he were carrying something heavy around his shoulders.

He stared straight at Wil, and then through her.

"This girl is claiming to be the princess, Your Majesty," the guard said. "Impersonating the royal family is a high crime. What would you have us do with her?"

Wil's breath hitched. *Your Majesty?*

Baren raised the latch and staggered through the gate. He stared at Wil, and she narrowed her eyes as she returned his scrutiny.

"This girl right here?" Baren said, sweeping his arm in gesture. "You mean to tell me that you see her? My little sister's ghost—you see her too?"

"She appears to be living, Your Majesty."

*Your Majesty.*

She hadn't misheard, then. Confusion and worry struggled for dominance, but she pushed all of it away. She had to get past Baren and speak to the queen before she would believe anything.

Baren laughed. "She comes here most nights. Sits atop the spires, or hides under my bed and whispers while I'm sleeping so I'll have nightmares. She's a ghost."

"Baren," Wil said, and at the sound of her voice he went still and silent. "I need to speak to Mother. Where is she?"

"You—" He unsheathed his sword and brought its point to her chin. "I told you not to come back here, and you tell Owen and Papa to stay away, too. I'm king now. Return to your grave."

"I am not a ghost," Wil said firmly, not allowing herself to hear the rest of his words. "And if I were, what good do you think your sword would be?"

He sank the blade into her flesh and drew it back slowly, coaxing a thin, bleeding line under her chin. She shuddered with pain but didn't move.

The young king held the blade before his face for inspection, and his eyes grew wide with hysteria as blood dripped from its edge. His breaths came loud and fast. "No," he said. "You're not my sister. My sister is dead. She drowned."

"That isn't true. Baren, listen to me—"

"You're a trick!" He brandished his sword anew, angling it at her chest. "You're a lookalike sent by my enemies to destroy me."

In a fluid motion she unsheathed the dagger at her thigh. The sleep serum would be more merciful than the guns at either hip; she didn't trust herself to shoot at him and not hit anything vital. She had already killed one brother.

He lunged at her, and she dodged the blow for her heart, holding out her dagger and letting his own momentum work to her advantage as the arched blade tore through his skin.

He staggered back, startled. The guards came forward with a clatter of guns, but Baren held up his hand to stay them. He regarded Wil, eyes wide. "You're the price I have to pay," he said, coming to a realization of some sort. "You were brought back to punish me."

His voice had grown faint, and he fell to his knees.

"Poison!" one of the guards cried out, and again they closed in on her. She would not be able to take on all of them, Wil knew, but if one of them so much as touched her, he would be dead, and she did not want to think what new horror that would evoke.

"Mother!" she screamed. The barrel of a gun was pressed into her chin, shoving her face upward. "Mother!"

Wil found Baren's eyes. Eyes that had never shown her a drop of kindness even when they had been children. He was on his knees, struggling to stay awake, glaring at her.

Then, from the dark mouth of the castle doors, she saw a white gown billowing on the cold breeze. Wil could just make out the long blond hair. "Mother!"

At the sound of Wil's voice, the figure began running for them.

"Stand down," the queen cried, gasping. "Stand down— she's—that's—"

"You are not in charge of my men," Baren said. He looked like a scared little boy. The queen saw this and held his shoulder to keep him from stumbling to his feet. Somewhere beyond the frenzy, Wil marveled that he was still conscious. Perhaps Zay had diluted the serum to compensate for what she'd used to put Loom to sleep.

"I'm the king," he said.

"Yes," the queen said. She was clutching the button of her capelet, twisting it one way and the next in compulsive sets. Three twists left, three twists right, five taps to its face with her index finger. "But you have not slept for days. You don't want to do something you'll regret." She smoothed back his hair, and his resolve crumbled.

The queen turned to Wil, who was forced now to understand the truth. Her father was no longer the king. He was gone.

There was no time yet for Wil to process her shock and all the things this would mean.

"Stand down," Baren mumbled, as though he were talking to himself, and the guards skeptically lowered the weapons pointed at Wil.

Now it was the queen's turn to look as though she had seen a ghost. But she did not ask Wil if she was dead. She did not ask who had sent her, or who she really was. For after all those years of wanting, she could never fail to recognize the child she'd nearly died to bring into the world. She would know her daughter anywhere.

"Wilhelmina."

Wil felt herself trembling. She would not cry. She would not.

"It's me," she said.

# TWO

THE CASTLE WAS HOME, AND at the same time it wasn't.

Winter's chill had snaked its way in through the stone walls. A fire was succumbing to a slow death in the hearth of the foyer. Ordinarily there would be servants in the winter to stoke it through the night.

But the feeble glow of the lone fire left the castle dim and bleak.

And it was quiet. The queen said nothing as she pulled the doors closed behind them, leaving Baren and his guards at the gates.

Wil barely felt the sting of the alcohol used to clean her wound. Her mind was numb.

It was late and the castle was sleeping, quiet but for the scuff of Baren's slippers against the stone as he paced outside the washroom. Wil could hear every step through the closed door.

Wil sat on the edge of the tub, her tunic unbuttoned and bloody, while her mother knelt before her, saying nothing.

"Mother, where is Gerdie?" If he were whole, if he were here, he would have come to her by now. He would have heard her screaming.

"In the basement, I imagine." The queen's tone was placid. "You know what an insomniac he is." She said this so simply, as though things were the same as they'd always been.

Wil searched her mother's eyes for any indication that this was a lie meant to calm her. All she saw was a woman eclipsed by the same dark pall that had been cast over this entire king-dom.

But Wil knew that her mother must be right. If Gerdie had been anywhere but his basement laboratory, he would have heard her scream. That place harbored a solitude of his own design. His work entranced him so much that he often didn't know she had descended the stairs until she was standing beside him.

Maybe this small thing hadn't changed. One piece of her world was still intact.

The queen dabbed a cloth under Wil's chin, and Wil flinched. "You can't touch me," she said, remembering herself.

"Wilhelmina." The queen's voice was gentle. "Look at me, my love." Wil did as she was told. All the Heidle children did as their mother commanded. It was their father they defied.

"Are you ready now to tell me what happened?"

"Yes," Wil answered, hoping she would come to believe it if she kept speaking. "And if you never want to see me again once you know, I'll understand. But all I ask is that you help me— someone will die if I don't have your help."

The queen rose to her feet. Her skin had lost its tan, and it was clear that the sunlight had not touched her in a long time. But she held a strong posture, and Wil could see that time had not weakened her. That losing two children and a husband she loved had steeled her in a way that made her nomadic soul burn bright.

"We can't talk here," she said very quietly. Wil understood. Baren was lurking the halls outside. "Go to your chamber," the queen said. "I'll meet you there."

The queen opened the door, and Baren flinched. "Mother, we can't trust this imposter," he said. "This ghost."

"Shh." She wrapped an arm around his shoulders and led him down the hall. "We'll find Nanny and have her mix something for you so you'll sleep."

Nanny. Another thing that had changed in Wil's absence. When she and her brothers were small, they'd had a nanny, with big, kind eyes and a head filled with stories. Volumes and volumes of them, from every kingdom, in every language. But she'd retired years ago, when Wil and Gerdie, the last in the line, stopped needing someone to look after them. Last Wil heard, the king had put her up in a cottage in Southern Arrod.

As their voices moved farther away, Wil crept into the hall-way, hoping not to encounter any servants. She could not bear to have any more pairs of eyes looking at her the way Baren's had. But the servants seemed to have been replaced by guards. The outside of the castle was under constant vigil, but the inside was empty, eerily quiet.

She entered her chamber and stood just inside the doorway, afraid to turn on the light.

Had the room always smelled this way? Of crisp, clean linen and cool air seeping through cracks in the ancient window. Of never-used perfumes whose scents faintly escaped their bottles along the shelves; her father had often returned from his travels with those bottles—the harsh, flowery scents didn't suit her, but they were proof that he had thought of her, however briefly, and so she had displayed them where the sunlight would find them and fill her room with colors.

It was night now, and the bottles were dark and lifeless. The castle was dark. The kingdom was dark.

Wil sat on the edge of her bed.

Then the room was flooded with light, and the queen came in and closed the door behind her.

The queen leaned against the door, her hands pinning the knob behind her. She was looking at the ceiling when she spoke. "Owen?"

Wil had learned to shutter out the pain before even the

notion of it could reach her. It was as though her brother had granted her permission not to wallow on his account. "He's dead."

"I knew it wasn't the rapids," the queen said. "All along—the way your father carried about. So many times, he stared at closed doors and I thought he was waiting for someone to return."

Wil grasped the lace of her comforter, her palms sweating despite the castle's relentless chill. "Don't blame Papa," she said. "It was me. All me."

Her mother did not move to sit beside her, as she had so many nights before Wil went to sleep. It occurred to Wil now that her mother had cleaned her wounds but not moved to embrace her. Called her "my love" but hadn't kissed her cheeks.

"Before that night," Wil went on, "something began happening to me. Something I hid because I thought I could make it go away. Owen and Gerdie knew, and they tried to help me. But I shouldn't have hidden it. Maybe then he would be alive, but I—"

Wil could not summon the words. She unbuttoned her tunic, until she had uncovered the stark white mark between her breasts.

For a moment Wil saw what Zay had described. The queen's face was fierce and commanding, and Wil saw herself in it.

The queen looked at her daughter's mark, which she had seen countless times before.

"This is the mark of a curse," Wil said.

The queen drew a loud breath. "I know."

"You know?" Wil rasped. "Why did you tell me it was a birthmark?"

"You seemed fit to outlive us all." The queen sat beside Wil on the bed, still maintaining her distance, making Wil feel like a damaged bird that had been pushed from its nest. This distance seemed to have nothing to do with her curse, Wil felt. "I began to think that whatever the curse was, you had defied it, as you had defied death."

"Why?" Wil said. "Why was I cursed?"

The queen shook her head. "I don't know. But in the weeks before we lost you and Owen, I knew something had changed."

Wil looked straight ahead, at her painted white desk. There was an ornithology book, still open, at its center beside an askew chair, waiting for her to sit in the amber glow of the blown-glass lamp and return to reading about spawnlings.

This tiny piece of the world that had once belonged to her now felt more like a memorial to a dead girl.

Without a word she stood and walked to the window. It stuck, as it always did, and she forced it open with the heel of her hand. The queen turned to watch as Wil reached along the castle's outer wall. It didn't take her long to find a tendril of ivy. Heart beating fast from the anticipation, she plucked a leaf and presented it to her mother.

The change was slower this time; there was a dull throb of

pain, like her curse had to wrestle its way out of her. But in one final bloom, the ivy hardened to emerald.

Sweat beaded Wil's brow from the strain, and this concerned her. Her curse had never been a conscious effort before.

The queen stared at it. She could see the lines of her daughter's palm through the stone. She was watching still as Wil's hand shook and the shiver shot up her arm and spread throughout. She saw the fierce change in her daughter's eyes, the way they brightened and glazed at the same time.

"It was an accident." It was as though someone else were speaking the words. "I didn't want Owen to come after me. He was always trying to protect me when he should have just let me go."

The queen understood now what the king must have done to hide this truth from her. She did not ask, now, for the details of her son's final moments. Later, she would have to. She would have to know what had happened to her son, so that his death could be a part of her the way that his life was a part of her.

But for now, she fixed her attention on her living child. Her daughter. She put her arms around her.

Wil shook with a sob. Her face was hot with tears. She was alive—despite everything, alive. Death had never been a match for this one. The emerald fell to the floor and Wil tried to back away. "You can't touch me. I'll kill you, too."

The queen tightened her grasp. "No one tells me I can't hold my daughter," she said.

"You can't." Wil's voice was pleading.

But the queen didn't let go, and it frightened Wil that her mother loved her so much that she would risk death just to hold her. It reminded her of Owen that night by the rapids. He'd stared at her with defiance, so sure of his decision.

Wil twisted from her mother's grasp. Her mother loved her too much to let go, and Wil loved her mother too much to stay in her arms.

"Please," she whispered. "I couldn't stand it if I hurt you."

The queen's sad expression said that Wil had already hurt her by disappearing, to be taken for dead.

"I'm sorry." Wil wanted to say more, but tears threatened and she knew that she wouldn't be able to hold them in if she tried to list all the things she was sorry for.

There was a strange heaviness in her blood, as though her curse was trying to surge forward. And then it receded. Later, she would experiment with the ivy. Perhaps it was just exhaustion from the travel and the confrontation with Baren.

The queen was twirling the ribbon of her nightgown. Three twists. Untwist. Three twists.

Wil told her mother about Loom, though she left out the part about his being a prince, but included his passion for helping the South nonetheless. She told of everything that had happened until it all came back to Loom, whose every heartbeat was now fated to her hands.

By the end of her tale, Wil had changed into a nightgown

the queen drew from her closet. Though she hadn't been gone for very long, it no longer fit her as it once had. The sleeves were too short. The hem no longer covered her knees. She had spent so much time in billowing satin trousers, loose in the Lavean fashion, it hadn't occurred to her that she'd gotten any taller.

Her bed still felt the same, though, as she sank into it.

The queen sat beside her, smoothing back Wil's hair as she had done when Wil was a child. "You've grown," the queen said at last. "I thought the chance to see you grow had been stolen from me."

Wil looked up at her. "I was a coward not to come back and tell you the truth."

The back of the queen's hand trailed down Wil's cheek. "I've seen my share of truths." She looked toward the door and back. "We'll keep this from Baren. If he were to know about this curse, I fear what he would have you do."

Wil's head rolled against the pillow. "Owen doesn't deserve for his death to be covered up."

"Owen would want it this way," the queen said. "I know well what he wanted for you. He and I argued many times on your behalf."

"I didn't know that," Wil said. Her throat went dry. "Why should you argue about me?"

"He wanted to bring you along sometimes when he traveled. He said your mind was like an animal held in captivity, rattling the cage. I didn't want to see how right he was."

The sentiment embedded itself into her heart.

"I don't know who anyone is in death," the queen said, "but I knew my son in life. And he would not want you to suffer more than you have. He always fought for you."

"Thank you," Wil whispered. She realized just in that moment how much she had needed for someone to tell her that.

"I don't know who would curse you," the queen said. "But I suspect the punishment wasn't for you to suffer, but me."

Wil studied her mother's face. The queen knew so much about the world; surely she'd met marvelers and seen the effects of their curses firsthand. The king had wanted his bride to have an easy life, a happy one. He'd outfitted her with pretty things and given her gardens to tend and children to love. But Wil had always seen who her mother was underneath all of that. She saw that they were the same.

"Who would want you to suffer?" Wil asked.

The queen swept a hand across Wil's brow. "I don't know, heart. Truly I don't. But birth curses are never about the child who was born with the curse."

# THREE

WIL DID NOT SLEEP, AS her mother had insisted.

Instead, she sat at the edge of her bed with the dagger at her thigh, the guns in their holsters at either hip. She was waiting until she was sure her mother and Baren had gone to bed before she made her move.

She had not wanted to remain in this chamber at all, had wanted to begin her search for answers immediately. But the queen had insisted that nights in this castle had become unsafe, and that this pursuit was one for the morning. Wil had not understood. She no longer understood anything about this place that had once been her home. Something was very wrong with it. Even her power seemed to suffer. The ivy leaf she'd crystallized before bed had only turned halfway, leaving a dull ache in her chest.

It wasn't just the absence of Owen and her father, or all the covered mirrors in the halls. It was something dark that had blotted out the sky over the entire kingdom.

Despite her mother's warning, Wil had to find Gerdie. Her worry for him surpassed her fear over what he might do when he learned she was alive. He was one who needed complete answers, and she would have to tell him everything. The whole awful, bloody truth of it.

Mustering her courage, she rose from her bed. It was outfitted with fresh linens, she noted. Even when she had been presumed dead, her mother had sent for a servant to outfit Wil's bed in winter sheets.

She looked at the carved clock hanging on the wall across from her bed, its patient ticking growing louder the more she became aware of it. She imagined her mother coming in weekly to wind it, even as she'd believed her daughter to be dead.

Her mother had no superstition about clocks, barely regarded them at all. And upon considering this, Wil realized her mother had kept the clock in this room ticking simply because she had missed her. Because having that small, steady sound in this room was the next best thing to a heartbeat. Despite its weeks of being empty, her chamber still felt like a place that belonged to the living. Made vulnerable by her half-sleeping state, Wil felt heartsick with guilt for what she had put her mother through.

She slipped out of bed. The thoughts followed her. What

had happened to her father? Where was her brother? What above all burning hells was happening to Baren?

Nagging as these questions were, their answers would not be the thing to save Loom's life. To pay Pahn's ransom she needed answers, and there was one person to whom she could always turn for those: Gerdie.

Still in her nightgown, she moved to her chamber door and opened it. Her mother sat in a carved chair in the hallway, her cheek rested on her fist, asleep. There was a tangle of yarn in her lap, and something partially knitted. Wil had always known her mother to have busy hands, but she could not recall ever once seeing her with yarn.

Had her mother camped out to protect her from Baren? Or had she meant to protect the rest of the castle from Wil?

Wil didn't wake her, but trod lightly across the flagstones of the hallway, toward Gerdie's chamber.

She was just about to turn the knob when she heard the motion behind her. She crouched, dodging a sword that meant to remove the head from her shoulders. In one fast motion she threw off her coat and drew a gun. Baren swung for her again and she curled her knees and somersaulted past his legs. She was up on her feet again before he turned to face her.

He had never been much with weapons, but even so, he had improved. She wouldn't have heard him coming if not for his hard breathing echoing throughout the halls.

She held her gun in two hands, steady as her gaze. She

would not shoot to kill, no matter what he might try next, she told herself. She couldn't do that to their mother. Not again.

But Baren lowered his sword. He laughed. A distracted, anxious laugh. His eyes gleamed dark with the madness of that sound.

Wil narrowed her eyes. They stood in silence for a long moment. Neither of them moved. And then Wil whispered, "What's happened to you?"

She did not lower her gun.

"You've been a plague since the day you were born," he said.

If only he had been the one to catch her the night she fell from the wall instead of Owen. It was an ugly thought, and it startled her to know she meant it. To know that she and her brother were matched in their hatred for each other. To know they had this much in common.

He let the sword fall from his hand. It clattered against the stone. He looked at it lying beside him. When he raised his eyes to her again, there was a snarl on his mouth, and his voice was a rasp. "I will have to kill you myself."

She fired a shot even before he had moved. It was no matter. It didn't stop him. Blood trailed from the wound in his bicep as he reached for her. She moved to take a step back, but he anticipated it, hooking her ankle with his foot, so that she toppled to the ground with him over her.

The gun flew out of her hands, skidding across the floor. Her wrists were pinned under his, his knee crushing into her stomach, making her breaths come in rasped, strained howls.

The shortage of air made her struggle even as she told herself not to give Baren the satisfaction. He pressed his weight into her as he leaned closer. In a few seconds, he would be dead from her touch. He would be dead, and her mother would find his ruby corpse and see for herself what a monster her daughter was.

Baren's face was over hers, so near that his features blurred. "You," he panted, furious and quiet, "were never meant to come into this world."

Wil waited for the crackle of gemstone. She waited for his grasp on her wrists to slacken. But he didn't let up, and her lungs protested how little air they were able to draw under his weight.

He drew one hand away from her wrist and punched her in the mouth. She felt the full weight of it, and then she tasted blood.

Gathering her strength, she twisted her hips and shoulders in tandem and used her freed arm to throw him off of her. But he had grown stronger, and for once, she felt how small she was under his broad frame. There was the sense that he could snap her spine in two if he had a mind for it.

She betrayed her bewilderment, and he grinned.

Then from somewhere far away there was the sound of footsteps, heavy and running. A blur of motion and blond hair, and Baren was thrown off her.

Gasping in the air she'd lost, Wil staggered to her feet,

grabbing Baren's dropped sword as she did.

Gerdie had Baren pinned to the wall, a dagger at his throat. As her vision sharpened, Wil saw the familiar pattern of the blade. The dagger—its blade simple and sharp and gleaming—had belonged to Owen.

Baren held his hands up, but there was no fear in his eyes. He was wheezing, until the sound turned into laughter. "Can you not simply be gone?" he said to Wil. He slapped his hand to his forehead, grasping his own skull so tightly his fingers turned white. "I can no longer remember a time before you were born. Before you condemned us all."

Wil might have wanted to know what he meant by that, if she hadn't been so confused by the rise and fall of his chest, the way he continued to live even after he had been so close to her. It couldn't be their shared blood; that hadn't spared Owen.

The sound of footsteps made all three siblings turn their heads. Their mother was running toward them, her gold night-gown bunched in her fists. She came to a stop and knelt to retrieve the gun that had slid across the floor, its barrel still facing her children.

Gerdie eased up on Baren only once his mother had retrieved the gun. Slowly, he returned the dagger to its hilt. He must have been sleeping, for that was the only time he removed his leg braces and monocle, all of which were absent now. As his adrenaline began to die down and his ragged breathing slowed, she saw the tremble in his left leg.

He hadn't looked at her once. Both her brothers were turned on their mother. Baren's arms were shaking. Blood oozed from his wound, stained his frilled white tunic. Wil could taste her own blood in her mouth, feel the sting of her split lip.

But if the scene was half as frightful as Wil suspected, the queen's eyes didn't show it. She touched Baren's arm. He hissed in pain and flinched away. The bullet had merely grazed him; Wil knew this because that had been her intention, and she could also see a crack in a wall stone where the bullet struck it.

"You will need to let me clean that so it doesn't get infected," the queen told him. "You can't afford to fall ill, not now with so much at stake."

Baren turned his stare on Wil. "I need to rid this castle of its ghosts."

"Come with me." The queen wrapped her arm around him and began to lead him off. When Baren's attention was on the hallway ahead, the queen reached behind her back, pressing the gun firmly into Wil's hands.

Wil was afraid to turn to Gerdie. She could sense his eyes on her now. Tallim powder and smoke all about him like an apparition. It was a sour, smoky, familiar smell. The smell of weapons, of war. Of home.

She made herself look at him.

His expression was wild, bewildered, as though she were a cauldron explosion. Those, at least, he could come to understand.

"Gerdie?" It was a cracked whisper.

He flinched as though the sound of her voice could kill him. She could hear the sudden haste of his breaths. His eyes—his bright, curious, brilliant eyes—were now guarded in a way never before directed at her.

For a moment they stood facing each other, the echo of their breaths in the stone hallway confirming that they were both alive and whole.

Maybe she was unwelcome now, Wil thought. Maybe after hearing of her and Owen's deaths, Gerdie had thrown himself into his work, reinventing himself as he invented things forged of steel and potion and powder, and now he no longer considered himself her brother.

Gerdie's jaw tightened, and in that small gesture he became familiar to her again. She recognized the change in his eyes, the way they always grew fiercer when he was fighting back tears. A wave of sorrow and something else—relief?—crested in his features.

"Where have you been?" he rasped. "Burning hells, Wil. Where have you been?"

# FOUR

GERDIE SAT ON THE EDGE of his bed, working a salve into his aching calves.

Wil was perched at the hearth, prodding life into the dying fire. In this way, things were as they had always been. The room was warm and quiet, all her brother's things neatly tucked into their shelves and drawers.

Outside, it had begun to rain. The wind skewed it sideways, and drops fell against the windows like desperate hands trying to beat their way inside.

With her eyes still on the fire, Wil began to speak. She told her brother what really happened that night. She told him about the blood squeezing from Owen's skin before it turned crystal. She told him about the shards in his hair, and the weight of him collapsing against her, and the moment she felt him stop breathing.

Gerdie didn't say a word to stop her, and so she went on, until she had told him about Loom, the boy to whom she had become inextricably fated. As ever, she confided in her brother more than she had with her mother, sparing no detail.

She took some comfort in Gerdie's predictable inclination to listen. He'd moved to sit beside her, the light from the fire causing his monocle to gleam when he turned his head just so.

Moments earlier, he had seemed like a stranger, but then, even that had not been so. He had recognized her the moment he saw her, even before her return could have possibly made sense. Gerdie wanted an explanation for her return from the dead, yes, but an explanation was not required before he'd moved to save her from Baren's attack. Not as much had changed between them as Wil had feared.

"I know I don't have any right to ask for your forgiveness," Wil said, finishing her story. The apology stuck in her throat, and she couldn't bring herself to say that she was sorry. The words were small and empty and unworthy of him.

Gerdie stared at the fire and his mouth twitched as though he couldn't settle on an expression. At last it was his turn to speak, and he weighed his words carefully.

"I read about drowning," he said, his voice soft. "About what it does to the brain, to the heart. How long it takes to die. But it never made any sense. I couldn't accept it, and I didn't know what was wrong with me."

Wil hugged her knees, sickened by her guilt.

Gerdie looked at her, and his expression was eerily blank. Whatever he was thinking, whatever else he wanted to say, he was hiding it from her. This was a side of himself reserved for their father, or for Baren. Sometimes even their mother, when he was trying to stop her from worrying. But not Wil. Never Wil.

She had no right to ask, though it chipped a hairline crack through her heart. She did not deserve her brother's trust until she had earned it again.

"You were there when the darklead attacked Cannolay," he said. This surprised Wil, until his face betrayed a moment of regret and sorrow, and she realized that of course this had been haunting him. The bomb that hit Cannolay was one of his own design, but he had hoped it would never be used.

"Yes," Wil said, her voice gentle. "I was there."

"Was it—" Now he was the one struggling for words.

"It did what it was designed to do," Wil said, giving him the courtesy of truth. "And Loom is the king his kingdom needs. As soon as he's on the throne, we could start to repair the relations between our kingdoms."

"You really believe that?" Gerdie asked.

"Yes," Wil said. She had spent weeks at Loom's side, but it hadn't taken that long for her to see how he loved his kingdom, how much of himself he was willing to sacrifice for it.

"I didn't want for that to happen, Wil," he said. "I thought I had hidden my weapons where Baren would never find them.

I thought he wouldn't know what they were even if he did. But one morning I woke in a fog. My body was heavy and I could barely think straight. I stayed in bed and I slept until it was dark outside, and when I went to the basement, everything was . . . ransacked."

"Baren drugged you?" Wil lowered her knees from her chest and sat up straighter. Anger surged, but she couldn't give in to it now. There was too much else to untangle first.

Gerdie shook his head, as though to free himself from the memory. "Something has changed in him" was all he said.

"Why didn't my power affect him?" Wil wondered aloud.

Gerdie reached for the aloe plant that sat atop his mantel. He always had them nearby. Ground with serlot oil and then boiled, the leaves created a salve that eased the persistent aching in his legs on cold days. He presented the potted plant to her now as though offering up an answer.

Wil took it and traced her finger along a fleshy leaf. It was soft and pliable. A dull ache stirred in her chest as something tried to fight its way out of her. Her heart sped in anticipation, but her skin turned clammy. Her temple throbbed with strain, and the more she tried to coax her curse into action, the more persistent the throbbing grew.

She thought back to her return to the castle, and how much effort it had taken to turn the ivy into stone. She'd felt a final push, as though her curse was letting out its last gasp of power.

"It isn't only Baren," she said. "This entire kingdom is

immune to my curse." She hoisted the potted plant to her eye level and studied it, Gerdie's face blurring in the background.

"You said that cursed things cancel each other out," Gerdie said, and his tone was as blunt and dreary as the rain outside. It worried Wil; without his hyper, eager curiosity, he could almost be a stranger to her. When she last saw her brother, the theory of her power being a curse had irritated him. It was too illogical to consider. But now he seemed to accept it, in some battered-down, resigned sort of way that said he'd witnessed many things once deemed impossible. "Maybe your powers don't affect things because this whole kingdom is cursed."

"That can't be true," Wil said, looking to the night sky beyond his bedroom window. "Can it?"

He laughed humorlessly. "Did you get a look at Arrod?"

He was right. Wil had noted the bleakness of her kingdom, but she had attributed it to being a projection of her own worries.

Gerdie touched her wrist, and she jerked back reflexively. Owen flashed through her mind. His veins hardening, his eyes glazing over with crystal. "What are you doing?" she cried.

Gerdie studied the hand with which he'd touched her, and then he held it out for her inspection.

Her curse had not affected him.

"Baren," Wil said, the speculation coming even before she'd thought it. Perhaps she had already known.

The conversation dissolved after that, each sibling lost in

their own thoughts and unwilling to share them. It was not from a lack of trust, but from the notion that speaking their fears might will them to be true.

Finally Wil asked, "Why did Baren attack the South?"

"I don't know," Gerdie said. "He's never needed provocation to do something needlessly cruel, but this feels different. Everything he does is so calculated and planned. I can't figure out what he's driving at."

It was a painful confession for Gerdie to make. He prided himself on finding solutions. Homing in on whatever thin thread of logic eluded everyone else.

Wil thought of the deftness of Baren's attack in the hallway. He had indeed changed. It was as though their father's death had transformed him into the sort of son their father had always wanted him to be—strong and cunning and fearless. But there was something wrong. Something sinister.

"I've tried to eavesdrop on his council, but he doesn't make it easy," Gerdie went on. "I was able to gather that he hasn't put out a draft notice for the war. He's recruiting soldiers."

"Could he be preparing for an evacuation?" Wil guessed.

"That's my thought," Gerdie said. "He's confident enough that he can evacuate the kingdom if there's retaliation from the South. Or he's so confident the South won't be able to retaliate that he isn't bothering to prepare."

It was unwise not to prepare, Wil thought, but Baren might have been right. The Southern Isles were ruled by a reclusive king who collected neutral allies at best, none of whom would follow him into war. He had no resources, no ability to strike back.

"Gerdie." Her voice was trembling and she tried to still it, and found that her hands and knees were trembling too. "What happened to Papa?"

"It was Baren," Gerdie said. "He'll never admit it, but I know it was him. Papa fell ill and he was gone within a day's time. His symptoms didn't match anything—anything." He was beginning to ramble, the way that he did when he was using facts to avoid emotions too big to contend with.

Wil stood. If her brother used scientific reasoning to ward off his feelings, she used perpetual motion to ward off hers.

"Where are you going?" Gerdie asked. He gripped the ledge of the hearth and struggled to his feet, his left leg shaking from the strain.

"To see if there are any wanderer camps moving through the woods," she said. "They'll know the gossip if anyone does. It may not be much, but it's a place to start."

"You won't be able to get out," Gerdie said. "Didn't you see the guards? No one gets in without Baren's approval, and no one leaves."

"I got in without his approval," Wil said, regretting her note of humor when she saw the exasperation on her brother's face. She had always been the exception to his logic, had always defied the order he applied to the universe. He could never predict what she was going to do, or the state she'd be in when she came back.

But for once, Gerdie did not argue. Huffing in theatrical resignation, he sat on the edge of his bed and fitted his braces around his legs. He worked hastily but deftly to tug the leather straps and their buckles into place.

The last time his sister had gone off into the night alone, she hadn't come back. If he couldn't make her see reason this time, at least he would accompany her on whatever disastrous endeavor she charged into headfirst. He even opened the door for her.

Wil knew all this as she strode ahead, turning her back on her brother so that he wouldn't see her smile.

# FIVE

Walking in silence was not uncommon for Wil and Gerdie. They had memorized each other's movements entirely, could anticipate the other's thoughts. Gerdie walked in the direction of the oval garden because he knew that was the point from which Wil frequently made her escape from the palace, and Wil deftly skirted the muddy patches slick with rain that often hindered Gerdie's stride.

All this was as it had always been.

Nonetheless something had changed. Their silence was not easy. Even if Wil could anticipate her brother's steps, she didn't know his thoughts. She sensed his eyes on her in the darkness of the rising, rainy dawn, and felt as though the real Wil had truly drowned and she was a clumsily painted replacement sent to deceive them all.

There was a dam about to break between the two of them,

she knew that much. She only didn't know when, or how to stop it.

Even the oval garden had turned strange—what little of it could be seen in the gloom. All around her were petals drooping like eyelids preparing for a long sleep, and bony branches pointing to each other in accusation.

She couldn't think of what words would set things right again, so she said, "The trees prevented the rain from drenching this part of the wall. It should be dry enough to climb."

In answer, Gerdie braced his boot into a foothold. Once he was partway up the wall, Wil followed after him.

It was nearly November and the sharp chill promised a characteristically early winter. Soon there would be snow, which would delay the ports. There was not much time.

Wil thought of what it would be like to bring Loom to this place. In her mind, in her cursed heart, he was with her. Loom had become a companion when he was beside her, and an instinct when he was not. He arrived in gusts, like wind in sails, filling her up with anticipation.

Her world had changed, but not all of it was for the worse.

Gerdie perched at the top of the stone wall, and Wil crawled up beside him. They had the morning's darkness to their advantage; it was easy for them to blend in. Not that there was any reason to hide: the only guards were stationed at the gate several hundred yards to the north.

Wil craned her neck to have a better view. "I thought you said there would be guards."

"There always are." Gerdie's voice was trailing.

Wil swung a leg over the outer side of the wall.

"Wait," Gerdie said. "Something isn't right about this. I've come here a hundred times and there are always guards."

Knowing that her brother had tried, unsuccessfully, to escape his own home so many times unnerved her. She forced it away. There was no time to go down the dark path of all her regrets and worries now with so much at stake.

She paused, trying to see through the thick forest that surrounded the castle wall.

Something moved between the trees, and she scaled a few steps to have a better look. By Gerdie's rigid posture he had seen it too. A flash of blond hair.

"Baren?" Wil whispered. She turned toward Gerdie. "Have you ever seen him wander off like that?"

"No," Gerdie said, and now he was also bracing himself to descend the outer side of the wall. Curiosity always won the battle against his cautiousness.

They moved quickly, quietly, all while trying to avoid protruding roots and fallen branches. The trees shed during Northern autumns, when the winds were so fierce they bent and severed the branches.

Wil kept her sights on Baren. He was moving faster than she'd ever seen him go, and he was unescorted. He must have dismissed his guards so that he could steal away from the castle, she thought.

He was not moving toward the Port Capital, but into the

thick of the woods, through which wanderers commonly tra-
versed. Only, there was no song filling the air. There was no
fire, no creak of caravan wheels. Wanderers always came awake
at sundown, filling the night air with their lively presence.

It was unusual enough that Baren would wander this far
into the forest. He hated going beyond sight of the castle, par-
ticularly at night. Wil had never seen him leave the castle after
dark; the woods were filled with things that lunged if they
smelled fear. But Baren seemed to know exactly where he was
going.

Thunder shook the morning sky. It didn't feel like morning. Nothing was chirping or moving around them. Nothing
was breathing or flying. Wil plucked a dying leaf from a branch
and felt a dull stabbing in her core. Her curse trying in vain to
break free.

Baren came to a stop several yards ahead. Beside her, Wil
heard Gerdie's labored breathing, and she worried what this
damp, cold air was doing to his lungs. But she didn't ask if he
was all right; it would only irritate him if she doted on him the
way she had when they were children. And the tether between
them was already so fragile.

"Do you know where we are?" Gerdie whispered.

"Yes," Wil said, her eyes fixed on Baren. He was standing
before a crumbling stone cavern overrun with moss and vines. It
was the tunnel of a railway that used to lead through to Northern Arrod. It had been abandoned more than a century ago
when an avalanche destroyed the hillside. Owen had taught her

that. He had known every inch of his kingdom, and given deep consideration to even its old and forgotten corners.

She felt another stab in her chest, and not from her suppressed curse, but from a loss so intertwined with guilt that she could not distinguish the two. Because of her, Owen was gone. Because of her, the entire kingdom was in the hands of the brother who was dragging it to ruin.

"You've been here?" Gerdie asked, pulling her out of her thoughts.

Wil shook her head. "I just know that it's an old train tunnel." She crept closer, keeping behind trees for cover.

Baren disappeared into the black mouth of the abandoned tunnel, and Wil moved to follow. She was just about to set foot inside when it flared to life with an eerie amber light. She ducked back behind a tree.

A sick feeling moved through her, pooling in her stomach and then radiating outward. The air hummed with a strange, unsettling energy, and it dizzied her for a few seconds as her body adjusted to the change.

It was starting to rain again, the sporadic drizzling turning heavy and unforgiving. Wil felt Gerdie sidle up beside her, their shoulders not quite touching. His nearness worried her, though she knew her curse had no effect on the living now. The tree she clung to would have been a mesh of gemstones if it did.

Baren was silhouetted against the glow, which had faded into a pale pink with roiling plumes of gold.

"You promised me that the dead could not return," he

shouted. His anger did not mask his fear.

Another figure emerged, as though from the stones them-selves. Wil could barely make out the shape—taller than her brother, and lean and cloaked. The figure's face was covered, and it spoke words that Wil could not hear over the driving rain.

The unease in her stomach churned.

The plumes of colored mist thickened until she could no longer make out either silhouette. Just a flash of Baren's golden hair—then nothing.

Beside her, Gerdie stifled a cough against his sleeve. The rain had drenched them both, and Wil became aware that she was shivering.

Still, she strained to hear what Baren was saying. It was no use; the wind was too loud and merciless; gusts of it tossed the rain like ships in a tumultuous sea. She moved for the cavern, and Gerdie snared her arm. The small gesture ignited a flurry of sharp pains where he touched her. She would have to find an outlet for her curse soon.

"What are you doing?" he rasped. "Baren will kill you."

"He won't know I'm here," she assured him, twisting out of his grasp. When she pressed forward this time, Gerdie didn't follow her. He was stealthy and strong, but she had a lighter stride and had perfected the art of going unnoticed.

Using the storm's cacophony to her advantage, she slipped into the tunnel, her back pressed against the wall.

"If she's returned from the dead, that is a very dark power," the figure was saying. The voice was soft, eerie, and it belonged to an elderly woman. Through the haze, Wil could just make out her pale blue eyes, a wisp of golden hair, and wrinkled skin. "That is a marvelry I do not touch, and I would advise you not to intervene."

"Not to intervene?" Baren cried. Wil scarcely recognized him. "You told me the dead couldn't come back. You told me my life would not be at risk so long as I was king."

"Has she tried to kill you?" The old woman's voice was calm.

"She will," Baren said. He was pacing now, agitated. "I need a way to kill her before she has a chance. My mother won't listen—she never listens. Neither will my brother. This undead *thing* has them all hypnotized. She was able to do that even when she was alive."

Wil had learned long ago to disregard her brother's disdain. She had learned that, for the most part, he was just words and murderous glances. But this rage shot through her skin and her bones and her cursed heart, because it was not a new side of him. No. It was who he had always been. It was the culmination of a lifetime of hatred he'd felt for her since the day she came into the world.

Perhaps Baren had always sensed that she was a monster. That she would be the undoing of their entire family, their entire kingdom.

All her life she had believed her second-eldest brother to be the villain in her life. But maybe, all along, it had been her.

"I'm sorry," the old woman said. "But I will not help you combat something undead."

"Then tell me what I need to do," Baren insisted.

"To kill something that has come back from the dead, you will need to sever the head and all the limbs and burn them. Bury the bones in separate graves, so that they cannot find each other and come back together. Do not bury them in water. Water is always moving and nothing in a watery grave is ever at rest."

Wil heard her own breaths coming hard and fast. She pressed her lips tight in an attempt to silence them.

Dazed, she moved back out into the rain and returned to the tree where Gerdie was waiting for her.

Over the churning of her thoughts, she barely registered his concerned expression. "What did you hear?" he asked.

Thunder shook the sky, but the clouds had thinned, letting in rays of pale morning light.

"I think I know how he's managed to curse the kingdom," Wil said. "I think he's become a marveler."

Her heart was thudding in her chest, each beat sending out a faint shiver of pain she forced herself to ignore. Loom. She had to get back to him. If Baren was as powerful as she suspected, the darklead wouldn't be the only attack on Loom's kingdom. She had to warn him.

# SIX

By the time they returned to the castle, Wil felt a pain that seeped into her bones like a chill. The sun was lurking behind the clouds, as though waiting for the rain to subside before coming out.

"You need rest," Gerdie said, after they'd both descended the wall.

He said this casually, out of habit. But the small bit of kindness in his words meant so much to Wil that she was startled. Gerdie owed her nothing, and she had no right to help herself to his concern. Not after what she had put him through, not while she was still broken by this curse that had cost them so much.

And then she thought of Loom, whom she'd left at Pahn's mercy, whose kingdom was under siege by a brother whose reign was her fault. She thought of Loom's heart stopping because she had failed to keep her bargain to save his life.

"I don't have time," she said. "I need to find the reason behind this curse or Loom is going to die. And if I don't warn him what he's up against with Baren, his entire kingdom will be destroyed."

Gerdie stared at her for a long moment, with the uncertainty he afforded strangers. And as she looked him over, she saw that he was not entirely as she'd left him. His eyes, usually warm and intelligent and kind, had turned steely and cautious. His face was leaner, his posture more rigid and guarded.

He looked gray, the way that Arrod looked gray. Had it only been September when they were laughing about the cauldron explosion that charred their eyebrows after they'd leaned too close? Had it really been only a handful of weeks?

He exhaled hard, a little white cloud escaping his nostrils, which were red from the cold. Then he seemed to come to a decision. "Follow me."

He led her back to the castle, to the back entrance of the servants' kitchen, where their mother was unlikely to spot them. The door that led to his basement laboratory was now marked with padlocks, which Gerdie set about unlocking. Wil supposed he took this measure after Baren had raided this place. The locks appeared common enough, but the complexity of the keys told Wil that they were no ordinary locks; they were yet another of her brother's brilliant inventions, like the trick triggers of her guns that prevented a would-be thief from shooting them.

The door opened, and the musty, charred smell of potions and cauldron smoke and dust flooded her. How she'd missed this place. It was comforting and familiar and it always carried the promise that whatever problem befell her could be fixed here. It still did, though that was impossible now.

Gerdie shut the door behind them, and Wil moved downstairs as he worked through another series of locks.

Rain leaked in through the cracks of the window, which was now welded over with bars. Droplets gleamed in a spiderweb woven across the stone, and a small puddle was forming on the floor.

The arrangement of things had changed, but Wil expected that, the way her brother was always toiling with new projects.

Gerdie descended the stairs and began rummaging through boxes, all of which were locked now, many of them chained to the wall. He seemed to be taking his time about finding whatever he was searching for, though Wil had never known him to misplace anything.

With his back to her, he began to speak. "I couldn't accept that you had drowned. And when the river itself gave me no answers, I began to wonder if your death had something to do with your newfound power. I wondered if Papa had murdered you, and Owen had tried to stop him and ended up dead as well. But that didn't make sense either." He slid a row of bottles to the right, revealing a small metal box that was dented and coated with rust. "I turned desperate. Maybe I'd lost my senses a bit—I don't know. I began searching your room for clues. I couldn't search Owen's things because Addney was always in there, and I needed solitude. I needed quiet."

He worked a key into the metal box, and it creaked as it opened. From it, he extracted a folded piece of paper.

Gerdie nodded for her to sit on the bench by the wall. She did, and he sat beside her. Gerdie never sat when he was in his laboratory, his body, like his mind, ever in pursuit of some great idea.

"Like I said, I went through your chamber," he said. "I began turning your things into dream serum. Little things—a bottle of perfume Papa bought that you had never cared for. A dulled pencil resting in the crease of an open book. I thought . . . if I dreamed of your things, maybe you would be there with an answer."

He looked to the paper in his hand, suddenly unable to meet her eyes. Wil ached, and she felt the crest of tears behind her eyes trying to break free. It was her fault that he had been in so much pain. All that time he'd spent grappling desperately for answers, and she had been off in the world and alive. She had been quarreling with Loom and meeting with marvelers and allowing herself to indulge in fleeting moments of some lie that felt like love.

"You never were," he said.

"Gerdie, I—"

"Eventually I began inspecting the stones in the wall," he interrupted her. "One of them was loose, did you know that?"

Wil blinked. "No," she said.

"I had to move the bed out of the way to find it," Gerdie said. "It probably won't make sense, but I just wanted to go over everything. Needed to."

It did make sense, but Wil didn't interrupt him.

"I found this tucked behind a loose stone." He handed the paper to her, and then he waited expectantly.

Wil unfolded the paper carefully. The center crease was torn, creating a slit across the image sketched on the paper.

She went still, staring at what she had just revealed. It was a drawing of a girl, done in charcoal, with a soft face, dark eyes, and dark hair done up in an elaborate series of knots that gleamed like silk.

If not for the utterly serene expression, this girl could have been her, Wil thought. But that wasn't possible. Portraits were forbidden and she had never posed for one. She didn't know anyone talented enough to work from memory.

She raised her eyes to Gerdie, who was looking at her now. "What is this?" she asked.

"I don't know," he said. "I could almost swear it's a portrait of you, but that's impossible."

"Did you ask Mother?"

"Wil." Gerdie's voice was soft. "Seeing this would have destroyed her."

Wil stared at the portrait, penitent as his words sank in. Royals didn't allow portraits. Since the night of their disappearance,

Owen and Wil had existed only in memory. And Wil knew what memory did to the face. It blurred the edges. It made the certainty of features go dull in some moments and too vivid in the next. Memories made dreams cruel, and waking hours harder still.

"But it must have been there for years," Gerdie went on. "Long before you were old enough to be its subject anyway."

"Right," Wil agreed, her voice trailing as she pondered. She had never thought to move her bed, and she would have noticed if the servants had. She knew when any of her things had been misplaced, even slightly.

"It must be a relative," Gerdie said.

Wil felt an odd kinship with the girl in the portrait, at that. Her brothers all bore a strong resemblance to both their parents, and to each other. But Wil could have been a stranger to them all.

"It might mean something," Gerdie said, as Wil traced her fingertip around the paper's edges.

Wil folded the portrait and tucked it gingerly into the breast pocket of her tunic. Then she stood and moved for the stairs.

Gerdie followed after her. "Where are you going?"

"Back to that marveler woman I saw in the tunnel with Baren. Maybe she'll be able to tell me what this portrait means."

Her brother folded his arms. "The one who just instructed Baren on how to kill you."

"To a wanderer caravan, then," Wil said, turning for the stairs. "Anything would be better than doing nothing."

"Wil, listen to yourself." Gerdie kept pace with her. "You haven't slept."

"Loom is going to die if I don't do something about it," she burst out. "I don't care about sleep. I don't care about guards, or about what Baren thinks he'll do to me. I don't care, all right? I can't afford to care about anything until I know that I've done what I came for and Loom is going to live. I won't have the death of someone else I love on my hands."

The words surprised even her. Love. She hadn't meant to say "love." Love was a lie and an illusion of her curse. Of Loom's curse. She had been so careful not to say it, not even when Loom had said it to her. She had been careful not to think it, lest she water the seed of its meaning and cause it to take root in her skull like weeds.

But, wrong as she knew it was, retracting it also felt wrong.

Gerdie didn't remark on it. Instead, he put his arm around her shoulders. His touch was the same as it had always been, gentle but solid.

But now, with the absence of her curse, the touch hurt. Everything was starting to hurt in this cursed kingdom. Wil didn't betray any of this, and she didn't move away. It meant too much to her, knowing that she could still return home and be embraced after everything she had done.

"Wil, we're on the same side," Gerdie said. "Nothing can ever change that."

She smiled. "Thank you."

"You're bleeding," Gerdie said.

Wil felt it a moment after he'd said it. She brushed her fingertips under her nose and they came back slick with blood. She stared at it. Since the emergence of her power, she had never gone so long without summoning it.

"I can't stay here," she said, holding up her bloody hand as evidence of this.

"Rest will help," Gerdie insisted. "You won't be able to do anyone any good if you collapse from exhaustion, or you get shot by a dozen of Baren's guards trying to climb the wall."

She stared at him, considering.

"You've never gone this long without crystallizing something, have you?" Gerdie asked.

Wil shook her head.

"All right, then how about this. Sleep just for a little while, and that will help you keep your strength up. I'll go through my formulas and see if there's some way to coax your power out."

It was better than any solution Wil could come up with at the moment. Her head had been foggy since her return to the castle, and it was only getting worse.

Hesitantly, she said, "One hour."

"Two, tops," Gerdie said as they made their way up the steps.

# SEVEN

GERDIE KEPT VIGIL AT HIS sister's desk, trying to concentrate on a formula that would aid in her predicament. But he often found himself glancing over his shoulder at her instead.

In her canopy bed, Wil looked small. Her head thrashed one way and then the other, and the pillow was dark with sweat.

He left her only once, to retrieve a cold cloth and drape it over her forehead, the way she used to do for him. And then he stood still to watch her.

He pictured the lungs inside her, imagining their motions as they drew and expelled air. He tried to comprehend that his sister's lungs had been breathing this whole time, and that the churning rapids in Northern Arrod were empty of her.

Wil had never seemed breakable, not even when she limped down his laboratory steps with a twisted ankle or a fractured rib; before this curse, he had believed his sister invincible. But now, suddenly, he saw how small she could be. He saw that she was just skin and muscle and organs. She was pieces that could fail, or be destroyed, or drowned. The river didn't kill her, but it could have. Baren would surely try, and if Gerdie left her for an instant, he worried that Baren would succeed.

It scared him.

When he and Wil were young, their nanny would wrap them together in a blanket by the fire and tell them stories. One of the stories was of changelings—children stolen from their cribs and replaced by a flimsy substitute that was all rot and decay and evil inside. It might fool the family for a while, but eventually it would reveal itself to be something ugly and wrong.

It might have been easier if this Wil, sleeping before him, were a changeling. Then he could hate it. He could cut it open from toe to crown and watch the illusion of Wil slide off its grotesque skeleton like a skin.

But this wasn't a changeling. There was no magic to her return, no dark marvelry that brought her back from the dead. She was just Wil, and all the lies that had been told in her absence. He would know his sister anywhere. The one he had spent his entire life trying to protect, whose bones he had set in plaster, whose bruises he had soothed with balms, whose questions challenged him, whose laughter echoed in the walls of a laboratory that was otherwise too still and somber when she was gone.

He was so furious and so relieved that he felt ill with it.

He had imagined a hundred other things that could have happened to Owen and Wil that night. A thousand. But none of them ever made sense by the end.

So when Wil told him what had really happened, Gerdie believed her, because although her absence had been an act of deception, his sister had never lied to him. But also because her story accounted for all the gaps in his own theories.

He had his answers now.

Burying Owen and Wil in his heart had been excruciating, but unearthing one of them proved to be even harder.

For nearly an hour, he held his heavy leather-bound journal over Wil's desk and he studied the notes for all of his potions. He had to flip several pages back to find them. Since Wil and Owen's disappearance, it had been impossible to concentrate most days. The more recent entries were notes about how long it would take to drown, and how long his father had been alone with Wil and Owen before his return to the castle. There were theories that had been scratched out before he'd finished writing them. And, as the result of one especially horrible day, the pages were warped by tears, some of the letters smudged and illegible.

The pages devoted to his potions seemed flaccid and useless, something penned by a silly child a lifetime ago.

The queen knocked at the door. It was early afternoon, and when she found Gerdie at Wil's desk, she stood still. It was a familiar sight. For as long as Gerdie could remember, he and his sister had always just orbited around each other. They kept each other safe.

The queen must have been thinking the same thing that had haunted Gerdie since Wil's return. This girl sleeping in her canopy bed—they had mourned for her. They had stood at the water's edge, hearts in their throats, as the king's men dove and dug for her body. And now she was here, as though she had just fallen from the sky. She was not an apparition that disappeared in the night.

"It isn't safe for her here," the queen said.

"It isn't safe for any of us," Gerdie amended.

The queen sat in the chair by Wil's bed. Even rumpled and worried, she was elegant and strong. She looked as though she hadn't gotten much sleep herself, but it didn't take the keen sharpness from her eyes.

"She can't stay," the queen said.

"I don't think she intends to," Gerdie said, unsuccessfully trying to hide his snap of anger.

"You can't stay either," the queen said. She wasn't looking at him. She was fussing over Wil and avoiding his stare, as though to say that she knew he wanted to argue but her decision was final.

Wil awoke, kicking as though she had been trying to run. Her chest felt tight, her face and neck and chest soaked with sweat.

She sat up and tried to calm her rapid breathing. Her cursed heart thudded in her chest like a caged thing, trying still to find a way out.

Her ticking grandfather clock said that she had been asleep for nearly three hours. Three hours wasted while Loom's life was cradled in her hands.

Across the room, Gerdie had fallen asleep slumped at her desk with his cheek resting on his arm. The fire's vivacity said that it had been stoked recently, so he couldn't have been sleeping for long. His monocle was buried in the waves of his gold hair. There were purple shadows under his eyes. His face had thinned, revealing cheekbones that had never been prominent before.

His sleep was fitful; she could tell by the way his eyes moved under their lids, the occasional slurred mumble. He looked so tired, drained of all the resolve he'd mustered since her return.

Seeing him now only confirmed everything she'd feared since her exile: returning to him had hurt him. This curse belonged to him as much as it belonged to Owen, who died to save her, and their mother, who had insisted upon having a daughter, and their father, and even to Baren, who had somehow always known that she was cursed and had tried so many times to destroy her.

And this curse belonged to Gerdie, to whom she was inextricably tethered, who had shared every gasp of excitement and pain of her childhood. Their hearts had always throbbed in tandem, until the day hers turned dark and vicious.

She stood and moved quietly across the room. Firelight lit up the side of his face, and he still looked like a child when he slept.

"I love you," she told him, for the very first and the very last time. She never would have said such a thing if he were awake. He might have said it back, and she did not want him to love her. Everyone who loved her was cursed.

Her mind felt too full, spinning and buzzing and reminding her of all her worries. She had to get out of this castle. She had to find a way to the woman in the cavern and seek answers. There was no promise that this woman would be willing to help her, but Wil had to try. As far as she knew, the old woman was the only marveler in the kingdom besides Baren; who else was there to ask about a curse?

Besides, if she busied herself, Loom would not seem so far away. Thoughts of her father's death and what had happened to him would not make her feel so powerless.

She moved through the castle, silent and keeping to the shadows—there was a wealth of those now, with no sconces lit on the walls, and no servants moving about with electric lanterns in hand. It was late morning, and this once would have meant noise and life.

Wil wore her dagger and guns sheathed to her hips and thigh, anticipating Baren's next attack. But no attack came. Perhaps her mother had managed to calm him, if such a thing were possible.

She reached the oval garden's partially frozen fountain when a retching sound stopped her. It had come from somewhere behind the rosebush.

It happened a second time, more violent than the first, and ended with a pained splutter of vomit hitting grass.

The figure spat into the dirt before shuffling out into the clearing. Bright winter moonlight in its cloudless sky lit the figure's face.

"Addney?" Wil whispered.

Even ill as she looked, Owen's bride was beautiful, swathed in a fur-lined suede coat. Her dark eyes were glassy with tears. Her hair lay over one shoulder, longer than Wil remembered, and her brown skin was awash with sweat, her cheeks flushed.

Addney lowered herself wearily onto the bench. "So it's true, then," she said, expressionless. "You're alive."

Wil took a step back. "I—"

"All I wished to know, when I heard the news, was if you had returned alone." Addney stared through the fountain.

"If you're sick, we ought to get you inside," Wil said, steeling herself against Addney's words. Again, she had taken Owen away from his wife. "This weather can't be good for you." It was Addney's first Northern winter, which would be a shock for her, given the South's perpetual summer climate.

Addney shook her head. "There are servants in the house. King Baren insists. He thinks I'm too stupid to know that they're spies."

The house. Addney was living alone in the house that had been built for Owen.

Wil sat on the bench beside Addney, maintaining a careful

distance. "Let me do something," she said. Addney wouldn't know how much Wil meant those words, how much she wanted to fix. "Can I bring you anything? Some water, or I could start a fire. I'm quite good at—"

"It will pass," Addney said. "The worst of it is gone by noon."

The world stilled around them. Wil heard her own raspy whisper, the words coming out as she understood. "You're pregnant."

Addney closed her eyes in a grimace, warding off another wave of nausea. "The queen has wisely advised me to conceal it from the king, a task which will be difficult in months to come—even for someone as dim as he is." She cast Wil a with-ering stare. "If I may speak so frankly about your brother."

"Does anyone know about this, besides my mother?" Wil asked.

"Gerhard," Addney said. "The first morning I was ill, he heard me and brought a cup of hot water with lemon to settle my stomach. He was . . . very kind. It was the first time I felt any sense of belonging to this place since Owen's death."

Owen's death. Addney said the words, trying to make them sound as though they didn't tear her world in two. Wil felt a sense of longing to be in Addney's presence. Here was the woman her brother had loved, and even if Owen was no longer here, his love for her still was. Addney wore that love the way she wore the moonlight on her skin.

Wil reached a gloved hand and laid it on Addney's knee, with great caution.

To her surprise, Addney gripped it. Her eyes were focused on the stone wall that bordered the castle, barely visible through the brush. "You were trying to get out there, weren't you? But you won't be able to with the king's guards."

"I've had a lot of practice," Wil said.

"I don't know what King Baren has done with your father's guards," Addney said. "They vanished. I can't imagine how he would have killed so many guards and servants so quickly and without a trace, but I suspect whatever he has done with them is worse."

Baren. He might kill them all if he had a mind to, Wil thought. Now that he was king, he could do this without consequence.

But Addney was carrying the rightful heir to the kingdom. In just a few months' time, Owen's child would steal the throne away from Baren, who would never relinquish it.

"You have to leave this place," Wil said. "Once Baren finds out—"

"I have tried." Addney's voice was fierce. "The guards have orders to kill anyone who tries to leave or enter that wall."

"That's what they'll have you think," Wil said. "But I know how to get around them."

Addney's words, though, turned out not to be an exaggeration.

Wil scaled the stone wall and heard the click of several guns before she'd so much as pulled himself up onto the ledge. She looked down at the unfamiliar faces several yards below. Her father's guards had rarely caught her sneaking out against the king's wishes, but when they did, they wouldn't have dared train their weapons on her. Her father had men beheaded for smaller offenses.

But these were not her father's guards.

She swung one leg and then the other over the outer side of the wall, letting them dangle as she sat. Beyond the guards, she could see the thick trees that stretched on for miles. Dead and dying with winter, they still clung to enough foliage to conceal her if she were to run. And beyond those trees, the ocean. And beyond that ocean, Loom.

Suddenly the guards seemed inconsequential. Just a row of men and guns and swords. They couldn't trap her here.

She pushed forward and began her descent.

# EIGHT

THE FIRST BULLET HIT THE wall and ricocheted back, searing the stone. Wil didn't stop moving. A fast enough target was not a target at all. She was in flight, her body finding footholds faster than she could think to command it. She and this wall were old friends; they knew the shape of each other.

Two-thirds of the way down, a bullet shot past her head, burning her cheek with its heat. She felt another bite at the heel of her boot.

She jumped, and the world became a blur of branches and snow and steel. The ground came up fast and she braced her arms, tumbling into a somersault and gaining forward momentum. She came up running. Behind her there was shouting, and she thought she could hear Addney.

The bullets did not follow her into the woods. The

commands being called out were far, far away. Baren had authorized his guards to kill on sight, but he had not authorized them to leave their posts.

It wouldn't be long before Baren found out what had happened. Soon there would be soldiers combing every foot of this place, and if they found her, not even the queen would be able to save her this time. Not when Baren had already made the decision to kill her, and there was no one in this kingdom to stop him.

It didn't matter, Wil told herself. In the grand expanse of sky and sea and land that stood between her and Loom, Baren was nothing. He was smaller than his guards had seemed when Wil sat high atop the wall. He was smaller than their bullets. Smaller than a winter bird up in the cloudy Arrod sky.

Mud from the morning's rain coated her hands and knees. This had been the thing to save her landing, Wil realized. She had a frenzied memory of sliding through it before pushing to her feet. That momentum carried her until the castle was long out of sight, and then she doubled to catch her breath.

Her vision swam. Her heart stabbed at her ribs.

*Focus,* she reminded herself. *You aren't trapped by your body. You are wind. You are everywhere.*

She made her way toward the abandoned train tunnel, moving at a slower clip, forcing herself to keep a less punishing pace. Gerdie was right; she was no use to anyone if she collapsed from exhaustion.

When she arrived at the tunnel, it seemed far less menacing

in the daylight. The sun was stealing through breaks in the clouds, giving a somber but crisp light to the world.

She walked several yards into the cavern, stopping where the daylight no longer touched the ground. Here, her blood turned cold. The hair at the back of her neck rose. Her skin prickled.

The air held a different current here. "I know you're here, whoever you are," Wil said. "I'm not going to leave, so you may as well come out."

The next gust of wind pushed into the tunnel, filling Wil's clothes, her hair, her throat with bitter winter cold. It set the branches and the leaves whispering, and the snow scurrying about in a panic.

The figure of an old woman emerged from the shadows of the cavern, towering over Wil. Her hair was visible first—long, thin wisps of gold that trailed halfway to the ground. And then her eyes, searingly bright and blue.

The wind stole into the tunnel, startling the leaves and causing them to swirl at the old woman's boots.

Wil had come to learn that marvelers carried an energy about them. It was subdued when they had a mind to hide it, but other times it was certain as the sound of breathing. This energy now was much like the energy Pahn had emitted when he healed Loom. A low, steady, keening little pitch that one would miss if one didn't know to listen for it.

The old woman was staring at her, and for a moment there was astonishment in her eyes. And then—nothing. Her face turned heavy lidded and impassive. "The princess who rose from the dead has come to see me," she said.

Wil might have felt fear a day ago, but the adrenaline from her escape was still coursing through her. She kept her posture steady, her expression neutral, the same way she would when dealing with vendors in the underground marketplace of the Port Capital. "You know that I'm alive," she said.

"Yes," the old woman said. "You smell like a living thing. No limbs tearing from their sockets. Eyes aren't decaying."

The woman reached forward and touched Wil's chin as though to inspect her. Her eyes changed immediately, flashing bright. It was an oddly gentle touch that reminded Wil of the way her mother had stroked her forehead when singing her to sleep. "You are certainly alive," the old woman said, "but not for much longer."

The words might have made Wil fearful if she'd had time for such a thing. Instead, she felt anxious. Loom returned to her thoughts with more clarity than this dreary cavern or the mud that caked between her fingers. She wasn't going to die. She was going to return to him.

"It's a birth curse," Wil said, her voice steady.

"Doesn't surprise me," the old woman said. "Not with your family."

"My family?" Wil echoed hollowly. "What do you know about my family?" Her father had been known throughout the kingdom, as had Owen. From Port Capital gossip, Wil knew her father's decisions were not always popular ones, whereas

Owen fulfilled his role as a lovable figurehead who could quell any tensions with his easy nature. But the rest of her family had been a deliberate enigma. Wil, her brothers, even the queen were the subjects of fabrications and rumors at best. The world knew nothing about any of them.

But this woman, this stranger, had the air of one who knew things the rest of the world did not. Wil began to worry over what Baren might have told her, and for what purpose.

The old woman leaned closer. Her breath was sweet and hot on Wil's skin. "Does blood ooze from the mortar between all those ancient stones? Do dead things whisper to you royals as you sleep?"

It took all Wil's resistance not to move away. "Of course not," she said. "Dead things don't come back."

"You did," the old woman said.

"I wasn't dead." Wil's adrenaline was waning. She felt tired, defeated. The distance between her castle and Pahn's cabin, which had seemed possible and clear moments earlier, now felt a lifetime away.

She didn't allow herself to give in to her sudden exhaustion. She didn't trust that it wasn't an illusion. This woman was a marveler, and marvelers were never to be trusted, Loom had said.

"You will die before this week is through," the old woman said. She released Wil's chin and canted her head to assess her. "Your heart will be the first to go. But not entirely. It will beat just enough to keep you alive. The lungs will be last. There will be just enough oxygen in your brain for you to feel every moment of yourself dying."

*Marvelers lie,* Wil reminded herself. But it didn't feel like a lie. The world had already begun to go dull around her. Her fingers had been numb since she'd awoken from her fitful sleep, and that numbness was spreading like snake venom up her arms and toward her heart.

"Death isn't my only option," Wil said. "You're going to propose some solution."

"Leaving the kingdom would be a solution," the old woman said. "In a kingdom that isn't cursed, your strength will return. But you won't leave. You're rooted here. The real question is why."

"Because I don't have what I've come for," Wil said. She rubbed her muddy hands against her trousers, trying to clear the caked dirt from her skin before she reached for the paper in her pocket.

Wil unfolded the portrait and held it up. She tried to conjure up some sort of explanation for why she had come here, some rational plea that this bit of paper and charcoal meant something to her, and that she was coming to a marveler to help her sort it out.

But when Wil saw the change in the old woman's face, she stopped herself.

The old woman held up a hand as though she meant to take

the paper from Wil's grasp. Instead, she lowered her arm to her side once more and said, "Where did you get this?" Her voice was hoarse.

It was the first genuine reaction this old woman had shown to Wil's presence, and Wil scrutinized it. That look in the old woman's eyes—this portrait meant something to her. This bit of paper with the image of a girl who looked like Wil had caught her off guard, though Wil herself had not. Perhaps she would not have to bargain with the old woman. Perhaps the old woman would be the one to bargain with her.

Wil folded the paper and returned it to her pocket. The air shifted around her, making the skin of her arms swell with gooseflesh under her sleeves. "It bled out from the walls of my castle," she said.

They stared at each other for a long moment, Wil and this strange old woman who spoke with Northern Arrod's distinct accent and yet did not seem to belong to this kingdom at all. Did not seem to belong anywhere.

"What do you plan to do with that portrait?" the old woman said.

"I intend to burn it," Wil lied. She had always been a smooth liar, and even in her waning state, her ability to haggle with seedy vendors was as strong as ever. And a vendor was all this marveler was; like everyone, she had a price. "My brother says that if you burn a portrait, the spirit of the subject will come to you in a dream. The girl in this portrait has the answer to my question, and as I see it, that's the only way to ask her."

The old woman lunged for Wil so fast that Wil barely dodged the blow. The woman was screaming now—a low, animal howl that shot through the air like a blade. She grabbed for Wil's neck, and Wil dodged. But even with the old woman standing more than a yard away, Wil felt the air getting thinner. Her throat felt tight, as though someone had pulled a rope tight around it. She took in a feeble, whistled breath before the air was stolen from her entirely.

Dully she was aware of the old woman hovering behind her as she clawed at the cavern wall, staggering, trying to reach the oval of light that marked the entrance.

"I told him to kill you because you need to die," the old woman hissed. "You, and your entire family. This curse needs to die with all of you."

Wil's legs gave way. Even when she hit the ground, she struggled. Her lungs burned. Her body bucked and twisted, begging her to breathe. She reached for the dagger at her thigh. She didn't know what she would do with it—the old woman was out of reach. She was miles away.

But the darkness was flooding her vision and her fingers were heavy and slack. She couldn't hold on to her life, much less anything else.

From far away, she felt the old woman reaching into the pocket of her tunic to retrieve the portrait.

A surge of strength came through Wil then. Just a last bit as it made its way out of her body forever. She grasped her dagger and sliced upward, digging into flesh.

Air flooded back into her throat, stolen by her lungs in a painful, stabbing gasp that made her convulse. She crawled backward, coughing, moving all her limbs to shake feeling back into her muscles.

The old woman didn't make a sound. She couldn't. Not with the bleeding gash Wil had torn across her throat.

Wil didn't stay to watch the old woman die. She ran the entire way back to the castle, her heart stabbing at her with every step.

She doubled to catch her breath when the castle was in sight. The world spun and tilted. Her breaths were ragged and loud.

The old woman may have been deceitful, but what she'd said about Wil dying if she stayed in this kingdom was true. Wil pressed her forehead against the trunk of a massive oak tree before her, trying to get her bearings. "Turn to stone," she whispered. "Please, please just turn."

A hand tightened around her wrist, yanking her to attention.

When Wil raised her head, she saw Baren standing before her. His eyes were dark and frantic, his mouth puckered. He looked like he had when he was younger and on the verge of tears. Wil had never seen her second-eldest brother cry, but she had seen him fight the urge away many times.

"Why are you back?" His voice was pleading. "Why couldn't you just stay dead?"

In that moment, she pitied him. Both of them broken by this curse.

"Say something," Baren demanded. His voice cracked. He let go of her wrist and tugged at his hair. "All these voices whispering in my head. You, whispering all night every night so that I can't sleep. And now you're standing before me and you won't say a word."

"What do I whisper at night?" Wil asked.

"You know what you say," Baren snapped. He gestured to the woods. "You tell me to visit her."

"Who?" Wil's brow furrowed. "The woman in the train tunnel?"

"Yes. Of course."

Wil looked at her brother. Truly looked at him. He was stripped of his defenses now. His sword was sheathed at his hip and his hands were trembling, and it was evident from his heavy eyes that he hadn't slept for days. Even the sleep serum from her dagger had not been enough to put him out.

It wasn't cruelty on his face just then. It was desperation. It was exhaustion.

"Baren." She kept her voice gentle, cautious. "What have you told her about our family?"

"I don't tell her," Baren says. "She knows all about us. She tells me."

It sounded like the utterings of a boy driven mad without sleep, but Wil believed him. Just as that old woman had formed an invisible vise around her throat, she had done the same to Baren's mind. But why? And why Baren? Because he was king? Because manipulating someone like Gerdie or her mother would have been impossible?

"Did she tell you to kill Papa?"

Baren's head whipped to her at that. His jaw was clenched, his stare suddenly vicious.

Wil didn't move. She braced herself for his next attack and summoned all her strength to combat it.

But Baren didn't attack her. His lip trembled. He was looking at her like she should have the answers, and he should be the one asking for them.

"Your Majesty!" Their mother's voice called from the castle gates. She moved through the guards with ease; perhaps Baren had given them orders never to hurt her.

The queen was breathing hard by the time she reached them. She was barefoot, the hem of her pale blue dress sodden with mud.

Baren canted his head toward her, but his eyes remained on Wil.

"You shouldn't be out here, Your Majesty," the queen said. Her voice was a coo. "You need your rest, remember?" She wrapped her arm around his shoulders, and he resisted at first, but she held firm.

"I want that thing—that monster—under surveillance," he growled.

"All right," the queen said. "Whatever you'd like."

The three of them made their way back to the gate, Wil several paces behind. She was listening for the music of wanderer troupes, but the woods were silent. If there were any wanderers moving through the woods at all, they didn't want to be found. She wouldn't be able to find any now, and even if she could, they wouldn't be able to help her by nightfall. The old woman in the tunnel—if she was still alive—was no longer an option. Leaving Arrod would return her power and restore her health, but the journey would use up the precious time she'd been afforded to save Loom's life.

She raised her eyes to the castle. There was Gerdie, watching her from the window of her chamber. She still had him. She always had him.

# NINE

W<small>IL SAT ON THE BENCH</small> in her brother's laboratory, nursing a bloody cloth she held bunched under her nose.

"Here." Gerdie sat beside her and handed her a flask of clear liquid. "I know it smells like varnish, but it might help. It's a crystallizing agent I use when I'm making jewels for sword hilts. There's nothing toxic to it."

Tentatively, Wil took a sip. Her stomach lurched, but she forced most of it down.

She had told her brother about the old woman in the tunnel, whom Wil may or may not have killed. She told him about the strange things Baren had said upon her return. Gerdie had listened to all of it with his usual thoughtful silence as he'd retrieved the flask from his trove of bottles. But he seemed more concerned about the state of his sister than about anything she had to say just then.

"Your neck is bruising. . . ." He was distracted, distraught.

"She wanted to kill me." Wil choked down a final sip of the potion. "She wanted to kill all of us. I think she's been using Baren to do it. I think you're right, that Baren killed Papa."

The words felt so strange to say aloud. Their father, dead. It still didn't seem possible. She still believed that he was in his throne room, merely ignoring her the way he always did. She would spend the rest of her life waiting—in some way—for his next order.

"If you killed her, it doesn't matter now what she wanted," Gerdie said. He took the bottle from her hands and returned it to the shelf. He couldn't stand to have things out of their proper places.

"I don't know if she's dead," Wil told him. "I'm not about to go back and check."

"You said that you slashed her throat," Gerdie said. "If you hit a carotid artery, she's dead."

"Marvelers don't follow scientific logic, Gerdie."

"Pray this one does, then. Here." He plucked a sprig from one of his herb pots and dropped it into her waiting palm.

The fine leaves hardened to diamond instantaneously, and Wil's head and eyes rolled back from the relief of it.

The crystallizing stopped before it could reach the stem, despite her frantic heart. But for now, it was enough.

"Thank you," she breathed.

"I can't do much for curses," Gerdie said. "But potions will have to do for now."

When Wil looked at him, he was frowning. She knew what he was going to say even before he'd opened his mouth. "You can't stay here."

"I can't leave without answers," she said.

"There are surely more marvelers in the world," Gerdie said. "And more wanderers."

"But not very much time," Wil replied.

"I thought you'd be eager to return to your prince," Gerdie said. She couldn't tell if he was teasing her. Either way, he was right. In addition to freeing Loom from Pahn's clutches, she needed to warn Loom about Baren.

If the answers weren't here in Arrod, she had to move on and seek them elsewhere. This thought pained her, and after a moment's consideration she said, "Have you been able to get into the Port Capital at all?"

"No," Gerdie said. "Unlike you, when weapons are pointed at me, I don't go charging forward." He broke into a smile.

"I wonder what the people of Arrod make of him," Wil said. She had always gotten a sense of the kingdom's climate by venturing into the Port Capital, but even if she could frequent it now, it would be harder to blend in. When she'd arrived, no one seemed to be lingering at vendors or before shop windows. Everyone was hurrying to wherever they needed to be.

"I think they're afraid," Gerdie said. "Their king is dead, and their new ruler is the heir they'd heard nothing about. But I don't think they know about the darklead attack on Cannolay." His voice had taken on a hush, even though they were alone.

Wil leaned forward. "Can you be certain?"

"He's playing that move close to his vest," Gerdie said. "By the time I'd discovered what was missing from my lab, he'd done it. He wouldn't have told me if I didn't already know."

"But people must know something is amiss," Wil said. "Imports have been drastically affected."

"I'm sure they have." Gerdie was sorting through the bottles on his desk. He didn't seem to be looking for anything in particular, and his eyes had taken on a worried, sort of dazed look.

"You could leave with me, you know," Wil said. "Mother would want that for both of us." She lowered her voice. "I know about Addney. In a few months, Baren will lose the throne, and then you can return—"

"Don't do that," he said. "Don't talk to me like I'm an infant, like you can just tuck me away in a safe corner of the world while you go off to save us all."

He didn't sound angry. He sounded practical and measured and certain that he was right.

Wil was quiet for a while. Was he right? Is that what she was doing to him?

"That isn't what I meant," she said quietly.

"Isn't it?" Gerdie's voice rose, and he began to speak rapidly, the way he did when he'd finally found words for all the things that had been building in his mind. "Isn't that what you did the night Papa exiled you?"

"What was I supposed to do?" she said. "Run home and tell you that I'd killed our brother? Throw myself at Mother's feet and beg for forgiveness?"

"You could have come to me, same as you always have," he said. "I would have *helped* you. I'd have fought for you. Don't you think I'd have stood up to Papa in a heartbeat? You're my sister, and you let me think that you were dead."

He cried out that last word, and it echoed from the walls. It silenced any argument she was going to present. He was right, and Wil knew it. She had always known it. After the panic and the shame of her exile, when she began to think clearly, she could have found a way to contact her brother. She could have returned and slipped past the guards the way she always had, could have hidden in the basement where no one but Gerdie would bother to go. She could have sent word, in code, or scaled the castle wall at night to slip a note through his chamber window. But she hadn't.

And now her father was dead, Baren was king, and Addney's life was in danger so long as she was carrying the next heir. There was so much to fix, and faced with the prospect of all she had destroyed and all that lay in pieces before her, she felt small, and powerless, and weak. That was part of why she hadn't come to him. She would rather her brother think she had drowned than see what she had become.

Gerdie had been bracing himself for her counterargument. They had always battled for the last word, but when none came, he turned and saw the look on her face. Some of his steely veneer softened and he came to sit beside her on the bench.

"Hey." His voice was soft. "This is my family and my kingdom, too. You're not the only one trying to save it."

"How?" she murmured.

"Do you think I've been sitting here alchemizing padlocks and bangles?" There was a little laughter to his voice. "You aren't the only one who's been coming up with plans all this time."

She looked at him now, and there was a wicked bright gleam in his eyes, so familiar that for the first time since her return she started to feel hope.

Making a decision, Gerdie reached for a leather satchel that was tossed rather unceremoniously against a wall. If there was something important inside it, Wil never would have guessed. Gerdie was so very good at hiding things, especially now that Baren had taken an interest in them.

"Baren is afraid of dead things," Gerdie said. "He wouldn't be in the room when Papa died, and he was wild-eyed at the thought of ghosts in the castle. You've seen how he gets when one of the snap traps catches a mouse. He'll yell for a servant to dispose of it, and he won't even look at the thing." He undid the fastenings of the satchel, reached in, and extracted something wrapped in cloth.

When he unwrapped it, Wil gasped and recoiled in shock. He was holding a human hand, the skin torn at the wrist, blood dark and gelatinous around a splintered bone. The fingers had gone wrinkled and blue.

She shrieked when he threw it at her. It landed in her lap, and a chill went through her.

He was laughing. "It's only leather, ink, and bones from a turkey drumstick."

All Wil's disgust and confusion dissolved, traded for fascination. She picked up the hand and held it against her own. The skin was textured, with thin cuticles framing the nail beds. There were fingerprints and pale freckles.

"How did you create the veins?" Wil asked, breathless.

"I painted them."

Another chill ran down Wil's spine and she deposited the hand back into her brother's care.

"I didn't think you of all people would be so squeamish," he said.

"I didn't think you of all people would pull a severed hand out of your bag and deposit it in my lap like a bloody hunting dog." She pressed her lips together, but a laugh escaped anyway. "Your talent terrifies me."

"It has the desired effect, then." Gerdie put the hand back into his bag. "I'm sure I can duplicate Addney's body and stage a murder scene. It need only be a passable likeness; Baren is too skittish to look very closely. And if he thinks I killed her, I'll earn his trust and he'll give me a spot on his council; that way I'll be able to keep him from doing anything to further this war. Meanwhile, when it's time to dispose of the body, the real Addney will be the one to go on the cart and be wheeled off. The guards can take her to the funeral pyre, but they'll have to leave her alone with Mother after that. They won't be allowed to see a woman's body undressed before cremation."

"Genius," Wil whispered, stunned. "How long did it take for you to come up with all this?"

"I've had it all figured out since the day I learned about Addney," he said. "Mother has been helping where she can by distracting Baren. And keep her in hiding until she gives birth to the new heir. After that, Addney will act as regent until the heir is old enough to rule. She could exile Baren to the moon if she sees fit."

Wil stared thoughtfully at the water as she considered all this, and when she looked back to her brother, he was grinning. "Sorry if this ruins your plans to save us all on your own."

"I deserve that," Wil conceded.

"Yes you do," he said, and then he softened. "Wil, we're on the same side. Nothing can ever change that."

Wil had nothing to say to this. She did not deserve her family's forgiveness. She didn't deserve their aid, and she didn't deserve to be welcomed back into their good graces. But this was not about her; it was about fixing what she had broken. Arrod would never have Owen as its king, but it would still have Owen's legacy.

"You're bleeding," Gerdie said.

Wil felt it a moment after he'd said it. She brushed her fingertips under her nose and they came back slick with blood. She stared at it, and all her worries from moments earlier came rushing back. She had managed to forget them for just a little while.

"I'll have to sneak into the cart with Addney," she said. "The only way to get out of this castle now is as a corpse."

She didn't register the words until after she'd said them. As a corpse. For the second time, the princess of Arrod would play the part of a dead girl.

"It's best if Baren doesn't see you and think you're dead," Gerdie said. "He'll try to detach your limbs. And your head—it would be a shame for you to lose that." He was trying to make light of their situation, and Wil laughed, playing along. It was a lie for both of them, but it lightened the air just enough to make things bearable.

"I can sneak into the cart at the last second," Wil said. She was still good at being invisible, even under Baren's intense scrutiny.

"Best to lie low until then," Gerdie said.

"Your lab is the most secure part of the castle thanks to your latest security measures," Wil said.

"That's convenient." He smirked. Then he stood and moved for his cauldron. "Let's get to work."

Alchemy in the modern world had become increasingly rare. Gerdie had brought life to a dying medium. With the rise of electric machinery and the instant gratification it brought, no one had the patience to forge a sword from scraps of titanium and a fistful of crushed obsidian. No one had the mind to think up bullets capable of seeking out the enemy's spine.

And Wil was certain that no one—in this life or the next— would ever think to fashion a corpse from bits of cloth and ink and bone.

Her brother had allowed her to assist in his work before, but he operated on a short budget of patience, and usually it wasn't more than an hour into a task before he was shoving her out of his way.

This time, however, they worked in tandem. The only words spoken were Gerdie's patiently uttered instructions. Wil cut strips of leather. She measured vials of ink. She coated bones with epoxy and sprinkled them with a glittering powder that would fuse them in the cauldron steam. And all the while, she focused only on the task at hand. She did not think of the old marveler woman who'd tried to kill her, or her father, or even Loom. All these thoughts were kept folded safely inside her chest, to be unfurled when there was something to be done for them.

By late afternoon, alchemized limbs began floating at the surface of the cauldron. Gerdie extracted them, laying each hand and leg on the metal table to cool. They looked strange, Wil thought, devoid of any veins or flush of color—which her brother would have to paint himself.

He used gallium for the blood at the fake wounds. It was a metal that melted at low temperatures and gave the appearance of congealed blood.

"Are you all right?" he asked her. "You look a little pale."

"I've seen worse things," she said. It was true. But this hollow, worried feeling that plagued her was not merely about these gruesome pieces laid out before them. Her entire kingdom had fallen ill. A strange girl with Wil's eyes awaited her in her dreams. Her father was dead, and she could not bring herself to mourn him; she was still angry with him for casting her away. That anger had been a dull ache she'd meant to contend with later, when less was at stake, but now she found herself clinging to it. It was the only thing that suspended her in her old life, in which she had believed that one day she could be redeemed. She had always known that her worth to her father depended on what she could do for him. She knew that she was a weapon he called upon when needed, same as his swords and daggers and guns. But still, she had thought, dumbly, that one day she would realize he had loved her—just a little bit—after all.

Gerdie handed her the flask of clear potion, and Wil took a sip. The sprig of mintlemint she reached for barely crystallized at her touch, but it was enough to keep her going.

"What do you need me to do now?" she asked.

"We're done," he said. "You should rest." She opened her mouth to argue, but he interrupted. "There's nothing more to do until nightfall. That's when I'll stage Addney's murder. It's what Mother and I have been planning. Until then, you need to stay out of Baren's sight. By the time he realizes you're no longer in the castle, you could be on a dirigible halfway to anywhere."

"I should at least look for wanderers," Wil said. "Before I leave."

"It makes more sense for you to save your strength," Gerdie said. "If you leave tonight, you can arrive in the Western Isles by morning. The kingdom is filled with wanderers. Much more than there are here. There's still enough time to make it back East."

He was right. Wil knew this, and yet the thought of sleeping precious hours away frustrated her.

Still, when she returned to her chamber and lay atop her blankets, sleep claimed her immediately.

Gerdie was the one to wake her. The sun was setting by then, casting pink light into her chamber. She pretended the rest had helped, for her brother's sake, but in truth she felt worse. Her muscles were stiff and painful as she moved. Her head felt stuffed with cotton. Sounds were far away and then very close.

She said nothing as Gerdie led her through a servants' channel hidden within the walls. Eventually it took them back out into the night air.

A cart was parked beside the door, covered in layers of burlap.

Gerdie tried to smile. "Your chariot awaits," he said.

"Mother will be along soon with Addney and then you'll be off to save your prince."

"Gerdie," Wil began, and found that she didn't have words for what she felt just then.

"I'll see you in June." He smiled. "You'll have to return home then to meet our new heir to the throne."

Wil threw her arms around him. It might be the last time she would ever have the chance. The next time she saw Gerdie, Baren would no longer be king and the only curse in Arrod would be her.

# TEN

GRIEF WAS NOT A LOGICAL thing. Unlike other emotions, it didn't come in any particular sequence. It shifted from a whisper to a roar without any warning.

In the weeks following his sister's and brother's supposed deaths, Gerdie had not allowed himself to be still. He labored in a fury over his cauldron. When thoughts of what had happened that night—what had *really* happened—overwhelmed him, he recited the periodic table of elements. He stirred powders into liquids, cast potions into cauldron steam. He became a creature of compulsion, of habit. In this way, he survived. He even made it through Wil's birthday.

By late October, the air had turned bitterly cold. Snow flurried in its early, noncommittal way, never sticking when it fell. It was on one of these cold mornings that Gerdie had awoken and found himself unable to get out of bed.

His legs had still worked. He hadn't been aching or running a fever. But he couldn't move.

The fire at his hearth was burning. A servant had come in during the early morning hours to stoke it. Warm orange light flickered on the stone walls, the ancient wooden floor.

Wil. His mind had hissed the word, taunting him. Owen and Wil would be skeletal by now, he had thought. Their soft tissue and their sinew worn away by the current. Perhaps bits of them would break away and float downriver. A decayed hand washing onto a distant shore, a tuft of matted hair being plucked up for a seagull's nest. He had the thought that he wanted to go out into the world and find these pieces of them. And he had the thought that he would never be able to.

"Wil," he had whimpered, his eyes filling with tears. "Oh gods, Wil." He rolled onto his stomach so that his face was buried in his pillow. But rather than muffling his sobs, doing this only made them come faster. His body had shaken with them.

He had not allowed himself to cry for his dead siblings, much less his father, or the life he'd had when all these things had been in place. Wil in her chamber, Owen out exploring the world, his father glowering down at all of them from his throne. He had been spoiled. He had been arrogant. He had believed that because he lived in a castle, he was immune to having his life shattered. He had believed his brother and sister to be invincible.

*You don't know everything,* Wil had said before she left him for good.

He heard her voice so clearly in that memory, and it made his grief flare like a flash in his cauldron. If someone had asked him about his sister while Wil was still alive, he would have remarked on her ability to fight, her fierce protectiveness over those she loved. Her stubbornness. Her irritating fascination with illogical things.

He wouldn't have even thought of mentioning her voice, or the way she swung her feet when she sat on his laboratory table and handed him things. But now that she was gone, it surprised him how important these inconsequential bits were. If he stopped remembering them, they would stop existing.

Why was he crying? Tears were useless. Tears would not water the earth and make the dead bloom back up like perennial flowers.

Calling the dead by their names was also useless, he knew, but he couldn't stop sobbing for her. "Wil. Wil. Wil."

No one had answered him. The pain had been so overwhelming that he had almost been able to believe it would change something. Change the rules about who lived and who died. But in the end, all that happened was that logic had come flooding back in. He found the strength to sit up and dry his eyes. The strength to wash his face and get dressed and buckle his legs into their braces.

"Wil is dead," he had told the fire in the hearth. "Owen is

dead." And then he'd left his chamber once again to face the world.

And now, he stood to watch his sister disappear under the cover of nightfall, and a bit of that old grief stirred in him anew. With no one there to see them, those traitorous tears came to his eyes again. It wasn't grief this time, he realized. It was relief. Even anger with his sister for having frightened him so much. Anger with Owen for still being gone. Anger with himself, because when Owen went after Wil that night, Gerdie couldn't be bothered to go with him. He was too busy sulking about his sister taking on their father's mission. He had been jealous of her value to their father. Jealous because he had agreed with their father: Wil was a valuable weapon. She was the kingdom's greatest spy.

Before Owen went after Wil that night, he had stood at the door of Gerdie's lab and said, "Please come. You'll be able to talk some sense into her."

Gerdie had not even looked up from his work. "Talking sense into our sister would be like pouring water into a sealed well."

If he hadn't been so bitter, he would have just gone with Owen.

He would have been able to save them both.

They had always been there to protect him, but he had left them to face the rapids alone.

# ELEVEN

By the time the horses began to pull the cart, Addney was shivering. She reached for Wil's hand. Maybe she just wanted the comfort. Wil took Addney's hand in hers, though she knew she had no right to. Addney wouldn't want to reach for her if she knew what Wil had done, that she was the cause of all this.

"Addney," Wil whispered. The name was heavy on her tongue. The name of the woman her brother had loved. The woman who was left to carry this child alone without him. "When all this is over, there's something I need to tell you. Something you have a right to know."

The approaching footsteps and voices silenced her.

From somewhere beyond the heavy layers of burlap, Wil could hear her mother directing the soldiers toward the pyre. It was deep into the woods and far from any trails frequented by wanderers, much less citizens of Arrod. The disposal of bodies was an ugly business best done out of sight, her father had said.

Without wanting to, Wil thought of Owen. What had her father done with his remains? Buried him? Cast him into the rapids?

She felt sick and weary and weak. She could not recall ever being so weak, not even when she'd crawled to her brother's lab bearing wounds from the Port Capital.

The cart rolled to a stop. Addney covered her mouth with her hand, as though she didn't trust herself to stay silent.

"Take your horses and ride a half mile west of here," the queen was telling the soldiers. "When you see the smoke over the trees, you'll know that it's done. Come back for me only then."

Addney held her breath until the sound of hooves had moved far into the distance.

"It's going to be all right," Wil whispered to her. "I promise you."

Then, the queen raised the burlap coverings, exposing Wil and Addney both to the winter chill.

"Move quickly," the queen said, helping Addney to the ground. "There's no time."

Through the darkness, Wil could just make out the shape of a wanderer's caravan through the trees. It was completely silent, save for the impatient whinnying of a horse that had surely not been there a moment ago.

It took Wil no time to recognize the woman who climbed down from the caravan to meet them. She was much older than when Wil had seen her last, and her graying hair was now completely white, but she was still the nanny Wil remembered from her childhood. The one who had tucked her and Gerdie in to sleep and stoked the hearth on winter nights, who'd spoiled them with stories and stirred honey into mugs of milk when they couldn't sleep.

Wil had missed her nanny horribly once she'd been sent into retirement, but now she couldn't even bring herself to call to her. Instead, she kept to the darkness and watched in silence as Addney climbed into the caravan, Nanny Blay behind her. She said nothing as the caravan hurried away into the woods.

"Wilhelmina." The queen took Wil's face in her hands, startling her with her sudden closeness. "Love, there isn't any time for you to stay either."

"I know." Wil's voice felt small. No, that timid tone wouldn't do. She would not give her mother more cause to worry about her. "Start your fire," Wil said, sounding more certain of herself this time. She hopped down from the caravan. "The soldiers will be suspicious if you don't. I'll be long gone before they get back."

Her mother held her by the shoulders, but she didn't move to embrace her. It was too much for them to say goodbye to her again. Too much for the queen to send a daughter out into the uncertain and cruel world after having already buried her once before.

Her mother kissed her on the forehead and said only, "Travel by air if you go west, and water if you go east."

She was speaking of the Northern winds and the way they moved the sky and the sea in the winter. It didn't matter how many years she spent as queen in a recluse's castle; the queen would always be a wild-hearted wanderer child. She would always know the world with a familiarity that even lovers did not possess.

Wil nodded. "I'll be back to see our new heir." It was a promise, and it was all she could give her mother just then.

The queen removed her shawl and draped it around Wil's neck, tucking it into the collar of her wool coat. She kissed Wil's forehead. "Go quickly," she said.

Wil turned without saying anything more. It was best this way. She sprinted toward the Port Capital, whose lights were not yet visible in the distance.

Once she was certain she was out of her mother's sight, she stopped to catch her breath. Each inhale came with a wheeze. She shuddered and coughed a mouthful of blood.

No time for that, she told herself, and began moving at a slower pace. Her own body felt strange to her. Never before had it pleaded so desperately for sleep. As Wil moved, she entertained fantasies of collapsing to the forest floor and sleeping forever. Of never moving again, never opening her eyes.

She gritted her teeth and persisted.

Something moved behind her—no, *around* her. The air took on that keening pitch, and Wil froze, dread coating her blood. No, it couldn't be. She was imagining things. She—

Something splashed at her face, thick and warm and sour. It

filled her eyes, blinding her, and her mouth, making her splutter and gag. Blood. It tasted like blood.

"You will have the answers you seek," the old marveler woman's voice hissed. Wil spun, swinging blind, but she could not tell where the old woman was standing. She seemed to be moving.

Furiously, Wil rubbed her eyes with her sleeve, trying to clear her vision.

"I will show you exactly what you are and why you don't belong in this world," the old woman's voice went on in a snarl. "And you'll come back to me begging for death. You'll beg for the death of your entire, wretched family, so that another Heidle will never curse Arrod's castle for the rest of time."

The old woman's voice was close now, a hot whisper in Wil's ear. "You will never be at rest until you're dead."

Wil managed to blink through the blood and regain her vision just in time to see the blur of her mother's golden hair rushing toward them. Then, her mother's arm coiling around the old woman's neck, jerking back and snapping it.

"Mother?" Wil gasped.

The old woman's body sagged, sodden and dead. The queen let it fall. "Run," she commanded Wil. "Hurry, before the ports stop taking their fares tonight."

The queen did not seem startled by what she had done. It had been an expert move, an easy break, and one that could only come from having been trained to do so. The queen spoke little of her life before she'd become a wife and a mother and a queen—all three of those titles were stacked in rapid succession. She afforded her children beautiful and ugly stories of warriors and knights and orphaned wanderers, but none of those stories had been of her own life. And now, truly, Wil began to understand that her mother was so much more than what she showed to even her own children.

The queen, with her pretty face and lace dresses, knew about all the light and shadows of the world. It was no wonder she was consumed by so many strange numerical compulsions, Wil thought. She needed to control whatever small thing she could—the placement of forks, the symmetry of paintings on the wall.

"But," Wil stammered, "she said—"

"I heard what she said," her mother interrupted. "It will be all right, but only if you go now."

Wil did as her mother said. Her mother rarely gave commands, and never in vain.

It wasn't until much later, after Wil had scrubbed the blood from her face and coat with seawater and she was on a ship bound east, that she thought of the old woman's words.

She would have the answer to her curse. The old woman had said that this knowledge would haunt Wil until she was dead, but didn't the old woman know that it already haunted her? Didn't she know it was already true that Wil would never be at peace with what she had done?

# TWELVE

FOR ONCE IN HER LIFE, Wil was seasick. She spent the first night of her journey sweating and vomiting belowdecks, burning with fever. Nothing would rid the taste of blood from her mouth.

Where had the old woman found blood? Had it been her own, from the wound Wil inflicted? Or had some poor forest animal made the mistake of crossing her path?

In her muddled state, Wil clung to the rough blankets and called out for Loom. She didn't know why exactly; she wasn't delirious enough to think that he would come for her now. But it soothed her the same way it made her restless, just like her mother's numerical compulsions. He wasn't here on this ship, but he was here in this world, and she would reach him soon.

When she'd reached the Port Capital and was faced with the decision of traveling west, to Wanderer Country, or east, to

Pahn's cabin, she'd chosen east.

When she finally found sleep, huddled on a pile of blankets in the cargo hold that had been fashioned into a bunk, the damp draft of the ship permeated her dreams.

She dreamed of Owen's chamber, only it was not familiar to her this way. The books lining the shelves did not belong to him. The chamber itself was large and mostly bare, conservatively furnished.

And she dreamed of her father.

Before King Hein Heidle was a husband or a father or a king, he had been a boy. At seventeen years old, he looked like Owen, the son he would one day have: tall and lean, with kind eyes and an easy smile.

He even slept in what would one day be Owen's room. For now, its shelves were stuffed with different books, sparse and absent of many trinkets. There was an easel proudly displaying a painting of the Port Capital skyline, and the floor stones were speckled with dry paint.

Hein Heidle, a prince not yet a king, sat at his desk sketching a girl. Her face was nothing but blank paper for now, but her hair was turning into something quite elegant.

A crash out in the hallway made him raise his head. Outside, the sky was dark and overcast with clouds, and the thunder growled out a warning. Something in another room fell and shattered.

"Hein?" a voice whispered, and the door creaked open.

The girl stood in the cold gray shadow of the hallway, her cheek warmed by the lantern on Hein's desk.

Hein rolled the paper and tucked it into his desk drawer. It was going to be her portrait, but it was too soon for her to see it. Her sixteenth birthday was still a month away.

"Papa again?" he asked.

She nodded. She didn't look frightened, but she did look unhappy.

The smell of spirits filled the dream like notes of a dismal song. It could be tasted as easily as breathed. The girl stepped into her brother's room and closed the door, sliding the iron bolt into place.

"What is he on about this time?" Hein asked.

"I don't know," the girl said. "But Mother is screaming right back at him."

Thunder shook the castle and all of the lights flashed and flickered, and then everything went dark.

The dreams turned tangled. Fragments of a smile. Bodies arching into a kiss before they tumbled to the sheets. Bare feet running through the oval garden, labored breathing. The smatter of blood on stone. A scream that made the stars go dull with sorrow.

Aleen.

In her dream, Wil heard the girl's name.

Aleen. It was Aleen's father's favorite word, because she was her father's very favorite thing. From the day that Aleen was born, her father doted on her. Her bassinet had dripped with crystals and ribbons. When she was a toddler, he carried her on his shoulders, showing her off to his loyal subjects, filling her head with promises. Her brother Hein would inherit the kingdom, but the world would all be hers.

Wil awoke, clutching a crystallized spider.

She rolled onto her back and held the thing close to her face to study it. It was of the larger, furrier variety—a spider she often plucked from sacks of grain and rice in the pantry. A stowaway spider, as they were commonly called, because they always seemed to find their way on cargo ships.

Its little fangs were bared as though it had been about to bite her. "Sorry," she told it, and tucked it into the pocket of her coat. The return of her power meant that she was out of cursed waters, at least. It had been a wretched night, but she felt better now. Her mind was clear, and the only pain she felt was a slight ache from a night spent on the cargo hold's floor.

Morning light stole in through the porthole. She wandered onto the deck and found a vendor selling day-old bread and hard cheese. She ate as she stood at the railing. Laid out before her was a perfect, clear blue. The water was calm, the winter sun beaming and unencumbered by clouds.

Everything since her return to Northern Arrod felt like a bizarre dream. The old woman, what had happened to Baren, what her mother had done. Addney, carrying the last living piece of Owen inside herself and fleeing with it into the night.

None of these were questions Wil could afford to resolve just yet. She had to tuck all of them away until she could return home. And she would return, she promised herself just then. She would not become what that old marveler woman had predicted. Even if she could never rid herself of this curse, even if she would have to live the rest of her days unable to embrace her family again, she would never allow those she loved to be destroyed. Not anymore. Not ever again.

Her thoughts returned to Addney, the girl in the portrait and in Wil's dreams. She had an aunt. Her father had a sister.

The entire dream had smelled of blood, and Wil knew that this was a parting gift from the marveler woman. But why had she wanted her to see these things?

Though Wil didn't have the answer for this, she was plagued by a lingering dread. Her father had kept his only sibling a secret, deliberately omitting any trace of her from the castle before his own children would come to fill it.

Whatever had happened to Aleen, it was surely awful.

The journey to the East took three days by boat. Wil did not dream of Aleen again until the last night of her journey.

In the dream, Aleen was thirteen years old, and she was pacing the hallway outside her father's chamber, worrying. When her father wasn't locked in his throne room and not to be disturbed, he wasn't in the castle at all. He left before dawn sometimes, and returned long after she'd fallen asleep waiting to hear the heavy sound of his boots striding down the hall.

He staggered about as though in a daze. Dizzy, appearing drunk. And when he was clumsy, he always seemed to break things that his wife loved. The porcelain urn containing her mother's ashes, or a painting of alber blossoms gifted to her by a loyal subject enchanted with her beauty.

Hein took over much of the running of the kingdom. He forged his father's signature when it was long overdue, and the guards all began bowing to his authority.

But Aleen—she often lingered outside her father's chamber, pleading for him to return to his senses. This was not the sort of man he was. While her brother had long given up on their father, she clung to the hope that he would be the man he had once been.

"Papa." She was wearing a brown dress, embroidered with pink and green tulips on swirling yellow vines. She leaned against the door frame. "Papa, you haven't eaten for days. Please come out."

Something stirred on the other side of the door. But it did not sound like a man. It was a sort of monster in the blackness of the darkest, most fearsome nightmare.

The knob slowly turned.

Wil awoke, grasping at empty air.

She felt impossibly alone, just her and a girl who filled her dreams but evaded her when she came too close to learning who she was.

The city of Grief in the Eastern Isles was on the horizon; if

Wil were to have looked to the porthole, she would have seen its carnival of electric lights and glowing wires and their shimmering reflections in the ink-black sea. But without having to look at all, she could sense it all. She felt Loom's presence like a breath to the back of her neck. Like his row of straight, smooth teeth taunting her skin with a smile, close as a kiss.

He was close. She had returned to him. She did not have all the answers Pahn demanded—not yet—but there was still time. It had not yet been a month.

She had believed that leaving Loom behind would give her the focus to understand her curse. His very presence confused her. His nearness made her own heart a stranger to her.

But distance had not given her clarity. Returning home had made her feel like a stranger meant to wear a dead girl's things. Even the word "home" no longer felt true. All the world felt like a desert, searing and hot and empty. Except for him. He was the place that made sense. Every ship she ever boarded would point in his direction.

She lay awake for the rest of the night, trying to sleep and finding it impossible. Aleen eluded her once more. She had not yet decided if she would tell Pahn what she had learned; it seemed too tenuous a thing to divulge until she understood how it related to her curse. She felt a strange loyalty to this girl. Though they had never met, they were blood, and Wil's father had loved her. That was more than she could be certain he had done for her.

She would tell Loom all of it the moment they were alone. It was his life that hung in the balance now, and she owed him that much.

By the time the ship arrived at the Eastern port, Wil had crystallized more than two dozen spiders and dropped them into the ocean, along with too many gnats and flies to count. It had been enough to maintain her strength, but as she exited the ship she was eyeing the trees hungrily. It made her feel less monstrous to compare this hunger to use her curse to something more human, such as unbuckling her boots in anticipation of scratching at an itchy heel.

Fortunately, there were plenty of trees between the city and Pahn's cabin. Once she had stepped into the thick of the woods, she crystallized a fistful of maple leaves, creating a bouquet of rubies and emeralds and diamonds, which she then tucked into her pockets. The city's electricity thrummed and throbbed, and she felt as though it were charging her as well. The smell of the sea and of things being cooked in the market all reached her with perfect clarity. The dying, bleeding girl she'd been back in Arrod was a stranger to her now.

Something rustled behind her and she froze, listening. Whatever it was, the sound had been faint. A breath. A step. She might have believed it was a forest creature if not for the sudden, strange feeling in her blood. Her heart felt heavy and sluggish. Something was trying to rend its way inside her mind to subdue her. The city—moments earlier loud and bright and alive—now sounded underwater.

Something reached for her arm and she twisted away, spinning on her heel. And there before her was Espel, flanked to her left by Masalee, her ever-loyal high guard.

Loom. The name burned through the haze that had suddenly, inexplicably worked to claim Wil's mind. His sister had come for him. To kill him for his crimes against his kingdom, or, worse, to throw him to their father's feet as a sacrifice. In a single moment she could vividly imagine his neck laid out on the guillotine, the rope being pulled.

Her heart should have been furious by then, but it would barely beat.

Loom. The name repeated itself inside of her over and over. Loom. Loom. She had to warn him. She had to get to him before it was too late.

She ran, ignoring the muffled shouts that came after her. Dodging branches, moving in erratic paths, she ran, even as her body protested. She felt as though she were falling asleep. Was this a dream? Would Aleen step out from behind an oak tree and show her a new vision of her fraught past?

A blade bit into her calf and she fell forward into the thin drifts of early snow. Arms wrapped around her own, hoisting her up.

"It needn't be this difficult," Espel said in Lavean.

Espel was on one side of her, Masalee on the other. They were fearless in handling her.

"What have you done to me?" Wil snarled. Her voice felt very far away.

Neither the princess of the Southern Isles nor her guard gave a response as they dragged her forward.

Wil had been accosted several times before, by market vendors twice her size, and she had always managed to free herself. She had the element of surprise; no one expected a small thing like her to put up much fight, or to manipulate gravity to her advantage. But here, now, she could not free herself from Espel and Masalee's hold. There was no element of surprise. They both knew exactly what she was.

By the time she had been dragged aboard the ship, Wil stopped struggling. It wasn't because she had given up, but rather because of what she saw awaiting her on deck. Loom stood flanked by guards, his wrists and ankles weighed down by iron shackles and chains. His eyes were a dark fire. Zay lay in a heap before him, unconscious, but by all appearances unharmed, save for the thin line of crusted blood at her forearm.

The scene told the story. Espel had come for her brother and anticipated his being able to escape, so she had rendered Zay helpless with one of her serum-laced daggers, ensuring his cooperation. He would risk his own life, but not Zay's. Never her.

Everyone had a vulnerability, and Espel knew how to find it.

Loom saw Wil and there was the slightest tension in his biceps, a rising tide in the sea of rage that already filled him.

But he was quiet, both of them waiting for the time to strike. It would come, shackles and all.

A new panic rose in Wil's chest, beside the place where her heart refused to beat harder. Where was Ada? Zay was never without her son.

She didn't dare ask. She didn't dare to draw attention to the most vulnerable among them. If Espel knew that Ada mattered to Wil in any capacity, it would only turn him into leverage.

Though Wil couldn't summon her adrenaline, Loom had plenty of his own. He was exhaling hard through his nostrils, sending white bursts into the frigid air.

Espel waved off her guards, and they stepped away from Loom. There were five of them in total, forming a half circle around them at a distance. Only Masalee remained, her hand ever at the hilt of one of her many blades.

Wil fought the persistent numbness of her limbs. She didn't betray her inexplicable weakness, and straightened her spine.

Pahn emerged from belowdecks, wearing thin olive-green linens, and unaffected by the cold.

"Ah, good, you've brought her," he said, as though Wil were an anticipated shipment of garden slugs. He regarded Wil with his arms spread out at either side. His smile was beaming. "I apologize for the ambush," he said, "but there's been a change of plans."

Wil felt at war with her body. Something tried to strangle her heart in a vise.

"Our deal is off," Pahn said. "It's come to my attention that you already belong to King Zinil."

"Belong?" she spat. "I don't belong to—"

"This is a time of war," Pahn said, "and you are a tool in that war. You presented yourself as a cursed girl, but you never told me that you also happened to be the princess of the Northern Isles."

The world went still around her. The air left her lungs. The sea stopped its shifting and turning. The howling winds went silent, and all she heard was Loom's soft voice. "Wil." His gaze had been on Pahn but now it was on her. Stunned and then desperate. *Tell them it isn't true,* that gaze said. Tell them it isn't true. Tell him that she didn't have the blood of his enemy inside her. Tell him he hadn't fallen in love with the girl whose family was destroying his kingdom.

She couldn't lie to him anymore. This was the truth, and it was the least that she owed him.

Loom was the one to look away first. He stared at Zay, the one true thing in his tragic world. Zay had hated Wil when she entered their lives, and it had not been jealousy. It had not been because Zay wanted Loom's affections for herself. It was because she had known that this strange, cursed passenger on their little ship would undo him somehow. She knew how purely and truly Loom offered up his love, and she knew even then that Wil did not deserve it.

Wil had known it too. That was why, when Loom offered

her his heart that night as they sat above the electric city, she had tried to give it back. She had tried not to let him love her, and she had tried not to love him back, but standing there with both their hearts raw and open and bleeding, she knew that she could not stop herself from loving him. In that way, too, she had failed him.

Somewhere far away, voices were talking, but Wil wasn't listening. One of Espel's guards snared her arm and pulled her toward the steps that led belowdecks. Wil staggered but didn't fight. It didn't matter where they were taking her. It didn't matter what they intended to do to her. Hang her by her ankles and try to bleed her curse from her veins, bottle it up for their own use. Lord her capture over King Baren, who would tell them to go right ahead and kill her for all he cared—spare him the trouble of doing it himself.

She would escape, one way or another. She would steal into the control room and break the captain's legs if she had to. She would dive into the open sea and swim for land. That was the least of her worries now.

As she was pulled down the stairs, she looked over her shoulder at Loom. He turned away.

# THIRTEEN

WIL HAD UNDERESTIMATED ESPEL. SHE had made the mistake of looking for herself in the Southern princess. They were both liars. They both knew how to prettily arrange their hair and paint their nails and dress brilliantly and smile. They both wore knives sheathed to their thighs beneath their ornate clothes. They were both only daughters of zealous kings.

Wil had expected Espel to be cruel. But she had not expected that cruelty to be equal to her own.

How had Espel known? Had she always known? Wil had been so careful. She had hidden herself so well that even she nearly forgot who she had once been, to whom she had once belonged. But the princess of Arrod would not die so easily. She still left pieces of herself to be found.

The rivalry between Espel and Loom had existed long

before Wil entered their lives, and it would exist long after she had left them. But in this battle, Espel had won. Loom would no longer want Wil. He would let them drain her powers dry, or kill her. He would let her escape. He would do nothing either way, because she was already dead to him.

Wil was shoved unceremoniously into a cabin and the door was locked behind her. This was not the same ship on which she had traveled with Loom all those weeks ago, but it was of the same Southern design. Ornately carved oak trimmed the windows, and on the bed were satin sheets with embroidered flowers in Lavean design, just like those on the clothes that hung in the closet—all of which belonged to Espel.

The cabin was smaller, though, and there was nothing but a bed and a tiny washroom with a standing shower barely wider than Wil's shoulders.

By nightfall, the ship was deep at sea. There was nothing to be seen through the porthole but blackness. Even the stars were buried. No one had come to Wil's cabin, not even to offer her food. She had nothing but time to sit, and fume, and plot her revenge. Loom would never forgive her, and she would learn to bear that burden. But he would become king, because tonight she was going to kill Espel.

In the washroom, a towel had been neatly folded and draped over the shower. The only other thing in the room was a glass dispenser filled with pale green soap.

Wil waited until it was well past midnight, when she was

certain the guards would be sleeping in shifts. It was a large ship, and Wil estimated that three of the guards would be patrolling it, as two others rested. To find Espel, Wil would have to look where those guards were not stationed; Masalee would be the one guarding the princess, and she would be the true challenge. Incapacitating the others first was key.

She wound the soap dispenser in a satin tunic to muffle the sound when she smashed it on the edge of the porcelain sink. She selected the largest shards, wrapping them in scraps of cloth to form makeshift hilts. She tied them to her wrists and around her waist, under the loose-fitting tunic she'd taken from the closet.

Next, she scraped handfuls of the green soap from the sink and ran the water, lathering it to a bubbling froth, which she smeared down the side of her mouth. It dripped against her skin, green and white and resembling a putrid sort of bile.

Then she screamed, a shrill, inhuman sound like an animal being slaughtered alive.

Footsteps pounded across the planks of the hallway. When a guard opened the door, he found Wil on the floor in convulsions, green froth coming from her mouth.

"Oh hells," he swore. He knelt at her side, and Wil could sense his hands hovering anxiously over her.

She went still as death. When he felt for her pulse, she struck, swiping his throat with a shard of glass.

It would be a fatal blow, she knew; Espel and Masalee

were the true challenge, and the fewer bodies she had working against her the better. There was no time to think beyond this.

She ran down the hall, summoning her memory of Loom's ship. If the layout was the same, then the control room would be to the left. She ran. Somewhere behind her, another guard had found the bloody mess in her cabin and was shouting.

An alarm wailed. The lights flickered, hot, bright white, then red. Chaos was good. Chaos could work to her advantage.

She spotted the captain at the end of the hall, swinging the door to the control room shut. She dropped her weight, sliding, extending her leg just in time for it to slam between the door and the threshold.

Subduing the captain was easy. He was no fighter. Wil had him on his back in an instant, her knees locked around his waist, hands pinning his wrists at either side of his head.

He stared up at her in bewilderment. The edge of the glass pressed against his wrist. In one sweep, she could end him. She needed to end him.

The last thing she should have done was look into his eyes. But she had done it, and now she saw that he was young, probably her own age. He was breathing hard, filled with adrenaline. If her heart were working, all this would be easy for once. This boy would be dead and she would not have to spill his blood. She could blame it on her curse, rather than on herself.

They stared at each other. His hands flopped helplessly under her grasp.

*Hells.* She was a coward.

When she shoved him into the utility closet and barricaded the door with his own chair, the captain did not put up a fight. He had seen the monster inside of Wil, and he seemed grateful enough that the human in her won out just long enough to spare him.

Lights flashing, sirens crying at a dizzying volume, she made her way down the hall again. Espel's cabin would be at the far end, near the staircase where it would be easiest to escape to the deck.

Would Espel be in her cabin, waiting for her assailant so that she could use the small space to her own advantage, or would she move to the deck and take her chances with her back to the open water?

All Wil could do was guess. She ran up the stairs. If Espel wasn't here yet, she would be soon.

Masalee was on her the instant Wil reached the deck, taking her down with a sweep across her ankles, pinning her wrists. Before Masalee was able to straddle her waist, though, Wil drew her knees up and landed a hard kick to her torso.

Masalee was off her and Wil wasted no time rolling out of the way of the punch being swung at her.

Her body should have been filled with adrenaline, but that peculiar sluggishness persisted. She could feel her curse buried in her blood, trying to break free.

She staggered to her feet. Something sharp cut the tendon

of her ankle and she screamed. The sound was stolen away by the sirens. She fell hard onto her back, hitting her head on the planks. There was a flash of white, then a weight on her chest. Masalee was on top of her, bits of loose hair spilling in rivers around her face as she leaned forward.

Bulbs lining the perimeter of the deck flickered and flared to life. The air was electric with marvelry. Masalee's eyes were bright with it, and in them Wil saw the little girl who had bested even the princess of the Southern Isles in a battle to the death. She saw why Masalee wore the silver robe of Espel's highest guard.

Masalee's lips were pressed tight, and Wil's heart drummed in response to their near-imperceptible straining.

It was her.

Masalee was the one controlling Wil's heart and subduing her power. Her face glimmered with sweat. Heavy drops of it fell onto Wil's cheeks and lips. Wil tried to draw up her knees and kick her away, but her muscles felt rubbery. Her lungs struggled to draw air. If Masalee had been controlling Wil's heart when she was nearby, it had been a fraction of what she could truly do, and now she held every muscle and vein under her command.

Wil clenched her jaw and met the high guard's stare.

"I knew that if I waited, you would give me a reason," Masalee rasped. Her cheeks were flushed. She was alight with power.

As though on a gust of wind, all the lights went out. The

sirens ceased. There was only the cold, unforgiving darkness of the sea.

Masalee was trying to slow Wil's heart further, to render her unconscious.

Wil fought it. She found the unwanted current in her blood and pushed against it. Teeth gritted, she strained and gasped. But she was a body drowning in a riptide. Any motion she made to save herself only used up oxygen and strength. She felt herself beginning to sink.

"That's enough." Espel's voice. And with that, Wil realized that Masalee had not been trying to subdue her. She had been killing her, squeezing her lungs and constricting her heart.

The pressure eased up just enough for Wil to draw in a gasp of air. She would not struggle, nor would she betray her frustration at being so easily controlled. She would not give Espel the satisfaction of having won.

Espel knelt beside her. The lights surrounding the deck flickered to a dim half-life, revealing the princess's soft, pretty features. Masalee was all fury.

"Let go of her," Espel told Masalee.

She had to say it twice more before Masalee seemed to hear. "Your Highness, I cannot. I will not leave you at the mercy of this—this thing."

"You will," Espel barked, her dulcet tone suddenly going low and sharp. "Or you will swim the rest of the way home."

Masalee pressed hard into Wil's wrists, her jaw tight, none

of her rage at all quelled. And then she let go and stood, grabbing her bloody sword and wiping it clean on her robe before sheathing it.

Wil didn't dare move; now was not the time to attempt another attack. She had just destroyed any chance of earning Espel's trust in the hopes that she could kill her. It had backfired horribly, and she would need to formulate a better plan.

Espel and Masalee had a conversation in glances. It was a language only they spoke, and with a look of absolute disdain, Masalee dropped to her knees and began unrolling the fabric at Wil's ankle.

Wil felt her skin fusing back together at Masalee's light touch, the torn veins and tendons reconnecting. There was pain and then the tingling relief of fresh skin.

"There," Espel said. Her voice was sweet again. It was eerie, Wil thought, how sincere Espel sounded. Not at all taunting. She held out a hand, and Wil took it.

Growing up in a castle of brothers, Wil was used to being the smallest person in a room. But Espel was smaller. She was short and solid with muscle. Silver tattoos gleamed against her skin, the lines appearing in glimpses as she moved against the ship's light.

This was the reclusive only princess of the Southern Isles. One of the world's few mysteries. In certain slants of light, she was a mirror image of her brother: the same heavy lashes, soft lips, round cheeks. But then she shifted just slightly and became a creature all her own, belonging to no one, having emerged into this world from some hidden springs from which no other living thing would be strong enough to survive. Her own mother hadn't been strong enough.

"Find whatever guards are still living and tell them to bring me the collateral," Espel told Masalee.

Masalee understood whatever this meant and she was gone in a swish of her silver robe. Even in her absence, Masalee protected Espel. The vise around Wil's heart tightened.

Wil's stomach clenched. She felt nauseous and dizzy from the strange current subduing her heart. Even as Masalee left her presence, it persisted. Wil had known Masalee was a marveler since the night she'd healed Zay's torn skin. But she had not known she was so adept at hiding the full force of her strength.

Espel and her guard had that in common, Wil supposed.

A cry pierced the air. It was loud, and somehow more shrill than the alarms had been. Wil's breath hitched. She knew that inconsolable cry, had listened to it nearly every night she'd spent on Loom's ship.

A guard emerged from the staircase, holding Ada unceremoniously under his arm like a sack of grain. Even in the dim, Wil could see how red Ada's face was, shiny with tears. He was crying for his mother, who was being dragged up the stairs by Masalee, just out of the reach of his flailing, open hands.

Zay watched her son, her mouth pressed tightly shut, her chest heaving. It was a silent, palpable rage. There was a dagger to her throat keeping her in place, but it appeared that her heart, too, was in a vise.

Wil betrayed nothing. She was trying to summon her heart to beat faster through her sluggish blood. She wanted to kill Espel; she wanted the last of her blood to leak out between fragments of crystal. She wanted to kill every guard on this ship.

The silent man held Ada under the arms and hoisted him over the water, as if to throw him in.

Zay turned into something wild. Somehow she had managed to throw the dagger from Masalee's hands, and now she struggled, willing to tear her arms away from her body to free herself from Masalee's grasp.

Ada was whimpering in Lavean and reaching for his mother. He couldn't understand why she wouldn't come for him.

This was a negotiation tactic. Wil knew this.

But no terms came. Espel gave the command with a curt nod, and the guard threw Ada overboard.

Wil heard his body hit the sea. The water was black and frigid, and it swallowed him immediately.

Zay screamed. And then she came undone, crying out words that Wil did not allow herself to listen to. Ada was the only thing in the world that could break her, and Espel knew that. But Espel did not know how to break Wil, and Wil would never show her.

"My father will meet with you," Espel told Wil, raising her voice to be heard over Zay's hysterics. "And you will make the journey without killing any more of my guards."

In the time it had taken for Ada to fall, Wil thought of her brothers and of her parents and of Arrod itself. She thought of Addney, and the child in her womb who would rule over all of it. Cooperating with King Zinil would give him the power to destroy them, just as easily as a boy in a hungry sea.

She would never betray her family. But Espel was not the only one who knew how to deceive, and so when Espel said "Do we have an understanding?" Wil said "Yes."

Espel's expression didn't change. She nodded to the guard holding Zay, and he let her go. Zay charged for the railing and bounded over it in a blur.

Wil held her breath until she heard the splash of bodies surfacing in the water, and Ada's cries once again filled the night, loud enough to stir all the souls in the Ancient Sea.

She didn't let her relief show. She wouldn't give Espel that.

"We don't have to be enemies," Espel said, taking Wil's hands in both of hers. The gesture was a cruel mockery of friendship. "We can be allies. You're more powerful than you know, Wil Heidle. We can save the world."

At that, Wil felt hope for the first time since her capture. She would never have Espel's trust, but she had something more valuable. She had her respect.

# FOURTEEN

THE DREAM BEGAN IN WIL'S chamber. Only it was not her chamber. Rather than white lace, the canopy was wrapped by little stars cut from bits of metal, strung together with twine. The entire room was pretty in that way: lacking frills, but displaying a talent for turning broken things into beautiful ones. There was a model of a windmill on the wall where Wil's grandfather clock would one day stand. Its rusted blades were painted a light blue, and they turned, moaning a song as a night breeze came through the open window.

Aleen knelt beside the bed, easing a loose stone from the wall. Once it had come away, she folded the portrait of herself and hid it under the stone.

She wasn't only hiding the portrait from her parents, but also from Hein himself, who had a tendency to create beautiful things, later decide they were not beautiful, and destroy them.

All she had wanted from him for her sixteenth birthday was a portrait. A forbidden likeness of herself. She often coveted the portraits drawn by artists in the Port Capital and wondered what it would be like to see her own face sketched from nothing but charcoal and paper. Her brother had done a beautiful job, and she hated to hide the drawing, but it would never survive otherwise.

Down the hall, something crashed, hard. The windmill creaked again, as though in warning.

The world broke into a riot of shards. Fragments of screams through darkness between trees.

Wil saw the silhouette of a woman moving into the arms of a man. She heard their eager lovemaking while her vision swam with bits of sunlight reflected from a metal wind chime in a window. She heard a heartbeat drumming in a womb.

And then she saw Aleen standing in her blue nightgown in the grass beneath the moon. She was beyond the castle walls, and something lurked in the dark forest ahead of her. The same something that had lurked behind the door in last night's dream. Aleen should have run, but she didn't seem to know this. She took one step toward the darkness, and above her, the moon disappeared.

Wil came awake, once again tasting the blood the old woman had thrown at her.

Her heart was pounding.

She sat up with a hand to her chest. Adrenaline surged through her, hot and wild and familiar. There was a tray beside her door. Wil crawled to it and lifted the silver cover. There was a luxurious Lavean breakfast of rice and pheasant, drizzled with jasmine. Beside that, a crystal tureen filled with wildflowers whose roots still clung to them. Masalee must have deduced that controlling Wil's curse for too long was detrimental to Wil's strength, and for whatever purpose, Espel wanted Wil to remain strong.

The flowers crystallized in bursts of emerald and ruby, and just enough gold to betray her thoughts of Loom. Creating gold did not hurt as it once had, which Wil found to be a cruel sort of irony, because loving him felt more painful than ever.

Still, she refused to let that love render her useless. She ate her entire meal, showered, and dressed in a pair of gold satin trousers and a matching tunic. And then she sat on the bed and plotted the possible ways to murder the Southern king and his daughter.

All the plans fell apart, thwarted by some consideration or other. Once her anger had subsided, she realized that it was not her right to kill them. It was not her battle to fight. That honor belonged to Loom.

Loom, who was trapped somewhere on this ship, hating her. She couldn't feel his nearness; he had hidden himself from her. Killed her off in his cursed heart.

It was for the best, she told herself. This lie they'd shared for all these weeks could never have lasted. Even their love itself had been a lie, an illusion of their curses. Wil knew that in her mind, and one day, if she worked hard enough, she would know it in her heart as well.

She did not owe Loom her heart anyway. She owed him her alliance, and nothing would change that. She would make sure that once he had claimed the throne, the North and the South became allies and this war came to an end. In that way, he would always have her.

There was plenty of time to plot and to scheme and to rebuke the idea of love. No one came to Wil's cabin for hours. Sometimes she thought she could hear Ada crying. Not the keening wail of peril, but the discontented mewling of a child who only wanted his mother.

This, too, was Wil's fault.

It surprised her to realize that the thought of Zay's certain and justifiable hatred toward her brought its own pain. By now, Zay was surely just as lost to her as Loom was.

The door to her cabin opened, mercifully pulling her out of her thoughts. Her heart began to slow, and when she looked up, there was Espel in the doorway, bearing a tray in her hands and a leather satchel over her shoulder.

Espel closed the door behind her, entombing them both in the small space. But Masalee was nearby. Wil could sense her.

Espel deposited the leather satchel on the bed beside Wil. "I wanted to return some of the things you left behind at the palace."

Wil lifted the flap. Waiting inside were her guns and dagger and sheaths and her steel gloves, all bunched together. The data goggles rested atop everything like eyes staring up at her, welcoming her back into her world of familiar things.

She was glad to see them, though they felt like relics from another lifetime now.

Espel nodded to the data goggles. "Do you know how those work?"

"They're powered by sunlight," Wil said.

"Sunlight, yes," Espel said. "But in order for the data to be correct, it's updated constantly. There are checkpoints all over the world, in the posts that generate electricity. The data refreshes itself and leaves a history of all the places you've been. It stores the things you've looked at and read about."

Owen had told her this, Wil remembered.

"My brother has told you how soulless I am, I'm sure," Espel said. Loom had never called Espel soulless, but Espel had labored to present herself that way. "But did he ever tell you how much I love electrical things?" Espel went on. "Telephones and lanterns. I love taking things apart and finding what makes them work." She nodded toward the goggles. "I took those apart, too. It was like climbing behind your eyes and looking at all the things you'd seen. I couldn't see images, of course, but I could read the data."

Wil gripped the leather strap of her goggles, but she didn't know why. Espel wasn't going to steal them. She'd already gotten whatever she'd wanted from them.

"In the data I saw fascinating things, Wil. I saw flowers

that grow wild and still bloom in the Northern winters. A trove of illegal powders and potions. I saw the royal garden tended by the Northern queen. Heidle family documents. Documents signed by the king."

So many of those things had belonged to Owen. They had been his goggles, before she took them the way that she had always taken things from him. And he should have been the one standing here now, defending his kingdom. Protecting its secrets. But it was only her.

"That's how you found out about me," Wil said. She was numb to it now. She had been so careful to hide her past, but it hadn't been enough.

"From the first time I laid eyes on you, I saw a girl made of secrets," Espel said. "Even now, I'm sure I don't know the half of them."

She didn't know about Addney. Wil took some comfort in that, at least. Wil had spent all day calculating her moves. Fighting Espel with brute strength hadn't worked. Earning her friendship may well have been impossible. And trust? Espel was far too smart for that. But Wil had her respect. And with her identity as the Northern princess revealed, she could create some measure of solidarity.

"What's going to happen to Loom once we reach the Southern Isles?" Wil said, careful to keep her tone dispassionate. No emotion, only logic. "He can't set foot in the palace without dying."

Espel considered this, and then she sat on the bed beside

her. She smoothed the wrinkles in her silk trousers. "Why does my brother matter to you?"

She hadn't called him "the Traitor"; she'd called him her brother.

It was as unexpected as anything else Espel had done on this voyage. Wil suspected Espel was altering her language to manipulate her. Humanize Loom and establish trust with her hostage.

"I don't understand," Wil said. It was the truth.

"You went to such lengths to conceal your identity from him, and yet you were his ally," Espel said. "Why? Why offer any sort of help to your enemy? Were you spying on behalf of your king?"

"No," Wil said. Her time spent with Loom had been the opposite of spying, she realized. "I helped him because he loves his kingdom as much as I love mine."

"He's a coward, you know," Espel said. "He tried to murder our father as he slept. He wanted the kingdom all for himself."

Wil shook her head. "He doesn't want anything for himself. He didn't want to steal your kingdom. He wanted to protect it." This was not a betrayal of Loom's trust. These were not things he had whispered into her open mouth between kisses. These were simple truths that anyone who spent a moment in Loom's presence would see. How big was the mountain palace in which Espel had grown up alongside her brother and never come to know him at all?

Espel laughed. She had meant for it to sound haughty, but

there was an uncertain waver to it.

"He may not know the best way, but he always tries to protect what he loves. I wasn't there the night that he tried to kill your father, but I know he did it to save Cannolay. He did it to save you."

Espel rushed to her feet, and for a moment Wil thought she would draw a dagger and kill her. Fury burned in her dark eyes. The outline of her tensed jaw jutted through her soft face.

"That's a lie," she snarled. "If he had succeeded in killing our father, I would have been next."

"No," Wil said. She recalled the knife Loom had thrown at Espel on the morning of Zay's near-execution. He could have killed his sister, but he'd only aimed to incapacitate her. "Whatever you might do to him, he would never kill you."

"You don't know—"

"I do know," Wil interrupted. "That day we fled the palace, he was on the roof. You were right there, defenseless. He could have thrown a blade and killed you, but he aimed for your leg to stop you from chasing us instead."

Espel's breaths were rapid, nostrils flaring. She looked so much like her brother, even in the littlest gestures. The tense shoulders, the way her mouth opened and closed because she was too enraged to form words. Her lovely, dark eyes that were now staring at Wil the way Loom had stared at her, as though every hope in the world depended upon what she would say next.

"It does not have to be this way." Wil's voice was quiet,

careful and slow. "You could have his loyalty anytime you might decide to take it."

"Enough." Espel's voice boomed. "You've spent a few weeks with the Traitor, and from that you think you know him better than I do. He was using you; that was all. Using others is all he ever does, because he's weak."

"And now you're using me," Wil said. "Bringing me to your father against my will so that he can force my hand. Do you really believe this will be more effective than what Loom and I were trying to do? Do you believe that my family will want an alliance with a king who holds me hostage?" She stood, venturing a step closer to Espel, whose anger was thrumming like a marveler's energy. "Loom broke away from your father. If he's the weak one, why can't you do the same?"

Wil thought Espel would murder her right there. She could have done it. She was armed, and every guard on this ship would come running if she called.

"I'm bringing you to my father not because he commanded me to, but because I want our kingdoms to come to a truce," Espel said, her diplomatic tone eerie and edged. "If you refuse to cooperate, I can't control what my father does to you."

Espel searched Wil's eyes, looking for some modicum of fear. She would find none.

"You can't control anything at all," Wil said.

# FIFTEEN

"Papa?" Aleen's voice was soft. She walked the hallway with bare feet, coming to a stop at her father's chamber door. She tried the knob, though she knew it would be locked.

Her heart was pounding in her ears.

The door opened, and there the king stood, looking haggard and pale. He had dark eyes, much like Aleen, but even so, their features weren't very similar. Where Aleen's eyes were wide and soft and curious, his were sunken and dull. Where Aleen's hair glinted with strands of chestnut and amber, his was blond and unruly.

"Papa?" she said. "I heard a crash."

He slid between the door and the frame, pulling the door shut behind him before Aleen could see into the chamber. He had grown thin in the past two years, and, it seemed, a decade older.

"Aleen." He cupped her cheek, and for a moment he looked at her the way he had when she was a child, when she was the thing that set the universe right. "You must think I'd forgotten your birthday, but I was preparing something special."

Aleen stood still, watching him. She could not reconcile this man, half stranger and half father. Despite his inexplicable absence from her life in recent years, she still remembered him as a kind man, a good one. And here she saw traces of that man in his words and face. But there was so much that she didn't recognize.

"What is it?" she asked, not letting her wariness show.

"Something I've meant to give you for a while now. Follow me. Be quiet. Your mother is sleeping."

Aleen followed him through the castle, not bothering with shoes, or to cover her nightgown. It was August now, and the air was heavy and humid.

When her father led her outside, she began to wonder at what sort of gift he wanted to give her. She had been asking for her own ship. Hein had one, complete with a crew at his disposal. Sometimes she tagged along on his journeys, but she might have liked to go off on her own, and had been saying this for years.

The night was balmy. Things chirped lazily in the grass, and the earth was soft against her feet.

Her father led her between the trees, so far into the woods that she could hear the river, which meant they were close to the Port Capital.

Here he stopped, in a clearing where the moon showed her his face. He was smiling, but his eyes were sad. They were always sad these days.

"Listen," he said in a hushed voice. Nearby, the clock tower was chiming its midnight song. "Three years ago, on this day, your mother confessed something to me. Do you know what it was?"

"No, Papa." Unease stirred in Aleen's stomach. She had been in these woods hundreds of times, but now they seemed strange like her father seemed strange, as though they were all in on a secret and she was not.

"She confessed that you do not belong to me," he said.

The words made no sense to Aleen. "Papa, of course I do."

"No." His voice was eerily calm—like all else about this night, strange. "Your real father is one of the castle guards. One of *my* guards."

Aleen stumbled a step back. For a moment the dream swam with images of the queen's laughing mouth pressing to that of a man. Shadows moving against a stone wall. Quiet conspiratorial laughter.

"That isn't true," Aleen breathed. "Mother loves you. She wouldn't."

"I could forgive anything," her father said. "Anything, except being told that you are not my daughter."

"But I am your daughter," Aleen cried. "Papa, I don't care who Mother had an affair with. I don't want to know. I don't want anything from him."

At the sight of her tears, her father softened. She threw herself forward and her arms wrapped around him.

It was as though no years had passed at all, the king thought. Aleen was still a child. She still adored him. It was not her fault. It was the queen who had done this. The queen with her weak, selfish heart.

He did not hold her. He didn't dare. All of his plans would be ruined if he allowed himself to love his daughter, who was not, it turned out, anything to him at all.

Instead, he said the words that he had been practicing over and over for the past three years. The words that would set things into motion.

"You are the thing that I love most in this world."

With that, he pulled his dagger from its sheath and drove it through Aleen's heart.

The dream turned frantic, like every color of ink dropped into still waters, spreading rapidly in all directions, tumbling into each other as they went.

The king, heartbroken and vengeful, seeking out a marveler who would teach him dark arts. The dagger he would have to forge himself from stone and steel. The nights he paced and plotted, and fell sobbing into bed. And the moment he finally worked up the courage, when Aleen came to his chamber door.

It took the king a moment to realize that, of the two of them, Aleen was not the one who had screamed. She only looked at him, her eyes never leaving his even as her legs gave way and he caught her in his arms.

It was a quiet death, and a slow one. Aleen seemed to be fighting it. Her lungs tried to find air even as they filled with blood. Her mouth moved as if to speak. Her eyes blinked even as they turned cloudy. He laid her on the grass, shushing her and touching his knuckles against her cheek.

He sat with her even after she was gone. And all he could think to say in his daze were the last words she had ever heard. "You are the thing that I love most in this world."

By sunrise, Aleen had long since stopped bleeding. Her skin had gone white, her body rigid and cold. All night, the king had been waiting for the daylight to come so that he could have a better look at her, at this girl whose existence had broken him.

But he didn't find what he was looking for. He didn't find traces of another man's face in her features. He didn't see a thing that had been conceived in a frenzy of lust and deception. He didn't see his wife's confession.

Rather, he saw his daughter. Only his daughter.

His chest began to heave. His body felt hot. Some new clarity entered him and he tried to combat it with whatever it was that had driven him to do this. Suddenly he couldn't remember. He began to panic.

It took him a long time to numb himself enough to lift her from the dirt. Blades of grass clung to her hair, and instinctively he brushed them away. He supported her stiff neck in the crook of his arm.

It was easier if he didn't look at her, and so he didn't. By the time he made it back to the castle, he had replayed everything the marveler had told him. He remembered everything he planned to say.

Guards rushed toward him as he approached the gate, and that's when he remembered that the dagger was still in Aleen's chest, and that, from a distance, she looked as though she could still be saved.

He clutched her tighter, unwilling to relinquish her to any of the guards. This was not for them. This was for his queen.

"Get my wife," he told them, but a moment later he saw that there was no need. The queen was running down the stone steps, her long, light hair flying all around her. The king could see what his wife's intentions had been when she awoke that morning. She had expected a pretty day filled with pretty things, as all her days had been. She wore a yellow dress with blue embroidered tulips across the skirt and ruby hearts at the chest. Her hair was brushed and curled and shining in the sun. Her lips were pink, her brown eyes painted in a way that softened her entire face.

The king presented Aleen to her as though he were offering up a gift.

The scream that she let out was unlike anything in the world. Inhuman. He wasn't sure which of them fell to their knees first, but suddenly they were both in the dirt, Aleen cradled in their arms between them, just as she had been when she was born.

The queen was trying to speak through her hysteria, but the king didn't listen to any of it.

"Look at me," he said, and she did. "Her blood was the only way to pay the price. As long as the Heidle name rules this kingdom, it will be cursed."

Sobbing, the queen shook her head. Her voice was strangled and faint. "You did this?"

"From now on," the king said, "any queen who loves someone more than her king will be cursed, and the one she loves most in this world will be the one who destroys her."

Nobody saw Hein, who had come running out to the gate when he heard his mother screaming. Nobody saw his little sister's body reflected in his eyes.

Wil awoke, stumbling out of bed before she'd even come to her senses. Her chest hurt, as though the blade that cut through Aleen had torn through her as well. She was so certain that her own chest would be bleeding that she pried her tunic away from her perspired skin and inspected the mark on her chest. But it was unchanged.

For the first time in her life, there, alone on a restless sea, Wil began to understand her father. She understood why he could never stand to look at her. Her father knew about the curse upon his family, and when Wil was born, plainly bearing the mark of that curse, he had known immediately what she was.

It was why he'd thought about killing her. He confessed that he'd entertained the idea on the night he exiled her.

Wil wondered what stopped him. She wondered if he had ever carried her to the bathtub when she was a wriggling little infant, intending to slip her under the water. It would have been a silent and easy way to do it. She had been helpless and at his mercy hundreds of times, and still he hadn't brought himself to spare his wife and his other children her curse. Perhaps that was his own curse.

Or maybe, she thought—shivering in her bunk as she curled up, alone—he had loved her.

Everything ached. She tasted blood. And she knew that they had approached Southern waters because, even in the dead of night, it was sticky and hot.

Somewhere in the depths of the ship, Ada was crying. No one came to soothe him, and Wil feared that he would be fed to the sea again just for the crime of interrupting Espel's sleep. She feared that Zay would hurt herself trying to break free from her own prison to reach him. She feared, selfishly, bitterly, that Loom was blaming her for all this and hating her more with each crescendo of Ada's mournful wails.

Everything was broken. No. Not broken. Cursed.

She closed her eyes, and there was Aleen, dead and ruined.

Wil had known that Aleen surely must have been dead, and that whatever happened to her would be awful—why else would her father have kept her hidden from their lives? Now she knew. The king had done far worse than just murder Aleen—he had turned her into a weapon, sharp and true enough to slice through the heart of everyone else who made the mistake of being born a Heidle.

# SIXTEEN

You're wind. You're everywhere.

Owen's words gave her strength even now, in a place where wind had not touched her face for nearly a week.

Cannolay shone like a beacon on the horizon. The mountain palace itself could have been crystallized, the way the sunlight hit all of its sharp angles and windows.

Wil watched it drawing nearer through the porthole of her small quarters. It had been two days of solitude. Espel had not come to speak with her again.

Wil felt the heat of the sun beating through the porthole. Land of Eternal Summer, even when the entire North was frozen.

The air smelled sweet, almost sugary, which Zay once told Wil came from the saybells—cascading white and lilac flowers with red stamens, which grew by wrapping their vines around the trunks of slender trees. All the palace gardens had them, and the sea breeze carried their scent all the way out to the boat now. They served no medicinal purpose, but Loom and Espel's mother, the queen, had favored them. She planted them along the trees where she used to sit and read, before giving birth to Espel killed her.

The saybells served as markers of some distant memory, Wil thought. Footsteps of a woman whose own children had never known her.

When Loom had lain in a cabin dying of his curse, Zay told Wil little stories like this to pass the time when they were alone. She knew quite a lot about her late queen, but she didn't mention her around Loom. He had never asked, and it seemed easier for him that way. Best not to mourn a woman he would never know.

Neither Espel nor Loom had ever acknowledged the saybells. Perhaps they didn't even know the story behind them. Espel and Loom had not been raised on stories; they were not given memories of their mother to collect in their pockets like buttons or shells. But the servants had adored Zay when she was a child and told her the history of the palace and all its souls, and she kept them tucked safely inside of herself— someone else's memories, someone else's stories—because she understood when something was precious, even if it did not belong to her.

When the door to Wil's bunk opened for the first time since she'd entered it, Masalee was standing on its threshold. Her jaw was tense and something burned in her eyes. Contempt or suspicion, Wil couldn't decide which.

Masalee was flanked on either side by two of Espel's guards. Espel herself was nowhere in sight, which was unusual; in the palace, one of them was never seen without the other. Something else was different about Masalee as well, or perhaps it was just that Wil had never been granted an opportunity to really study her. Proficient in battle as Masalee was, she couldn't have been more than seventeen years old. She was tall, corded with slender, solid muscle. Despite the youthfulness of her face, she had the stare of a soldier who had lived a hundred lives; it was the same look that had been in Owen's eyes, as admirable as it was devastating.

Today, though, she seemed weary. Even pallid. Her black hair had lost some of its sheen, and sweat beaded her brow.

Wil pretended to take no note of this. Her heart was especially sluggish today, and now at last she saw that she was not the only one affected by Masalee's skill. Masalee herself was making herself ill trying to maintain this hold over her.

Saying nothing, Masalee stepped to the side, clearing a path for the guards to shackle Wil's wrists and her ankles. The men pulled her to her feet and prodded her forward. Wil shuffled down the hall and onto the deck, chains clinking.

Masalee was two paces behind, her silver guard's robe

sighing around her as though in indignation.

They had not arrived at Cannolay's main port, but at the castle itself, in an area that was blocked from view by a high channel carved directly out of the mountainside.

From where she stood on deck, Wil could smell the water where the sun warmed it. It was so blue, candied and shimmering. She felt, for a breath, that Owen was standing beside her, whispering something she couldn't quite make out.

Espel was ahead of her, facing the palace as they docked.

More shuffling. Wil felt Loom's presence, as ever. She heard the rattling of his chains. Guards hauled him to stand beside Wil, and she turned her head to look at him.

He stood rigid, jaw set defiantly. But Wil saw how dark his eyes were, how sunken and beady with exhaustion. She could smell the salt of his sweat, hear the rattle of his breaths. He did a good job concealing his weakness, but Wil saw it just the same. The closer they drew to the castle on the horizon, the more his curse strengthened. Already there was a rash of fever across his cheeks and nose.

Wil was worried that his precarious state was something Espel had anticipated. Espel knew that her brother wouldn't be able to survive entering the castle. He'd be dead long before he could be locked in any of its dungeons, surely. Was that part of her plan? Was Loom thinking about any of this? Did he know how worried she was for him just now?

The tether between her cursed heart and Loom's had not

frayed at all in their time spent apart. Their hearts did not care which of them belonged to which kingdom. Their hearts did not care that Loom was furious with her, or that she deserved every drop of his ire. Their hearts did not care. They reached for each other just the same.

She wanted him to look at her. Begged him with her thoughts. But he didn't afford her so much as a glance.

That was it, then. He had declared her dead to him forever. This enemy princess. This liar.

*Tell me something true.* That was what he had said to her before he kissed her. What would have happened if she had told him the truth then? Would he have sent her away? Would she have gone? Perhaps then neither of them would be standing here before King Zinil, whose broad shadow spread out behind him like a corpse.

King Zinil had boarded the ship and come to assess the prisoners his dutiful favorite child had brought him.

Espel's eyes went to Masalee just for a beat before they moved to Wil.

Espel was one who existed to survive. Wil had seen Espel command her own army of guards using fear, and she had seen her feign compassion. She knew that this was a girl who had fought for her life and won, leaving bodies in her wake when she was just a child. And though Espel now stood regal in gold satin whose bright embellishments sharpened her beauty, Wil knew survival when she saw it.

The king stood beside his daughter as though he alone was

to credit for creating her. His pride was its own presence, filling up the entire kingdom, and everyone could feel it.

Wil's pulse was thready. King Zinil walked for her in broad, heavy strides that echoed into the open air. He grabbed her chin, jerking her face upward so hard that Wil thought he might break her neck.

Loom tensed beside her. He had never been so silent. So impossible to read.

"We'll see if you're worth the trouble," King Zinil told her. Wil met his stare with coldness. She would let none of her terror show. Fighting this man now would mean certain death. The chains weren't what stopped her. She could use them to her advantage; they were long enough that she could pin his arm behind his back and then use the chains to garrote him before he threw her off. But they were surrounded by guards. Guards who could shoot her, impale her with blades, or throw her into the sea to drown. Or worse. Espel could poison her with sleep serum, and when Wil awoke, she would be chained to a dungeon wall as Masalee manipulated her heart to the king's advantage.

The king let go of Wil, and she could feel the imprint of his grip still clinging to her bones. "Everyone leave us. Send for my high guard to fetch the prisoner," King Zinil barked to the guards standing behind him.

All the guards made their exit, even the ones who had been flanking Wil. Only Masalee was left standing beside Espel, who raised her chin.

Wil recognized the high guard who boarded the ship next.

He was wearing a silver robe, like Masalee's, which denoted him as being the king's highest guard: Zay's father, the man who held his own daughter's neck under a guillotine.

This time, he was carrying a different prisoner, pulling him by the arm so that the man skidded to a halt before the king. Immediately the man dropped to his knees and fell forward into a bow. "Your Majesty, I—"

"Can't you keep your prisoner silent?" the king snapped at his guard. His gaze fixed on Wil. "This man was peddling stomach tonic in the port. It contained mercar. Do you know what that is?"

Mercar was a fine red powder that her brother often used to create an adhesive for metals. When boiled in water, it created a rich purple ideal for dyeing fabrics. If this man was putting mercar in his tonics, it was likely in small doses to give them a rich color.

But Wil said none of this. Mercar was not fit for consumption and had no place in medicine, and there was no reason a wanderer with no alchemy experience should know what it was. She shook her head.

"In large enough quantities, it's poison," King Zinil said. "He sold this tonic to one of my guards and the man was dead that same night."

"It couldn't have been my tonic," the man cried, pressing his forehead to the floor. "Please, Your Majesty—"

The king's guard jammed the hilt of his sword into the

man's kidney. The man gritted his teeth and fell silent.

"Step forward," the king told Wil.

She did as he commanded, her chains dragging on the floor between her bare feet. Her heart began to kick up a faster rhythm, independent of the rest of her body, as though it were a puppet being drawn on its strings. Masalee.

The guard pulled the prisoner to his feet, and the man stared at Wil. He was nearly two heads taller than she was, and twice as old. At a glance she was nothing that should have been able to harm him—just a girl, whose hands and ankles were chained, no less. But Wil knew that look he gave her. It was the same one Baren had been giving her all her life. It was the look of one who could see past even her best impression of innocence. It was the look of one who could see the monster she truly was.

She felt as though her skin had been removed and there was her heart in plain sight, black and putrid, pumping her cursed blood into motion.

"Take his hand," the king ordered her.

She thought of Loom and Zay, who would surely pay the price for her small acts of defiance. There would be bigger battles to wage. This king would not have what he wanted from her, but if he had small victories, he would not see it coming when she struck. And she would strike. If she had to learn every thought in his head and every inch of his palace and every scrap of gossip from every servant in his charge, she would strike.

But it would come at a cost, and this man was nothing to her. Wil had to remind herself of that. It was either this man's life, or the lives of everyone she loved.

She reached out and took the man's hand in both of hers. He was trembling.

Her heart's strange, forced rhythm persisted. The sun brightened in her vision. Wil could smell whatever sweet fragrance Espel had used to bathe that morning, and the sweat from the heavy Southern heat in Espel's hair and Loom's labored breathing. She thought he whispered something then. Something she couldn't hear over the rush of blood in her ears.

The man cried out in pain as his hand began to harden. It was crystal, and it spread from his fingertips to his palm. By the time it had begun to reach his wrist, Wil felt her pulse going sluggish again. Blood dripped from the spot where crystal met flesh, pooling between her fingers.

"That will be enough," the king said, and Wil allowed the man to jerk his hand out of her grasp. She saw all the tendons and muscles inside of his palm, the spider cracks of arteries.

The king drew his dagger, and in a single motion, the crystal hand was severed and lying at Wil's feet. Espel's eyes went dark with the sound of the man's scream. Her posture was rigid, and her mouth quirked.

Wil did not let herself react. With her eyes fixed on the man writhing in pain, she thought of Owen. She thought of the king he would have been, and of his child, who still had a chance. All that was more important than this man, she told herself. This man who could save no one, not even himself.

With a nod, King Zinil summoned two of his guards to haul the man away. He was still holding the severed hand.

Beside her, Loom stood with his head hung low. Thick, perspired waves of black hair curtained his face. Wil wished that he would look at her. She wished that he would show her his eyes again. If he did, it would give her the strength to endure whatever awaited her in that glittering palace. It was foolish to hope that a mere glance would fix all that had gone wrong between them, but still, she wanted the chance to try.

"Bring her to the dungeon," King Zinil said. Wil went rigid when guards grabbed her at either arm. Her mind, in contrast to her heart, went frantic. *Think,* she commanded herself. She was too outnumbered to fight, surrounded as she was with weapons, and still shackled. But somehow she knew that if she entered that palace, she would never be free of it. She would never be without chains.

Loom struck out with a cry, hooking the king's ankles with a sweep of his leg, knocking him to the ground. Guards charged forward. Blades glimmered in the burning-white sun. Wil dodged an arm meant to snare her neck, jabbed her elbow into a guard who tried to coil an arm around her waist. Without the ability to move her legs freely, she misjudged a step and a guard slammed her to the deck, hard. She landed on her stomach, groaning, struggling to breathe.

Several feet away, Loom had also been taken down. He was on his back, and it was Espel who stood over him, a foot pinning his chest and a blade in her hand.

It was not one of Espel's usual blades. It was black, glimmering with bits of metal. Zay's jeweler's knife—the one she used to carve gemstones as though they were butter; Loom had once said it could cut through anything.

Now Espel held that blade to her brother's throat.

Everyone went silent, watching the siblings. Waiting for the kill.

The king was picking himself up now. He took one staggering step closer to his children, and for the first time, Wil saw all three of them together. The boy she loved and the sister he couldn't save and the father who had ruined them both.

Espel did not take her eyes away from Loom. He stared back at her without fear, either because he knew she wouldn't kill him or because he knew that she would—Wil couldn't be certain.

"Kill him," the king said. "Kill him for crimes committed against this family and this entire kingdom. This is your time to avenge us all."

Espel's chest rose and fell more quickly. Her grasp on the hilt flexed and tightened.

Wil could not bring herself to scream. She could not summon the strength to watch Loom die. Not him. And yet, when Espel raised the blade and swung down hard, Wil didn't look away.

No blood spilled. There was no cry of pain. There was no tear of flesh.

For a moment, Wil didn't understand what she had just seen. Then the chain that had bound Loom's wrists and ankles broke apart, and she understood.

Espel whirled on her father next.

Beside her, Loom rose to his feet. If he was stunned by her decision, he didn't betray it. He assumed a guarded stance, prepared to fight anyone who charged at his sister.

No one did, though. The guards had formed a bewildered half circle around the royal family, unsure whom to strike and whom to defend. Their king? Or the murderous princess who may have been seconds away from becoming their queen?

The king laid a hand on the hilt of one of his many daggers, but he didn't draw it. How could he kill this brilliant legacy he had created? This was the moment he had always feared—the child who had killed her own mother finally grown and strong and capable enough to kill him as well. He had turned her into a monster of his own design, thinking that would keep her at his side always. Wil saw the fear and the hurt in his eyes now as he realized that he had made a mistake. Espel had not wanted to be his monster. She had not wanted to be any sort of monster at all.

If she killed him, it would end now. She would be queen. The guards would drop to their knees and swear their loyalty. The palace and the kingdom and the implications of this war would all be in her bloodied hands.

She could have done it. She should have. But she wasn't moving.

Her arm shook just enough to jar the blade, revealing her vulnerability to everyone on the ship. She took a step back, shaking her head. She couldn't do it. Even after everything, she couldn't.

Seizing the opportunity now to strike, the king drew his dagger. When he threw it, his aim was absolute. It sailed past his daughter and tore clean into Masalee's chest.

# SEVENTEEN

Masalee crumpled.

In a rush, Wil felt her adrenaline flood her body as she was freed of the marvelry's grasp.

She didn't move. Didn't dare.

Espel cried out and fell to her knees at Masalee's side, as surely as if her father had torn open her own chest instead.

The king stood over her, clenching his fists, glowering. He stared at his daughter as though she were a flame consuming his entire palace, as though everything in his world was being destroyed. There was a strange sort of heartbreak in his powerful face.

The king's men charged for Wil. She swept low, dodging a hand that tried to snare her. She braced for a fight. But, to her surprise, King Zinil didn't order them to take her down. He spun around to his guards, who all stiffened to attention. "Cast this ship out into the sea," he shouted to them. "If you ever see it again, destroy it at all costs."

This was wrong, Wil thought. He had wanted Espel to bring her back to him, and now he was letting her go? Had he anticipated his daughter's betrayal? Was he forming a new plan?

There was no time for her to suggest this to Loom or Espel, not with Masalee bleeding to death before them.

Espel didn't regard her father as he stormed away from her, flanked by all his guards. She was holding Masalee's face, saying words that Wil was too far away to hear.

Wil was so entranced by Espel's sudden vulnerability that she was startled when the jeweler's knife severed her own chains. Loom spun the blade around to offer her the hilt. "Zay is locked somewhere belowdecks. Find her. She'll be able to steer us out of here."

There was no anger in his voice, but no affection either. From those words, Wil could not tell where they stood, but for now it didn't matter. It couldn't matter. Blood was pooling at the heart of Masalee's robe. "What about—"

"I've got this," Loom said. He put his hand on her shoulder and, oh, that familiar way he held her, gentle and protective. "Hurry," he said. "My father will sink this ship if we stay."

The Southern king had only needed one blade to punish his daughter for her betrayal, and he'd done it. He had aimed for the one thing in this world she needed more than her own heart.

Espel did not turn to see her father standing ashore and watching her as the ship departed, though she felt his eyes boring into her. She did not see the falter in his proud shoulders as he turned his back on her.

But Masalee still had life in her, rapidly draining out though it was. Details forced their way in. Her chest was torn open. *No. No, no.* She peeled away the folds of the robe, trying to find the source of the red current. Masalee had gone pale and waxy, but her eyes were focused. She was watching Espel intently.

"Your Highness," she gasped. "I—"

"Don't talk." Espel tore away the silk to look at the damage. Her hands were steady when she consulted the vials hanging around her waist, searching for anything she could use. None of them had been damaged in the scuffle, and she was awed by the cruelty of that. All these small, replaceable things were unharmed, while Masalee lay broken.

Loom was kneeling at Masalee's other side now, pressing his fingertips over the wound. Her back arched and she gritted her teeth. He was going to kill her, Espel thought. He wanted to take Masalee away from her out of revenge for all she had taken from him. She had made a mistake in choosing to help him— what was she thinking, cutting the chains of a traitor?

But he only said, "It's deep, but it missed her heart. I don't think there's any internal bleeding. Her lungs sound clear." He poured something that caused the raw flesh to sizzle and hiss, and used his hand to wipe away the froth and the blood, revealing the gaping wound.

"Espel." Masalee was still trying to speak. Her lids were heavy. "Listen—"

"Stop it." She took Masalee's cheeks and leaned down to kiss her. Her lips were so cold. "Stop trying to say good-bye to me," Espel demanded. "Just stay with me. Look at me."

Masalee did look at her, the same way she always had: like Espel had set the stars and the moon in the sky. She looked at her in a way Espel had never felt worthy of, and which filled her with so much love it changed the staccato of her heart. It did. Every time.

Espel pressed their foreheads together, and Masalee canted her head to kiss her again. Their mouths barely touched, and then Masalee's eyes fluttered back and she went limp.

"Masalee?" Espel grabbed her chin. "Masalee!"

For the first time in her life, Masalee did not answer her.

Espel commanded herself not to succumb to the hysteria clawing at her mind. Of course she had imagined something like this happening. Masalee was her guard; it was her duty to die for her if it came to it. Espel had pictured Masalee dying many times. She had tried to prepare for it. But, kneeling there, seeing the life drain from Masalee's cheeks and lips, hearing the creaky gasps of her breath, she refused. *No. I will not let you leave me.*

Somewhere in all of this, Loom was using one of Masalee's

daggers to cut scraps from Masalee's robe and then setting them aside to use as bandages.

"Do you have any saline?" Loom asked. Espel blinked at him, her mind processing the words several seconds after she heard them. Saline. Of course, to irrigate the wound and stave off infection.

*Do not panic,* she reminded herself as she drew the vial from her belt.

Loom moved deftly, pouring the solution over the gaping hole in Masalee's chest, carefully tracing it so that the liquid dribbled back out of the wound, flushing it clean.

It wasn't just about stopping the bleeding. Holes could be patched, but infection was the lethal part.

Espel knew all this. But still, she watched on, useless as her brother plastered wayleaves over the dampness. Espel could smell the tang of blood and the burning menthol of the plant, and she felt sick. This was not merely blood; this was the shreds of the girl she loved. This was death, hovering over their heads with fingers outstretched to steal her away.

"I need your thread," Loom told her. He would have been carrying his own, had she not stripped him of all his weapons and vials and tools when she took him captive. They were always prepared, both of them, for anything. But even as Espel did as he instructed, and even though Masalee was not the only dying body to ever lie before her, she felt unprepared for this. Her father had struck Masalee out of revenge; she broke his heart with her betrayal, and so he in turn broke hers. How had he known? She had been so careful to hide her heart. She had been everything he had demanded. Cold. Solitary. Ferocious and cruel. She had disowned her brother, frightened her tutors, frightened herself. And still he had found it. The one thing that she wanted for herself. The one person in this world to look at her and see a girl, not a monster.

Espel cleaned the drying blood and Loom pierced Masalee's skin with his needle and thread, pulling it taut. Somehow they had come to an unspoken understanding that he should be the one tasked with this. The needle pierced the spot on Masalee's chest where Espel had so often laid her head.

Masalee's breathing was labored and quick; her brows knotted and she began to struggle for consciousness, but she settled when Espel poured a careful measure of sleep serum into her mouth.

Loom worked at stitching the wound and Espel could hear it each time the needle punctured Masalee's skin.

Blood, Espel had seen. She knew the smell of it, the way it hid itself in her hair and under her nails so that the bathwater bloomed with red clouds.

As a child she had trained herself not to be bothered by it. But she saw Masalee in every bit of it now. She saw the smiles that went from soft to wicked when they were alone. She saw her hands, callused and small and strong, grasping the hilt of her sword when she assessed a room. She saw something precious being spilled.

When the most gruesome of it was through, Loom gingerly wiped the wound clean.

Masalee's chest was still rising and falling.

Espel felt as though a piece of herself had just been repaired as well. Something broken that had been bleeding for years.

She looked at her brother.

"We should get her belowdecks," Loom said with trepidation, and it occurred to Espel that he was asking for her permission.

She stared at him. His face was solemn and eager. Masalee's blood was smeared across his arms.

Espel nodded her assent, and Loom gathered Masalee up. He was so gentle with her, taking care to tuck her head against his chest, covering her exposed skin with the shreds of her robe.

Neither of them spoke as they made their way to Espel's bunk. Espel drew back the blankets, and Loom set Masalee down. Her body was limp and heavy; Espel had never seen her this way. The girl she knew was all muscle, always rigid unless they were alone, ready to strike. Even her lips—soft and small—were always in a tight line. She could hear the flutter of a bird's wing from across the garden, could reach into the sea and catch a fish with precision. She was always grasping at a sword hilt. She was tall and proud and strong. She was everything that mattered.

"When you change her clothes, try not to lift her too much," Loom said, pulling Espel out of her thoughts. "Those stitches pull easily."

"I know," she snapped, her habitual edge returning before she could stop it.

"She might take a fever," Loom went on with patience. "I'll bring you some lyster just in case."

Masalee's fingers were knotted in Espel's, and Espel wondered when this had happened. She had never dared to let her brother see that she was capable of caring for anyone; it was the same as admitting that she had cared for many people, for many things, all her life. For her mother and her kingdom and for him. For the children they'd been forced to kill on that sweltering afternoon Masalee became her guard, and the bodies lost in the darklead explosion. It was too much, and she forced it out of her mind. She focused on the girl who lay before her.

Sweat beaded Masalee's skin. Her lips and lashes twitched. The night would yield no promises—Espel knew that—but Masalee could make fire from stone. She could control hearts and still an ocean current. And she could fight her way to morning.

Loom moved for the door and Espel caught his wrist. Both of them were bloody and wan. She could feel how frail his curse had made him; she could feel how much the palace had slowly drained him of his vigor, even from here. And she could sense his confusion that she had gone through all this trouble to help him, the brother she had disowned all those months ago. The brother she had never shown even a drop of kindness.

"Why did you help her?" Espel asked. Her voice was hoarse

and stripped of all its pretense.

"Because I understand," he said. "Our father tried to take away someone I love, too."

He gave her a small smile, as though their startling loyalty to each other was the most natural thing in the world. As though it had always been there. Maybe—Espel considered—it had.

With that, it felt as though the world was being set back on its axis again.

Loom left the lyster plant on the bedside table with a bowl of water, and he didn't linger.

Once he had gone, Espel rested her head on the pillow and kissed Masalee's feverish temple. It was a hard kiss. A steady one that Masalee would feel even in the grave of her darkest dreams.

They were children when they met, both of them gasping in the summer heat, drenched in sweat. Bodies were strewn around them. Lives that Espel and her brother had been forced to take. The blood of an orphaned boy was splattered across Espel's face and she could feel the weight of it on her lips.

She had been tired, and she had marveled that she still had the strength to maintain her stance, because her insides felt shaky and weak.

Masalee was battered by exhaustion, filthy, her hair a tangled mess. But she did not look frightened. She lunged forward with a scream unlike anything Espel had ever heard—even in combat.

They were fighting for their lives, both of them, and somehow Masalee gained the upper hand. Whether she wanted to live or was merely unwilling to lose, Espel couldn't tell. She still didn't know, even now.

She remembered being pinned on her back, stunned by the strength of this untrained orphan who looked as though she hadn't eaten for weeks. She felt every bit of her fire, her anger, her hatred. Espel realized in that moment that she was not alone in feeling these things.

She could have outmaneuvered Masalee. She could have twisted and rolled on top of her and strangled her. But she didn't. She wanted this girl to be the one who lived, because this girl was the only one to understand her.

If Masalee were to leave this world, there would be no one left to believe that there was any good in her, the wicked girl who killed her own mother on her way out. She would be nothing but a girl fighting for her life until the day she died, the taste of blood on her lips.

# EIGHTEEN

EXHAUSTION HAD NOT STOLEN ZAY's ferocity. There was grit even to her sadness.

Wil sat by the control panel while Zay paced the length of the room. After a sizable tantrum, Ada had finally fallen asleep slumped against his mother's chest. Now, Zay was the one in need of comfort. She kissed his hair and bounced him gently as she moved.

"It doesn't surprise me," Zay said, after Wil had finished the story. "Killing Espel would have been too merciful for him. He wanted her to suffer."

"Did you know?" Wil asked. "That she's in love with her guard?"

"I'd assumed she had a barbed boulder where her heart should be," Zay said. "So, no. But Loom was the same way in the palace unless we were behind closed doors."

Wil could not imagine Loom playing the part of cold and emotionless for very long. He was so filled with words and ideas and emotions, all of them brimming over. When he learned who she was, he turned away. Wil had been so certain he was lost to her forever, but now she wondered how much of it had been playing a part.

"They were what they had to be," Wil said.

"I still think she'll try to murder us all if we let our guard down," Zay said. "Best to sleep with an eye open." But she had not seen the way Espel fell to her knees. She did not see the desperation when she kissed Masalee. Espel knew how to play a part, but that had not been a role. That had been Espel, truly Espel, when all her armor had fallen to her feet and turned to dust.

"I don't care who you are, you know," Zay said. She was sitting now on the ledge of the porthole that stretched nearly floor to ceiling.

The words, coming from Zay, meant more to her than she could have known before she heard them. Wil stared past her, at the sunlight lazily burning the surface of the Ancient Sea.

"It's a relief, actually," Zay went on. "Now I can pinpoint why I never trusted you."

While Loom had looked at Wil through the shroud of both their curses, Zay had seen Wil clearly. Wil couldn't fault Zay for not trusting her; she didn't deserve trust.

"You were trying to protect Loom," Wil said. "I understood."

"That boy," Zay grumbled, shifting Ada in her arms. "How did he seem, up on the deck? We were too close to the palace. I know we were."

"However he's feeling, he's trying to shrug it off," Wil said. "It isn't nearly as bad as it was the last time. He was still on his feet."

"How were his eyes? Glassy?"

"Not very."

Zay stared ahead for a moment, anger and worry wrestling in her features. The injustice of what King Zinil had done to someone she loved. It wasn't enough that Loom had been cast away; now the thing he loved would kill him if he came too close.

"Why didn't you tell us the truth, though?" Zay went on, changing the topic back to something she could bear. Her tone was softer now. She drew Ada closer to her chest as he slept. "Did you think we would kill you?" There was some playfulness to her tone, but it wasn't entirely in jest.

"No," Wil said. "I wanted to protect my family. I know what my father has done. But my family aren't monsters. My brother is—" She paused. "He's brilliant, and kind. He wants to save the world, not dominate or destroy it. And Owen—"

Here she stopped speaking. She had thought, after all these weeks, that his loss would cease to consume her so entirely. She had hoped to draw strength from her memories of him, and the gentle, near-imperceptible whisper of his presence she felt when she was in open waters. But if it had been a hundred years since losing him, it had still only been a day.

Zay drew one of her legs onto the ledge. "What really happened to him?" she asked, with the gentle coo of a patient mother trying to dislodge a splinter.

"Owen is dead." Wil made herself say it. "If he had just—let go of me, he would still be here, and I'd be the dead one."

She tried never to relive that night by the rapids. Owen wouldn't want her to. There's no point, he would say. No point turning to something that can't be changed and letting it interfere with what's left to be done. And thanks to Owen, she had a lifetime left of things to do.

If he hadn't come for her that night, if he'd ignored the nettling premonition that something terrible was going to happen to his kid sister, she may have even made it across. She didn't believe it, though. She believed that she would have fallen in. Her mind would have been a frenzy of panic at first, and then, she supposed, a resigned sort of calm. The burning in her lungs would have faded. Her vision would have tunneled, and she would have gathered the most relevant scraps from her life like dying flowers. She would have seen her mother especially, and then her brothers. She would have wished full lives for all of them. She would have felt how certainly and brutally she loved them. And then she would have left.

Zay didn't ask anything further, and when Wil finally worked up the courage to look at her, she saw sympathy in her light brown eyes. Not pity or the detached remorse of a stranger who has just been told a sad story, but the look of a girl who understood this pain. Wil had the thought that Zay might have even walked over and embraced her if the contact wouldn't have turned her to stone.

When the door opened, they both started, lost as they had been in their thoughts.

Loom stood at the threshold with water dripping from his freshly scoured arms. He still smelled of blood and sweat. His eyes were weary and dark from the toll his own curse had taken on him.

The last time he'd been in Cannolay, it nearly cost him his life. This time, he'd at least remained on a ship in the sea. He looked as though he would recover. Wil wouldn't be put at ease until she saw the light in his eyes again, though. Right now they were dull and heavy lidded.

"It doesn't look good," he announced in a tired, hoarse voice. "But if she manages to survive the night, she'll have a chance."

Zay looked between Wil and Loom, each of whom was staring at the floor. She stood. "I should put Ada to bed." As she squeezed past Loom in the doorway, she patted his shoulder.

Wil swiveled in the captain's chair and studied the controls with renewed interest. Zay had set them on a northern course, and now the tiny gray blip of their vessel was trailing through a tiny screen of blue. Zay didn't know where they were meant to be going, only that they needed to move fast. Now there was a sheet of electric blue between Loom and his palace, and Espel, for the first time, was on his side of it.

"How much of it was true?" Loom asked. His voice was quiet. He was still standing in the doorway, as though he hadn't yet decided whether he would stay. He let out a rueful laugh. "Was anything true?"

Wil drew her brows. She made herself look at him. "Everything I told you was true."

"Lying by omission is still lying."

"All right," she conceded. "I won't pretend I'm not a liar. I'm a good liar." For the duration of her captivity on this ship, all she had wanted was to speak to him. To have him throw the full force of his anger at her and be done with it. To know whether there was anything left between them to salvage. But suddenly his scrutiny made her angry. Who was this boy to begrudge her her secrets? This boy who had tricked her, dragged her into his conquest, and then made her fall in love with him? She was angry with him for wanting so much, and angry with herself for wanting to give it to him even now. Angry with herself for wanting him to pull her into his arms and hold her the way his brief touch on the deck had implied. Angry with her cursed heart and everything else that had led to her wanting to kiss this enemy prince.

"How can I trust anything that you tell me?" Loom said. "How can I ever know?"

"Is trust easy for anyone?" Wil answered coolly. "It wasn't easy to go along with you at every turn, Loom. Sometimes I felt like I was betraying my family."

"Because you were," he blurted. "We're enemies."

The words hit her like a slap, and Loom seemed to realize it the instant he'd said them. Enemies. Never mind everything they had been through together. Never mind all the things he had said to her. Loom's easy faith in her had not only reminded her that she was still human, but given her the promise that she would still be human tomorrow, and in ten years, and in fifty. That this curse would not turn her into the monster she feared becoming.

"You really believe that we're enemies?" Wil's voice came out as a whisper.

He stared off to the side. "I don't know."

He didn't know. After everything, he didn't know. She stood, shoving him roughly out of her way as she exited the control room. "Come and find me if you ever figure it out," she said.

She went to the deck and spent more than an hour pressed to the railing that separated her from the water, brooding.

Belowdecks, Espel kept vigil over Masalee. Zay sang to Ada as he dreamed. They did these things easily because they knew with such certainty to whom they belonged.

Wil used to belong somewhere. For all the tumult in her family, she had always been theirs, and they had been hers. She'd freely flitted in and out of Owen's chamber as she pleased, stealing little pieces of his adventures for as long as she pleased. Gerdie invited her into his laboratory, but more than that, he invited her into his mind—a place so sacred to him that he sometimes retreated there for days. And her mother had always loved her with a fierce loyalty of which most living things were incapable, Wil was certain.

And her father—he had lied to her about who she was. About what she was. Loom hadn't been right to think that telling a lie was the same as committing a wrong. Sometimes lying to someone was the only way to love them.

She fought the desire to tell Loom about Aleen now. To not present the story of her curse and her slaughtered aunt to him like a bloody, desperate offering to prove that she was capable of being honest. Before, she had wanted to give him all of herself. Now, after what he'd said, she wanted to lock him out of her world completely. It wasn't just that he had called them enemies. It was that he said it with uncertainty, as though she meant nothing to him. Wil was no longer Wil. She was just some unfathomable princess from a warring kingdom, no more and no less.

Her thoughts turned to what would come next. Brooding was useless. Being practical would magnetize the needle on their compass. Whatever existed between herself and Loom, their kingdoms still needed help. Espel had cast herself free of her father's hold, and now neither of the royal siblings had any claim to the Southern Isles.

Wil had little to offer on behalf of the Northern Isles, being a spare. Even if Baren got himself killed with his destructive ventures with marvelry, Gerdie would be next in line until the new heir was born. Gerdie would not be partial to putting her at risk to end this war.

But maybe he wouldn't have to.

King Zinil didn't want his children, but once he'd gotten past his outrage, perhaps he would still want something from Wil. He had, after all, sent Espel halfway across the world to retrieve her. Wil knew kings. Kings did not let emotions dictate prosperity—even if said king would have to bargain with his estranged children. King Zinil wouldn't turn Espel or even Loom away if they presented him with something he wanted.

# NINETEEN

"Drink all of it," Zay said, when Loom's expression turned sour. She had brewed lyster leaves into a tea, even throwing in some mintlemint leaves to offset their bitterness. The taste wasn't unpleasant, but Loom's stomach had grown intolerant of everything as his fever spiked.

He forced down the tea to appease Zay, who was drawing back the blankets on his bed.

"I don't care how much your sister loves her guard, I still think her heart is shriveled up like a moldy peach pit," she said.

"Do peach pits shrivel?" Loom mused, lying on his stomach. He closed his eyes. "Espel is . . . obtuse, I'll admit. But she's still in there somewhere. I can still get through to her. I have to believe that."

"You could have died," Zay said, spitting fire into that last word. "The ship pulled right up in front of the palace. It's a wonder you're even conscious." She was laying strips of damp cloth against his back. His skin was pink with fever. This was a routine she'd performed dutifully in the first months of his curse, when he still insisted on returning to Cannolay with food and coins he'd managed to accrue in his travels. He was so determined to help his kingdom even if all he could offer was a crate of pears or a bottle of eyedrops he'd bartered in Brayshire.

"I never left the sea," he said. "I'll be fine."

She wrung a cloth out over his hair, dampening it. "Tell me you aren't stupid enough to trust your sister, Loom."

He smiled. It was a warm, sleepy smile that reminded her of when he was a child. "Now, now, there's no need to be jealous, *ansuh*. You know you're the only one I trust."

"At last, you speak sense," she said.

He chuckled, burying his cheek in the crook of his arm.

Zay straightened her spine. There was still the cloth in her hand, dripping onto the satin sheets from between her fingers. "Am I really the only one you trust?"

"Well, I suppose Ada has never betrayed my trust either," Loom said. "But he doesn't say very much, does he?"

"And Wil," Zay said. "You've hinged a lot of hopes on her."

Loom was silent for several seconds, and then, very softly, he said, "That was a mistake. You were right about her."

"No I wasn't," Zay said. "The two of you are exactly alike. Banished from your kingdoms and trying to save them nonetheless. You're both stubborn, and if you ask me, you both care far too much about the things you choose to pursue." Her voice softened. "And you've both lost a lot. I always knew that much about her, right from the start."

Loom opened one eye to peer up at her. "Who are you and what have you done with Zaylin?"

She flicked at a wave of his hair. "I'm serious."

"So you like her now?"

"'Like' has nothing to do with it," Zay said.

"Uh-huh."

He turned away from her. He was still and quiet for so long that Zay thought he must have fallen asleep. Just as she stood, he said, "All I know about that girl is that she's a liar."

"Speaking as the only one you trust," Zay said, gathering up the mug and the bowl of lyster water, "you are acting like a fool."

That evening, Wil found Loom in the galley. The pair of them were the only two passengers on this ship not to be currently occupied with someone else. Therefore, they were the only two who had the time to entertain the idea of food.

It had been hours since Wil ate her last meal, which had been slid on a tray into her cabin before the door was shut and locked.

Loom was staring intently into a bowl of mashed grains and apple slices. His appetite was feather light at sea, Wil remembered. He ate distractedly, small, infrequent portions, too restless to be still longer than it took to chew.

Sweat beaded his brow. There was a damp towel draped across the back of his neck, fragrant with herb water. But his breaths weren't as labored now. He had slept for several hours, Wil knew. From her cabin she had listened for him. She had heard Zay arguing with him when he'd tried to refuse whatever tonic she'd brought him. And then, later, Zay shushing Ada when he fussed after Loom had fallen asleep.

But even the exhaustion of Loom's curse had not been able to keep him down for very long. His restless mind had inevitably awoken him.

And now both of their restless hearts—Wil's and his— came back together like waves.

She sat across from him and waited for him to stop pretending he hadn't seen her come in.

At last, without looking up, he said, "You have an idea."

She leaned back. "How can you tell?"

"You're fidgeting," he said. "You fidget when you have something to say."

"I do not."

"Yes," he said practically. "You're a statue when you're listening—especially if you're scheming about something. You pout when you're thinking, but once you have something to say . . ." He trailed, and looked once again at his bowl. He was trying not to smile. This gave Wil more hope than it should have; despite his efforts, he wasn't nearly as angry with her as he'd like to be.

"I think we should go to the Northern Isles," Wil said.

"In a Southern ship, that would be certain death," Loom said. "Our kingdoms are at war, remember? He said that word, war, with its own fire, as though it were her fault.

"We go somewhere neutral first," Wil countered. "Sell this ship or abandon it. Get a new one and head to Northern Arrod."

His muscles tensed at that. His guardedness when he looked at her was jarring. He had never been this way with her. He had been cocky and a bit pretentious when they were strangers, though he hadn't been unkind. Somehow, in their short weeks together, they had moved past even that, into the familiar sort of ease that Wil supposed could be called friendship. She'd never had any friends other than her brothers, so she couldn't be certain. But now all that was gone. He had reduced her to something less than even a stranger. Strangers at least got some share of his warmth, and Wil could see now that he was trying to be cold.

"Why would I want to go there?"

Wil pretended that this exchange wasn't breaking her heart. "Because I have an idea to get you on the throne."

Loom looked past her, and Wil spun around to follow his gaze. Zay was standing in the doorway, apprehensive. "Bad time?" she said. "I don't mean to get in the way of your battle of angst, but I'm starving."

"Not a bad time at all," Loom said. "Wil was about to share her plan for us to sail into enemy territory and get ourselves killed."

"It isn't enemy territory," Wil snapped. "Not to me."

Although she couldn't be sure how true that was with Baren on the throne. He would kill her sooner than he'd kill Loom or Espel, even if they were the children of his enemy.

Loom's stare had gone flat. Zay inched onto the bench beside him and helped herself to his lunch. "Why would we go to Northern Arrod?" she asked with her mouth full of grains.

Wil pressed on. He could be angry with her if he pleased, but they had larger matters to contend with. "Don't you think it's strange that your father let me go?" she said. "He sent Espel all that way to capture me, and I was right there. He didn't even try to take me down."

"He was distracted by Espel's stunt," Loom muttered. "He had expected her to kill me."

"I'm sure that's true," Wil said. "But he still could have tried to take me regardless. Instead, he called his men down."

Zay blinked at that. "He did?"

"Yes." Wil gripped the edge of the table as the ship listed.

Zay exchanged a look with Loom, and something went unspoken between them. Some deep worry they shared. For once, Wil understood their secret language, because she had already thought the same thing. "You lived," Wil told Loom. "And now your father wants to punish you for it. He let me get away because he's planning something worse."

This got Loom's attention and he finally met her eyes.

"Before, he wanted me for my curse. I'm sure he still does. But I'd wager he's planning to kill me for it. Not just that, to torture me to death while you're made to watch."

Loom was working hard to maintain his neutral expression. But his fingers—just his fingers—betrayed him, tightening into a fist that made his knuckles white.

"He'll use Pahn to do it," Wil said. "I'm not sure how. That's the thing about marvelers, isn't it? One never knows what to expect."

"What do you suggest we do?" Zay asked, for once in earnest.

"We get ahead of whatever he's planning. King Zinil wants me for two reasons," Wil said, pushing aside the messy ordeal of emotions and sticking to the facts. "Because of my curse, and because I'm the daughter of his enemy. He's just exiled both Loom and Espel, and ordered for them to be killed on sight if they return." She looked from Zay to Loom. "But if you bring him something he wants, as a show of penance, he'll welcome you back. If not you, Loom, then certainly Espel."

Loom had gone rigid. "What do you propose we give him?" He seemed to already know the answer.

"Me," Wil said. "Before he can send Pahn after me. Before whatever he's planning, we give him what he wants."

"No." The way Loom said the word wasn't loud or sharp,

but it was absolute. He said it again. "No. We don't know what he would do to you. He might carve out your heart and put it into his own chest to have your power."

Wil shrugged. "Let him."

Zay lowered an eyebrow. "Did you hit your head?"

"My brother is an alchemist," Wil said. "The best in the world, from what I've seen. He knows how to alchemize a corpse in anyone's likeness. I've seen him do it using nothing but cloth, ink, and bones he pilfered from the kitchen after dinner."

The tension hadn't left Loom's shoulders. "My father won't want a corpse."

"So we'll make it breathe," Wil said, waving this detail off as inconsequential. "It'll look like I'm comatose. Say you knocked me out with sleep serum."

"He's going to figure it out eventually," Zay said.

"Yes, so we'll have to move quickly," Wil said. "Loom, this is your chance at earning his favor again. He'll allow you back into the palace. From there, you can finally have your chance to kill him."

"What about Espel?" he asked. "Even if my father were to lift the curse, he's not going to make me his heir. He would never choose me over her even now. You saw it. I betrayed him and he wanted me dead. She betrayed him and he wanted her to suffer. Do you think he stabbed Masalee just to punish her? It was more than that. He wanted Masalee to die so that Espel would have no one left, and she would come back to him. He still wants her to return."

"Then we pretend Masalee is dead," Wil went on. No emotion, she reminded herself. Just facts and logic. She could not contend once again with the horrible methods of kings. "Espel returns with her tail between her legs. She brings you with her."

Zay squinted. "How convincing could an alchemized corpse really be?"

"I screamed the first time I saw one," Wil said. It wasn't her proudest moment, but confessing such a thing was easier now than it would have been weeks ago, when she had labored to present herself as invincible.

What she didn't add was that her last venture to Northern Arrod had not just been perilous because of Baren. The curse set upon the kingdom suppressed her own. She couldn't stay for long before it weakened her. Two days, maybe three. It wouldn't take that long. Gerdie was quick, and he knew what he was doing. This would work; it had to.

She was less concerned with Baren. She had spent her childhood evading him and she could do it once more.

She feigned nonchalance about the way Loom was watching her, his head absently canted, lips parted at the center, like he was going to ask a question but kept thinking better of it. Was she so foreign to him now? She wondered. Did knowing her lineage change that much?

He stood, and when he breezed past her and made his exit

without another word, Zay surprised Wil with a sympathetic smile.

"I think your plan is a big gamble," Zay said. "But I also think it's the best one we've got. We can't float around in the middle of the ocean forever. Let me talk to him."

Again Wil felt that bitter jealousy to which she wasn't entitled. This time, it wasn't jealousy that Loom trusted Zay, but rather that Zay was worthy of his trust.

# TWENTY

THE SUN WAS MELTING INTO the Ancient Sea, setting the waves on fire with a flourish of oranges and pinks. It, too, was cursed, Wil thought, filled with all those dead spirits. It brought her comfort—her and the sea, both cursed, both still pushing forward and ever restless.

Wil knocked gently on the door to Espel's cabin. "I've brought some dinner," she said. No one had told her to do this, but the door had remained closed all day, and despite all Espel had done, Wil found herself worrying for her.

When the door opened, Wil drew a deep breath through her nostrils. She was trying to detect that ominous smell of death, that foreboding that Masalee's situation was grave.

But rather, the cabin smelled of blood and a citrusy salve that was medicinal but not unpleasant. Masalee was splayed on the bed, the bunched sheets proof of her fitfulness. Her mouth was open, her skin glistening and wan. She had been changed into bright purple linens, with a gold peacock embroidered up the left sleeve. Her bloody, shredded robe was neatly folded and tucked against the wall, betraying Espel to be one who organized and sorted things when she was anxious.

Espel had become statuesque. Steely. More vibrant in defiance of her father's attempt to break her. She stepped aside to allow Wil into her cabin.

"Did Loom send you?" Espel asked.

There was nowhere to set the tray. The bedside table was covered in vials, all neatly arranged around a bowl of lyster leaves floating in water. Wil knelt to place the tray on the floor, and Espel knelt before it, nodding in invitation.

"No," Wil said, taking a seat. Might as well get comfortable. "Loom is currently not speaking to me." *Thanks to you,* she thought, but didn't add. She couldn't put all the blame on Espel for exposing her identity; it would have had to happen eventually. Maybe it was for the best that it had happened now. Maybe a week on a ship with a boy who now hated her would cure her of this irrational love.

In the lantern light, Espel looked almost sympathetic, but even at her most vulnerable she was too stoic to betray such a thing. Just for a moment Wil caught a glimpse of the girl Espel truly was, under what her father had turned her into.

In the murky swamp of her delirium, Masalee let out a

pained cry. Espel was up and by her side in an instant; she traced Masalee's mouth with a fingertip drenched in sleep serum.

Wil envied Espel, and she even envied Masalee, who lay torn open and burning with fever. She envied them for being so certain of their love. For having tumultuous lives but such uncomplicated hearts.

"I don't need to know what someone's secrets are to know that they have them," Espel said, sitting on the floor again. "I look at you and I see a girl who's made of secrets. But you don't betray a single one."

"I thought so," Wil said.

Espel regarded her food with the sort of weary stoicism of one who needed to persist with human tasks in the face of tragedy. Wil couldn't tell whether she mourned more for her father or for Masalee. The only thing about which Wil could be certain was that this princess was not to be trusted. She wouldn't tell Espel of her plan yet. It hadn't been decided anyway.

What startled her, though, was the empathy she felt. She knew what it was to be banished from her kingdom. So did Loom, but Wil supposed it was different for spares. And especially for only daughters. To have everything taken away was like being erased. Like floating in the darkness between stars, not existing at all.

Wil didn't seek Loom out before she retreated to her cabin for the night. Zay announced that she was setting them all on a course for the Western Isles, pending plans notwithstanding, because it was neutral territory and they would need more than solar panels for fuel if they drifted aimlessly forever.

Even if Loom was too stubborn and hurt and angry to speak to Wil, she knew him. She knew that if she waited another day, his resolve would weaken and he would be more open to her plan. It was more practical than anything he had proposed, but more than that, he was too congenial to let this go on. Too diplomatic. Too kind.

She wrested in the sheets. Zay was all about conserving a ship's energy when she was at the helm, which meant no temperature modifications, and the night was stiflingly hot.

She missed Northern waters. She missed winter, and snow, and crystals of ice on her windows. Strange that she would feel this homesickness now of all times. But when she first left home, Owen's death had rendered her too numb to feel anything beyond her own guilt and sadness.

When she'd met Loom, in an unanticipated twist of fate, he became her ally. He became an anchor.

Getting wistful about him wouldn't help, Wil reminded herself. She would never be his enemy, as he had put it, but she would no longer indulge this illusion of love. That's all it was. An illusion. A curse.

When she slept, she saw Aleen's body laid out in the grass. Her eyelids had shifted, revealing the dark, lifeless pools of her eyes.

The queen screamed, and she didn't stop screaming. Not really. Even when the queen went silent, that scream was still inside her, muting out all else.

The king had the audacity to return to his castle. He locked himself in his throne room for days.

The queen did not sleep. She did not speak. In her head, her own scream turned into Aleen's. Both of them being murdered over and again.

The guards did not stop the queen when she moved past the castle gate. They bowed, offered to escort her wherever she was going—barefoot, in her nightclothes, hours before sunup. She ignored them. Dead eyed and somnambulating, she disappeared between the trees.

In the morning, the ocean tossed her body against the stone wall that separated the water from the Port Capital, as though it was returning a rejected offering.

Wil awoke with the queen's screams in her mouth. Hands were grasping her shoulders. She had propelled herself upright, gasping.

"Hey." Loom's whisper silenced the frenzy. "Hey, hey, it's okay." He touched her forehead, her cheek. He swept the hair from her face.

She couldn't see him at first, and then her eyes adjusted to the moonlight and she saw his eyes, dark and blinking.

His thumb pressed at the hollow of her throat, where her pulse thudded wild.

"You sounded like you were trying to scream," he whispered.

"It wasn't my scream," she said, still delirious. For a moment she thought they were in Northern Arrod and that her grandmother's body would crash into their boat. She anticipated, with dread, the soft thunk. She could hear how cruel and small and wet the sound would be.

But there was no death. There were no bodies. Aleen and her mother were long since passed. It was just Loom.

She eased herself back against the pillows. "I didn't mean to wake you."

"I wasn't sleeping," he said. He knelt beside the bed and laid his head on his folded arms. It may have been the darkness deceiving her, but Wil could see the Loom she knew just then. No guard. No coldness.

"What was it?" he asked.

She hesitated. When she'd set out for Pahn's cabin, she had meant to tell him what she had learned about her curse. She had hoped he would have the answers somehow. He would help her to navigate this horrible thing she had inherited.

But now she realized he couldn't.

No one could.

She stared languidly at Loom. "You should go back to bed."

"Wil." He wound so much frustration into that single word. Somehow he had loaded her name, a single syllable, with all the things he hadn't said since learning her true identity. She felt all of it rushing out of him at once.

"Hells." It was unlike Loom to be so ineloquent. She relished that she was the cause. Pretending to hate her had not worked, but he had convinced her that he didn't care about her at all. Since he'd turned away from her that horrible day on the deck, she'd felt cast out of his orbit. Loom had a passion for everything—for his dead mother and his ruthless little sister and his tempestuous wife and a toddler who wasn't his. For the tiniest sprig to blossom out from the boulders of Cannolay's mountains. But he had jettisoned her away. She had felt less than even his kingdom's foliage.

"You called us enemies," Wil said. Her voice was cool, but the recant flustered her.

"I—" Loom's voice caught. His fingers laced together in the same desperate sort of way Wil had seen in vendor slaves pleading for their lives. "I shouldn't have said that."

Wil said nothing.

"My father has done awful things," Loom went on. "And you never confused his wrongs for mine. Not a single time."

Wil pushed herself upright. "Why would I? You have enough wrongs of your own." It was an unfair jab, and she knew it. Loom had fought harder for his kingdom than anyone; he cared about every bit of it. He'd even cared about her. But she was too wounded to say she was sorry.

He glared up at her, the whites of his eyes shining against the dark. "I get it, Wil. I shouldn't blame you for what your father has done. For what your family has done."

"My family isn't what you think," Wil said. "My brother Gerdie is the most honest, the most loyal, the most *good* of us. And Owen—" She made herself go on. "This war wouldn't have even started if he were still with us. He would have been the king Arrod needs. And my mother truly was a wanderer, Loom. She had no mind to be a queen, but she couldn't help that she fell in love with a king."

"I understand the sentiment," Loom mumbled.

Wil crossed her arms. "I love my family," she said, guarding her tone, careful not to let her softness show—not because she wanted to hide that part of herself from Loom, but because he hadn't earned it back. "I was only trying to protect them."

"Were you ever going to tell me?" Loom sat on the edge of the bed. She turned her face away from him, and he tilted her chin. "Hey. Were you?"

"I don't know," she confessed. "Maybe I would have just left one night while you were sleeping. If you had your kingdom back, it wouldn't have mattered."

"How could you say that? How could you think it wouldn't matter if you just disappeared?"

Wil didn't want to say anything. She didn't want to breathe. She didn't want to do anything that might make him realize their sudden closeness and pull away.

It did matter. That's what she wanted to tell him. But what came out was, "You matter. You matter to me."

He pushed forward and kissed her. She exhaled into his mouth. His familiar, warm mouth that she had not allowed herself to miss while they were apart.

He tugged on her arm. And with that small, gentle act, she felt herself drawn to him. Again. Always. She had felt his pull from halfway across the world and through all the spirits in the Ancient Sea.

She slid down until her stomach was pressed to his, her hands at either side of his head. The dark curtain of her hair fell over her shoulder and shadowed his face. He looked at her hair, and then at her.

He raised his head to kiss her again. Her hands clenched into fists against the mattress and then slackened. All of her went soft, and weak, and eager.

She thought of what he had told her on the cliff overlooking the electric city, windmills spinning and winking at them as they gleamed. *I love you.* The words played over in her mind until she wasn't sure whether they were his or her own. Her knees around his hips and his fingers touching her jaw, uncertain at first, then rising up to her hair. He wasn't just touching her, but winding himself around and around her, until she could not remember what she had been before this curse. Could not remember that she had ever wanted to be rid of it. All she wanted was this sudden feeling of belonging, of being wanted, of *wanting*.

He was beautiful, she thought. He had always been beautiful, but it had changed now into something that made her greedy. Something that hurt even as she craved it. Something that made everything wrong and everything make sense.

Her heart—her cursed, insolent heart—beat at his command. He traced his knuckles down her arm and her nerves fluttered and followed, her skin rose with gooseflesh. She felt warm where he touched her and cold where he'd been.

She dipped her head down for another kiss. She wanted him. Needed him.

No. She drew back as if emerging from water. She once again heard the creaking of the ship as it rocked and drifted in the dark waters.

He *didn't* need her. Curses made liars of hearts, which weren't especially prone to telling the truth as it was.

She sat with her legs around his waist. This was how it had been that day on the deck, when they were strangers to each other and she'd held a blade to his throat. She still held that blade to him. He still fell under her command. She still couldn't let him go. Why couldn't she let him go?

"What is it?" Loom's voice was sleepy with desire. His sudden concern only made her want him all the more. His hands opened, fingers outstretched at either side of him, as though he was trying to prove that he could stop touching her if that was what she wanted.

"I don't want us to lie to each other anymore," she said.

He sat up, causing her to slide back against his hips. "Are

you going to tell me you're the princess of another kingdom now, too?"

"I'm talking about this." She gestured to her heart, and then his. "Pahn said that cursed hearts are drawn to one another. That's what this is."

"Is that what's bothering you?" He reached out his hands, and despite all reason she took them.

"You don't sound surprised," she ventured, uncertain.

"I told you, I know a lot about curses." He squeezed her hands, and something within her fluttered.

"Then you've known this whole time that it's a lie," Wil said. "All of it."

"It isn't a lie." His brows drew together. "Of course it isn't. Wil—how could you believe that?"

"Because it isn't real." She saw the sudden hurt in his eyes, but she kept going. She kept going because if she didn't say it now, she would never have the courage to say it at all. "You would never fall in love with a girl who turns things to stone. It's monstrous. You look at me as though I'm some sort of wonder, and you don't see the horror of it. You don't see my curse for what it really is."

"I see your curse," he said. "And I see you. How dare you tell me that I don't? I see blood and fight and fire. I see the way your eyes change when your mind is someplace far. I see the way you laugh, like it's a confession you're giving up. I see how desperately you love your family even though you've hardly said a word about them before tonight." He sounded so honest. He looked so honest. "I see all of what you show me and some of what you don't." His voice softened. "And if you don't love me, then fine. But you don't get to tell me that I don't know what I feel."

When she looked away from him, she felt something rip. Some artery or muscle or maybe time itself. Something that could no longer be mended. She should have told him that she didn't love him, but the words wouldn't come.

She disentangled herself and sat on the end of the bed, away from him. "Tell yourself whatever you need to."

His stunned silence filled the cabin. Neither of them moved for a long time, and then he stood, smoothing the ruffled satin of his trousers.

"You're right," he said. "You are a good liar. You've managed to fool yourself."

"Wait." She stood and paced after him as he went for the door. "This morning you wanted nothing to do with me because I'd lied to you. Now you're mad that I'm telling you the truth?"

"I may not always know what you're thinking," he said. "Hells, I'll admit that you turn my brain upside down and make my heart beat sideways. But I know curses, and you're not a curse to me."

He pulled the door open and stormed off before she could say something to prove him wrong.

# TWENTY-ONE

W<small>IL AWOKE WITH HER HEART</small> beating erratically. It slowed for long seconds and then burst into fits.

She supposed this was Masalee's doing. She lay still in bed, staring at the ceiling, and focused. Masalee's presence was a dull, throbbing, invasive thing in her blood. It was gentle but forceful at once.

Wil found the source of the marvelry like the beat of a drum echoing through her blood, sending ripples. She pushed back, gently at first, casting the sensation away from her heart like a paper boat on a soft breeze. She pushed until it was gone.

She wondered if Masalee had any control over her marvelry now, or if it was shooting out of her as she thrashed and dreamed. When Gerdie was in the throes of his fever, he often muttered fragments of equations and chemical properties.

For now, the force of the marvelry had stopped, but as Wil went about the routine of showering and brushing her teeth, she experimented with her heartbeat. It refused to listen to her, but sometimes—just for a fraction of a second—she could feel the curse's claws wrapped around her valves and arteries. She could push against it. And then it all collapsed around her, and her heart once again became traitorous. Masalee hadn't controlled Wil's heart on the night Wil was taken hostage in Cannolay, but then, Masalee didn't do a thing unless Espel commanded it. And Espel was one who thought carefully about every move. Wil suspected that Espel didn't want to reveal Masalee's power to Wil right away; as it was, she had described Masalee's powers as barely competent, when they were profound.

She made her way to the kitchen. Loom and Zay were huddled on either side of the table, so close that the crowns of their heads nearly touched. Loom looked up when Wil entered, and whatever secret thing existed between him and his wife disappeared.

It hadn't been this rigid even when they were strangers, Wil thought. Of course, then she had been too busy plotting to overtake his ship and maybe throw him overboard for good measure.

"Hi," she said. Had she ever bothered with a hello when it came to him? It seemed they always met when they were desperate. There was always something to be done, something that needed saving. There were always wounds that wouldn't stop bleeding or cities that wouldn't stop burning.

Ada was crawling under the table, trying to befriend a long-legged spider that kept awkwardly ambling just out of his grasp.

"You came up with a good plan," Zay said by way of greeting. "There's only the matter of what to do with Espel." She lowered her voice when she said her name, as though it was something to never be uttered.

"She wants to be queen," Loom said. "I want to be king. We've both been disowned, but if we returned, my father would still want to murder me and reinstate her."

"I assumed that the plan was to kill him," Wil said, hopping up onto the counter and skinning a banana.

"It is," Loom said. "If I kill him, the kingdom will be mine. His guards will swear loyalty to me."

"That sounds like enough of a plan to me," Wil said.

"In case you haven't noticed, Espel can be competitive," Zay said, scooping a giggling Ada into her arms. "Soon enough, she's going to come out of her cabin, and we need to have something to tell her."

"You want to lie to her?" Wil was looking at Loom.

He hesitated, as he always seemed to when it came to his sister. For him, it was in irreconcilable balance. He had no mother and may as well have had no father. The only blood he truly had was a sister who had been raised to rival him. They were mirror opposites, matched blow for blow, equally skilled, equally frightened of what it might mean for them to care for each other.

"If she knows I plan to kill our father, I wouldn't put it past her to kill me and take the kingdom for herself." Loom said this with renewed steel. It was the truth. Whether or not he wanted to betray his sister was not as important as the logic behind it.

"What are we going to tell her?" Wil asked.

Here Loom averted his eyes. He looked at his steepled fingers. "I'm going to fight her for it," he said. "And I'm going to win."

"It doesn't seem like Espel to admit defeat," Wil challenged. "She'll want a duel to the death, or not at all."

"No she won't." Loom's voice was soft. "She's stubborn, and she might have once been stubborn enough to die, but not now, with Masalee to consider. If she dies, there will be no one to stop me from selling Masalee off to the highest bidder. There's no shortage of kingdoms in need of a marveler that strong."

"You would never do that," Wil said.

"It doesn't matter what I would do," Loom said. "Only what Espel thinks I would do. Espel and I will duel for the kingdom. She'll agree because she believes she'll win. But when she loses, she'll concede."

"And if she wins?" Wil said.

Loom shrugged. "Then this will all be a lot easier."

"What would stop her from killing you?" Wil said. Loom was a skilled fighter, but Espel was skilled and cunning. Unpredictable. Even now, Wil was trying to sort out whether Espel truly panicked on the ship with her father, or if it had been her plan to betray him all along.

Zay crossed her arms and looked to Loom. "It's entirely possible she'll try that."

Loom smiled at Wil. It was the sort of sleepy, cocky smile that lured her heart to him every time. "Then I hope you'll avenge me. Bring guns. My sister is a crafty one, as you've pointed out."

"I'm being serious," Wil snapped. "We can't trust her. I never thought I'd be in a position to remind you of that."

"There's no need to remind me," Loom said, pushing himself to his feet. "I may not know the life story of everyone on this ship, but I'm well aware of Espel's."

There was thunder in his steps as he moved past her and made his exit.

For the rest of the weeklong journey to the Western Isles, Wil barely encountered Loom, and when she did, it was always with the guarded politeness of strangers. It irritated her, but she could find no way to break it.

Some nights, she dreamed of Aleen. Other nights, she dreamed of nothing at all. Wil found herself grateful for Espel's presence on the ship at night. The Southern princess had proven to be a relentless insomniac. Once everyone had retired to their cabins for the night, and after even Ada had ceased his nightly mewling, Wil would hear Espel pacing up and down the hall, foraging in the kitchen, and tending to Masalee.

It was a welcome sign of life on an otherwise silent sea.

By the final day of the journey to the Western Isles, Masalee was on her feet again. A brush with death had hardly lessened the ferocity of her gaze. She moved slowly but deftly, all her weapons sheathed.

Masalee was at Espel's side as they all stood on the deck to watch the land coming into view. It was late night now, and the timing had been Zay's idea. Even though Southern ships were welcome in the West, they couldn't afford any unwanted attention.

Masalee should have been resting, especially on this ship where Espel was hardly in need of a high guard to protect her. Espel had told her this, but Masalee wouldn't return belowdecks. The cold night air made her shiver, and Espel muttered, "Hells, you're stubborn," and wrapped her own scarf around Masalee's neck. "You're of no use to me dead, you know."

"You don't think I'd make a good ghost?" Masalee said. "Haunting you all throughout the palace, stirring the curtains and such?"

"No," Espel said. "I order you to live forever."

"As Her Highness wishes."

Wil saw the smile Espel gave her guard. It was full of gratitude and relief and warmth, because for once in their lives, the winds of fate had granted them mercy. The king had surely aimed to kill, and for a while it had seemed as though he'd succeed. But on the third day, Masalee's fever broke and she had been fighting her way back to her usual self ever since.

Masalee was just the right height for Espel to rest her head against her heart. That's precisely what Espel did in that moment, and Masalee wrapped both arms around her, enveloping them both in the wolf pelt blanket that puddled at their feet.

In the palace, love was not an option for anyone in the king's shadow. Love was a weakness that the king would use to twist his children into compliance. But out here, they were safe. They were free.

"We'll sell the ship first," Loom murmured against Wil's ear. She nearly jumped. She hadn't heard him approach—stealth was one of his infuriatingly smooth abilities. She turned to face him. His eyes caught the lights of the distant port, like the reflection of the moon on black water. "You and Masalee should be the ones to make the deal while the rest of us lie low," Loom went on. He didn't have to explain further. Wil and Masalee weren't of Southern descent, and ship vendors would likely assume they'd obtained the Southern ship through theft, given how rare Southern ships were on the general market. This would lower suspicions. Stolen ships passed through ports and changed hands every day.

"I'll trade this ship for one with a more Northern design," Wil said. "So it will make things easier when we make our way to Arrod." She kept her voice even, as though she weren't desperate to talk to him, as though her stomach didn't feel sick with all the tense silence that had plagued them for this whole trip. She spoke to him as though she didn't want to kiss him, or punch him, or both.

"Where are we going to dock?" she asked.

Loom nodded ahead, to the docks that presented as shadows beyond the streetlamps. The port was cluttered with ships; very few people traveled by dirigible during the winter months.

There was also a fair mix of wealth in the Western Isles. Affluent families sent their children here for its universities, so a ship as ornate as Espel's was less likely to stand out.

"We should get some rest once we arrive, and then everyone should leave at first light, so it will seem like I traveled alone."

"Masalee will be with you," Loom said.

Wil narrowed her eyes. "Where was I when all these plans were being made?"

"It was Espel's idea." He averted his eyes, a gesture so unlike him that Wil couldn't help being concerned.

"You've been speaking to her?"

"Not much," he said, his gaze flitting briefly to his sister, who stood on the opposite side of the deck, fretting over Masalee's blanket. "I think it's important for Espel and me to establish a tentative sort of trust. We have to work together on this."

Loom was right; he and his sister did need to work together. But all this was leading up to the day they would inevitably betray each other for the throne.

"Loom," Wil whispered, wrapping her arms around his

shoulders and rising on the tips of her toes. To anyone else, it would seem that she was bringing herself in for a kiss, murmuring platitudes. "I'm always on your side. You know that. But she's going to betray you. I don't know how or when; I only know that she'll kill you for the throne."

He was staring at her mouth as she spoke. When their gazes finally met, the sadness in his expression threw her.

"I know," he said. "There's something I have to ask of you."

"What is it?" Wil asked.

"If Espel has to be killed, I'm the one to do it."

Wil caught herself tugging at one of the sweeping waves of his dark hair. She was winding the lock around her finger, worrying it. She wanted to tell him that he and his sister would surely survive this. She wanted to tell him that he would be able to save the sister who had been lost to him the moment their mother died bringing her into the world. She wanted to say that he and Espel would be able to rule their kingdom together, and that he would not lose the only family he had left.

But he deserved better than empty promises.

She took his face in her hands and she kissed him. It was a soft, small kiss. Only an instant. He bowed his forehead to rest against hers and he closed his eyes.

"I promise," she told him.

# TWENTY-TWO

THOUGH THE WESTERN ISLES WERE neutral territory, and though the ship arrived silently and without incident, Wil was too uneasy to sleep.

While everyone else retreated belowdecks to salvage what precious hours remained before sunrise, Wil paced the length of the deck. When this did nothing to settle her, she descended and strolled the line where the water met the sand, keeping the ship in sight.

Though she hadn't inherited her mother's gold hair or blue eyes, Wil did have her restless and nomadic spirit. An insomniac's soul. She couldn't help it. Back at the castle, Wil often slept deeply and dreamlessly, worn from whatever mission she had carried out for her father or brothers. But without that accomplished exhaustion, her thoughts came alive at night.

Now, she thought of Loom killing Espel. If it came to that, Wil knew it would be necessary. Loom would try to spare his sister's life by any means. But he was not above claiming his kingdom at all costs.

She thought of Owen. Of the heavy and horrific loss that sat forever in her chest, fossilized by guilt. Owen's loss was fused to her bones. What she had done to him would never leave her.

She didn't want that for Loom. But she had made a promise and she'd meant it; it was his decision and his alone.

She sat on a sand dune some distance from the water. She liked sand; it was soft and malleable, yet immune to her curse. It didn't splinter and stab at her the way grass did.

When all this was through, she might spend the rest of her life traveling between beaches. Northern Arrod's Port Capital was waterfront, but it was all sidewalks and city, no real beach to speak of.

She turned her head when she heard the gentle whisper of footsteps kicking away sand. Loom was approaching, his stride uncertain and tenuous. She smiled to let him know that he was welcome to join her. The smile felt wrong and forced and fake, and she cursed herself for it.

He was shivering when he sat beside her, but he unwound the knitted blanket from his shoulders and fitted it over hers.

"Thought you might have frozen to death by now," he said.

"Not a chance." Wil raised her head into the forthcoming breeze. "Cold is good for you. Gets the blood flowing."

"I'm not sure how well my blood will flow if it's frozen," Loom said.

She laughed, and threw half of the blanket around him. He burrowed into it gratefully.

Wind blew her hair across her face, and Loom snared it with his finger and tucked it behind her ear.

They had orbited closer to each other now. His eyes held hers. They were dark and lovely and as endless as the sea. Wil forgot whatever it was she had been about to say.

The curse that bound their hearts was a cruel one, but it was not nearly so cruel as the burning white stars and the whispering wind and the night that lied and told her she could have what she wanted. She could have him.

She should have been the one to pull away. She should have known better. But she raised her hand and traced her finger across his lower lip. She only wanted to touch him the way that the starlight did.

His eyelids were heavy now. The cold burned a red blush across his cheeks. His finger trailed from her ear to the side of her throat, stopping at the place where her pulse thudded. A pulse that meant death for so many, but not for him.

Wil felt like a fool for wanting to give in to her curse, and then in the next breath she felt like a fool for trying to fight it.

She moved to kiss him, but he was the one to draw back. He started, the daydream gone from his eyes. He was alert now as he craned his neck and scanned the beach.

"What is it?" Wil asked. "What's—"

He threw her back onto the sand just as the arrow shot over her head. Another followed. It embedded itself in the ground beside her.

She looked up, breathless, but there was no one in sight.

Loom was the one to act. He must have seen something she'd missed. He grabbed her wrist and pulled her to her feet. The blanket fluttered and fell like a corpse as they started to run. They moved for the grass, where the solid earth wouldn't slow their footsteps.

Another arrow. Another. Wil and Loom were moving in a zigzag pattern, but it wasn't throwing off their attackers as well as it should have.

The next arrow confirmed Wil's suspicion that she was the target, not Loom. She pulled him into the cradle of a giant tree's roots.

She pressed her palms to her eyes and tried to think. Who had she angered? Heaps of underground market vendors, but none of them would have tracked her here. Or if they held that much of a grudge, they would have come for her months ago when she was traveling alone and at her most vulnerable.

"Could this be your father?" she whispered through labored breaths.

"I don't think so." Loom leaned forward to scan their surroundings. "We might have lost them. Are you all right?" He was grasping her shoulder now, inspecting her. "Were you hit?"

She shook her head. "I'm fine."

Grass stabbed at her legs and palms as it crystallized.

"High winds," a voice cursed. "Look at that."

It was a Northern Arrod accent.

"The king was right," another man said. "She really is some sort of evil witch."

The men were standing over them now. Lumbering and tall, with thick arms and armor that glinted cruelly against the night.

Wil stood, but Loom was faster. He moved a pace ahead, his arm spread out, shielding her.

She considered her weapons but didn't move. Her assailants would have plenty of time to drive an arrow through her before she finished reaching for her gun, and Loom was stubbornly prepared to take that arrow for her.

"We could kill them both," the first man said.

"The king was very clear that nobody else be killed," the other man said. "Some superstition about ghosts."

"Winds, he really is a mad one, isn't he?"

Baren. Baren had hired assassins to kill her; but how had they tracked her here?

The men laughed, and one of them nocked an arrow, pointing it tauntingly at Wil's heart. "Shame to kill such a pretty little thing," he said. "I hope the king lets me keep your corpse. Would make a lovely figurehead for my ship."

The words had only just left the man's mouth before the

knife came at him. He was on the ground, empty-eyed, a burst of blood at his temple. The other man had no time to react before he shared the same fate.

There was fire in Loom's eyes as he stood over them. His teeth were gritted. Blood dripped from his dagger onto his boots.

Wil's shoulders dropped. She stared at the corpses of the men who moments earlier had tried to take her life.

Loom wiped the blood from his weapon and sheathed it. Wil didn't realize that her hands were trembling until he took them in his own, covering them completely with his fingers.

"You aren't injured," he said. "Come on. This isn't the first time someone's trained a weapon on you." He tried to laugh.

Wil shook her head. "He knows." Her voice was shaky, like the rest of her. Loom was right; this was not the first attempt that had been made on her life. Nor, she suspected, would it be the last. But if Baren was willing to expend resources on tracking her across the ocean, then the old marveler woman must have told him what Wil truly was. Had he dreamed of Aleen, too? "Baren knows."

"Wil?" Loom touched her chin, her cheek. He sought her gaze until at last she looked away from the hapless assassins. "What is it? What does he know?"

"We have to get rid of their bodies," she said, awakening from her daze. "Before anyone sees. My brother knows about my curse and he's sent assassins to kill me."

Disposing of the corpses was the easy part. The Western port slept at night; it was the woods that lived, far off in the distance and filled with the shanty songs of wanderers. In the darkness, Wil and Loom dragged the bodies to the sea. They would wash ashore eventually, but Wil and Loom would be long gone by then.

Wil slung the crossbow over her shoulder while Loom picked the bodies of their knives before casting them to sea.

It was gruesome but methodical work, and as Wil watched Loom crouch at the water's edge to wash the blood from his arms, she felt as connected to him as ever. He was not one to balk at horrible things when they needed to be done, but moreover, he did not expect her to cower or retch or complain. They were equals. Equals when things were ugly. Equals when things were not ugly at all.

He reached over her shoulder and slid an arrow into its place in her new quiver. The gesture was gentle and intimate, as if he'd swept the hair from her face.

"You all right?"

She nodded. "For now," she said. "But there will be more. We can't stay here. The second we get a new ship—"

"That isn't what I meant," Loom said. His voice was soft. "You said that your brother knows something. What is it? Why is he so desperate to kill you? If he wants you gone, he could simply banish you from the kingdom."

"He isn't trying to save the throne," she said. "He's trying to save our family. This curse—it doesn't only affect me. It's meant to destroy all of us. My mother, my father, my brothers. Anything that happens to them is all my fault."

"That doesn't make any sense," Loom countered. "Of course it isn't your fault."

"Why do you think I want to help you?" Wil snapped. "You have this idea that I'm kind and—and good, but I'm not. I'm trying to repair the damage done to your kingdom because it's my fault that Cannolay was attacked. It's my fault that Baren is on the throne, and it's my fault that he's trying to destroy both your kingdom and mine."

She had begun pacing for the woods now, as though she could escape the truth of it. Loom kept up beside her. "How?" he demanded, unbelieving. "How could it be your fault that your brother attacked my kingdom when you had no communication with him? When you couldn't have possibly anticipated—"

"Because I killed Owen," she cried. Her voice was tight, but she would not let herself cry. She couldn't afford to fall into that dark hole of grief. Not now. "You hate my family, and for what my father has done, I don't blame you, but Owen was *good*. He was going to unite our kingdoms. He was going to fix everything, but because of me, he can't, and everything is broken."

They had stopped walking, surrounded by rows of half-dead trees. Loom offered no words of condemnation. He merely waited for her to go on.

So she did. She told him about Aleen and the curse meant

to destroy her entire family, with her as the weapon. Her crime? Being the daughter her mother had always wanted. Being the one thing the queen loved more than her king. She told him about the old marveler woman's attempt on her life, and the dreams that showed the bloodbath of her late aunt in vivid detail. Love as a weapon. Love turned into hatred.

By the time she finished the tale, she had backed away from him, as though subconsciously anticipating his disdain.

"You were right," she said. "You were right to think the worst of me for lying to you about who I am. You were right to be angry—"

In two broad strides, Loom bridged the space between them. He put his arms around her.

The embrace silenced her. She closed her eyes, shutting out the world and all the words she had been prepared to say. The apologies she had been prepared to give. Loom had a way of making the world feel still and calm. He had a way of making her feel like she was still a part of it. Her arms coiled around him and she gripped his shirt.

"Before we kill my father, it sounds like we should kill your brother," he said at last.

Wil shook her head against his chest. "I can't do that to my mother a second time."

"He shouldn't be on the throne," Loom said. There was a strange comfort to hear him talking once again about practical things.

"He won't be for long," Wil said. She drew back just enough to look at him. "My family is planning something."

"What?" he asked.

"That I can't tell you," she said, and hastily added, "Not yet, but you'll know soon."

He didn't press her for more, but she could see the perplexity in his stare. He didn't know what it would be like to have a family with whom he could share a secret. There was no loyalty shared between him and his sister and their father.

"But we do need to move fast," she said. "If we leave by late morning, we can be in Northern Arrod in a day."

"A day might be too ambitious," Loom said.

"Not the way Zay pilots," Wil said.

Loom laughed.

It had been more than a week now since she'd seen her mother and brothers, since she'd been in the castle that had become too silent. It felt like a lifetime ago, with all that had happened.

He tucked the hair behind her ears. Clouds of breath escaped him and dissolved in the frigid winter air. He was starting to shiver, though he hadn't complained about the cold.

Wil led them back to the ship. Neither of them could sleep, so they spent the last hour before sunrise on the deck, wrapped in the same blanket and perched back to back, scanning the horizon for any other assassins. None came. Wil almost wished that an assassin would come. This time, she'd demand answers.

She would want to know how they had tracked her here, and what Baren had said. Was he telling the entire kingdom about her curse? Then again, who would listen? Something had clearly overtaken him. Something dark and shifty and all-consuming, and anyone who'd had an earful of his ramblings would dismiss him as mad.

Loom didn't try to discuss it, and she was grateful for that. She was grateful for the comfortable silence that existed between them now. He canted his head until it touched hers, and in that small gesture she knew that things were okay between them. They didn't always need to understand each other. Riddles and secrets and all, they took each other for what they were. It was enough.

Before the sun rose, Loom set about to rouse everyone.

Wil and Masalee found themselves alone on the deck; it was the first time this had happened without Masalee managing Wil as a hostage.

"I'll stay with the ship," Masalee said, decisively but without her usual edge. "You find a buyer."

Wil supposed this was Masalee's way of giving her orders, but in truth this had been her own plan as well. Vendors, she knew. Con artists, she could handle. Besides, she had a Northern accent and it would raise no suspicion that she might want a Northern ship and be headed toward Arrod.

Wil nodded to a man standing several yards away. He

looked to be in his twenties, and he had ash-blond hair tied in a ponytail. Despite the cold air, he wore a leather vest over his tunic, and no coat. "I'm going to ask him," Wil said. He was clearly Northern, and he was so clearly at ease with the port, Wil suspected he had spent a great deal of time in the Port Capital.

"What ship are you going to trade for?" Masalee asked.

She had a quiet voice, though not entirely soft. It pulsed with a quiet strength that she kept at bay until the moment she dealt her blow. This was the first time Wil was able to really observe her not as a guard or an enemy. It surprised Wil just how much she liked her. How much she suspected they had in common and how well they would work together in a fight, assuming they were actually on the same side of one.

"I'm going to try and haggle for that large one," Wil said, nodding toward a massive ship with a black exterior and the Northern flag emblazoned on its side. "I'll pretend I'm cocky enough to fool him. I suspect he'll end up giving me that one." Her gaze flitted to a Northern ship that was smaller than Espel's but had been outfitted with solar panels, hinting it had been modified with an electrical system not common in Northern ships.

"It sounds easy enough," Masalee said.

"Don't sour our luck with optimism," Wil said, and Masalee surprised her with something resembling a smile. "Try to look helpless and dumb," Wil told her. "It really helps." To demonstrate, she batted her eyelashes.

Masalee's stare hardened, and Wil couldn't tell whether she was rejecting her suggestion or trying to put it into action. In any case, Masalee was too stalwart and strong to give even the barest illusion of weakness.

All Masalee said was, "I'll steady your heart so you don't kill him."

Wil made her way toward the man. He was a captain, by the looks of him. Though she was far from home, it comforted Wil to realize how at ease she felt in this port town. It wasn't very different from home. She felt herself stepping back into her old role of the nameless wanderer child, who had never met the royal family, much less shared a drop of blood with them. She was meek and helpless and timid. Lost.

"Excuse me," she said. The man spun to face her, and his quizzical expression at once brightened with a jovial smile.

"Morning, young lady," he said, in that familiar Northern Arrod accent. "Looking for a ride somewhere? I'm closed for fares, but I can direct you to—"

"No," Wil said, her voice coming out with a stutter. She hunched her shoulders and looked back to Masalee, who was fidgeting anxiously. She had buried her swords in the folds of her robe, and her expression had softened. She was using her young features to her advantage.

"I'm a university student," Wil said. "My grandmother— she's taken ill, and I'm trying to return home with my maid."

The story began forming in her mind, all the pieces weaving together in a sudden surge of inspiration. She had always been an excellent liar, but more than that, she enjoyed the lie. She was enchanted by the idea of being someone else and living an entirely different story.

She was prepared to tell this man the rest of it. She was going to say that her fare had been stolen—her fault for being so careless—but she had managed to acquire a ship. The man wouldn't ask questions about this, not if he wanted to barter. She was going to blush and avert her eyes and beg him to trade her for that lovely Northern ship in the distance, so that she could make it home. He was going to take pity on her and trade the smaller one instead.

It was one of her more inspired sob stories, Wil thought.

But she didn't get to tell it. Before she could go on, the man put a pitying hand on her shoulder.

"Young lady," he said, "I would be happy to do business with you, but you won't be able to sail to Northern Arrod anytime soon."

She raised her eyes, and her genuine confusion blended perfectly with her act from a moment earlier. "Why not?" she said.

"I suppose you haven't heard," the man said. "The South just waged an attack on the Port Capital. Even if you could get through the war zone, there would be nowhere left for you to dock."

# TWENTY-THREE

FOR ONCE, WIL WAS GRATEFUL for Zay's overzealous piloting. Wil had bartered for the smaller ship with the modified electrical system, as anticipated. But it was a joyless accomplishment. Her mind was in a frenzy. She felt dizzy and sick. The light glinted off the water and the sun was shrieking in its sky. Her heart was pounding. From somewhere far away, she felt Masalee trying to calm it. But Masalee's strength was still fickle, and she couldn't control Wil's heart for very long.

Only Loom could touch Wil now, but he didn't. He stood beside her on the deck, watching her. She clutched the railing hard, her knuckles white.

"Hey," he finally said. His voice was not soft. It was not soothing or placating or calm. "Whatever waits for us on the other side of this ocean, we'll handle it."

"'We'?" Wil looked at him, incredulous. "My entire family could be dead right now, and you're saying 'we'?"

Wil made herself say those words. Her entire family could be dead, and she had to face it. Her mother and Gerdie, and even Baren gone. She tried to picture it. She tried to see Gerdie, bloodied and dead in a smoldering castle. But the image wouldn't form.

Her breathing had grown rapid. Her vision blurred. Loom put his hand over hers, prying her fingers off the bar.

"Wil."

"This is my fault." She shook her head. "None of this would have ever happened to your kingdom or to mine if Owen were alive."

"Wil." His voice was firm. He took her shoulders, forcing her to look at him. "You aren't going to fall apart. That isn't going to help them."

Wil knew, in some small, faraway part of herself, that he was right. Panic was of no use to her family, or herself. But for once in her life she couldn't help it. Her breath came in short, erratic gasps. Her vision tunneled. Her ears filled up with wind. The ocean, once beautiful and inviting, was now cold and menacing.

Loom put something into her hands. A smattering of leaves. They burst into crystals. Jagged blooms of red and crystal. A rush of calm moved through her. Her thoughts cleared. Color returned to the sky and sea, and to Loom's deep brown eyes.

He wasn't looking at her with worry. He wasn't going to console her. He was instead reminding her of her own strength. It still persisted inside her, despite everything; it was what made her run for the Port Capital when she was banished, and what kept her breathing as she flew away from home on a dirigible after Owen's death. It was that bizarre force that kept her lungs breathing and her eyes blinking and her world orbiting its sun.

Owen's death had knocked the wind from her chest. Her father's loss had left her hollow and still too stunned to even cry for him. But a world without Gerdie would be pointless. Empty. Cruel. Without Gerdie, everyone in the world would be a stranger. There would be no due north on her compass. She would never be home again.

She didn't have words for this. She dropped the crystals into the sea and watched them disappear.

"How will we arrive?" she asked. "If the ports are destroyed, I mean."

"Masalee will hide the ship," Loom said. "She's done it for Espel a hundred times before. That's probably how Espel was able to make it to the Eastern Isles undetected."

"How can she hide an entire ship?" Wil asked, though she couldn't bring herself to care about the answer.

"She creates an illusion of the ocean and skyline," Loom said. "If you were to look very closely, you might see that the seams with the waves and the clouds are off, but at a glance, it's just sea and sky."

Wil leaned her arms against the railing and slid forward, as though the weight of her body could push the ship faster. They were already going at top speed. She could hear the engine straining under her feet.

Her anxiety drained away, taking everything else with it. She couldn't wonder at the power of marvelers, or think about warring kings. She couldn't even muster any anger. Nothing mattered until she was home and her family was in her sight again.

Sometime after nightfall, Wil's exhaustion caught up with her. She fell asleep sitting upright against the ship's railing. A gentle touch woke her. She bolted awake with a start to see Masalee crouched before her.

"You shouldn't sleep here," Masalee said. "You'll fall through the slats and drown."

Wil turned to look at the sea below. She was dazed, her mind foggy with sleep. What Masalee said seemed improbable. Wil couldn't imagine falling or drowning. She couldn't imagine dying at all. It seemed that, despite the world's many attempts to kill her, her destiny was to live a long life and wreak havoc on everyone she loved.

Her heart was slow in her chest. She felt the tendrils of marvelry in her blood, and she didn't fight it. She eased back against the railing with a deflating breath.

"Please let them be alive," she whispered. She didn't know

who the words were spoken for. Maybe her words were a prayer.

"You love them," Masalee said, settling into a kneel beside her. Her presence was calming when she allowed it to be.

Wil stared skyward without answering. She wished that she didn't love her family, or Loom. Maybe then they would be safe.

But it was no matter. Masalee didn't need Wil's words. She could sense them. Just as her marvelry moved through veins and arteries, she had a way of entering minds, too.

"We think our family is the center of the world," Masalee said. "But that's a mistake. We're all the center of our own world. There's always something else on the horizon if we keep walking."

"You don't believe that," Wil challenged.

"My family is dead," Masalee said. "My father was killed by Gray Fever. I was too young to work, and my mother couldn't afford to keep me. She was going to sell me to slavers. She changed her mind, so they killed her. Took me anyway."

Wil drew her knees to her chest. Masalee spoke her story with brevity and calm, as though it were a recitation from an old book.

"I'm alive because I wanted life," she went on. "Even with nowhere left to go, I was willing to kill the Southern princess if it meant I got to survive."

"You didn't kill your family," Wil said. "That's the difference."

"You're pitying yourself," Masalee said. "If they're alive,

you fight to keep them alive. If they're dead, you fight to keep yourself alive."

"Would you say that if Espel were dead?" Wil said. She was just bitter and angry enough now to say such a thing.

Masalee closed her eyes just a beat too long; it was the only small betrayal of pain she would afford. "Yes."

Wil believed her. Espel and Masalee had a love that was built on strength. On survival. But even if one could survive losing the other, it would be a hollow existence. Wil had seen the light leave Espel's eyes when the dagger tore through Masalee's chest. The air in their lungs could never take the place of the love those two shared.

"You and I don't have much in common," Masalee said. "But King Zinil has used us both as bait."

"What do you mean?" Wil asked.

"He tried to kill me so he could manipulate Espel. Make her weak. Make her return. And he attacked your family to lure you right where he wants you, with Loom at your side. No matter what happens, you can't stop fighting. You can't let him break you." She grabbed Wil's chin, forcing her to look at her. "No matter what," she repeated.

Wil's heart tried to pound, but it couldn't. Wil held her tongue. Masalee wasn't her enemy. Masalee wasn't the one who had done this to her family, to her kingdom. It wasn't Masalee's fault that what she said was true. Wil hated that most of all. Even if her family was dead, she could not allow herself to crumple in her grief. She could not let King Zinil weaken her, make her malleable, and steal her curse.

"I know," she said, but the words, like all else, meant nothing. Until she found her family, the entire world meant nothing.

Wil forced herself to retreat belowdecks to sleep. She had been awake for the better part of forty-eight hours, and what Masalee said was true: her mind needed to be sharp for whatever awaited her.

The ship had distinctly Northern designs—glossy oak beams that bordered the interior, and plaster walls that resembled cottages that framed the cobblestones in Arrod's villages.

She had been searching for an empty cabin, but instead she found Loom. He was sitting on the edge of a cabin's small bed whose flannel sheets were still neatly tucked in place.

His hair was damp and dripping. The room smelled of shower steam and root soap—something found in Northern Arrod, made from roots and lemongrass.

On Loom's bare chest, Wil could see the inked fable of his tattoos. Stories that blended one into the next. Somehow, these were more familiar to her now than the patterns on this ship, which were patterned after her home.

"Hey." His voice was soft. "Are you going to try and sleep?"

She slumped, with her shoulder against the door frame. "I'm so tired," she confessed. Her voice felt small. "How can I rest, not knowing if they're all right?"

He stood, made his way across the room, and rested his hand on her shoulder. Wil thought that he might speak some words of wisdom. Something profound that would get her through the night and leave her stronger for it.

But Loom must have known that any platitudes he offered now would be unworthy of the air used to speak them. Instead, he kissed her forehead. The kiss was gentle and sincere, and from that small thing, Wil knew that the love he felt for her was not entirely a curse. He saw something in her. Something good. Something she could not find in herself.

"Good night," he said. But when he moved for the hallway, she caught his wrist.

"Can you stay with me?" she said.

In answer, he put his arms around her. She pressed her head to his heart and heard his breathing and the rush of his blood. She felt him tremble and tighten his hold; she felt the way that her body steadied his.

She ran her hand up the length of his back, feeling the warm skin still humid from the shower. She felt the spot where his skin curved in along his spine.

He reached past her to turn out the light and close the door. He felt what she did: that the world was big and vast, and somehow they had found each other. There was no promise for how long.

There in the dark, love felt possible and honest and easily conquered. Soon morning would come and shed light on all the jagged edges, all the places to fall and to drown, but for now they were both here, and they were safe, and it was all right.

When he kissed her, it was nothing like all the times before when they had been curious and unsure. This time, there was the certainty that came from two hearts that now knew each other well. They first met in a fit of blood and fire and passion; they had fought and failed and triumphed alongside each other, and from the start they had always matched each other, muscle for muscle, move for move.

He sat on the edge of the bed, drawing her down with him. Her knees locked around his hips, and she sucked in her breath when his hands traced the length of her sides.

Wil rested her forehead against his, their shallow breaths colliding.

"I love you," she said. It was a confession.

His cheek curved with a smile in the moonlight. When he fell back against the sheets, she followed, pinning his shoulders as he rose up to kiss her. It was almost like fighting, she thought, but gentler. When his hands slid under her tunic and moved along the curl of her hips, her heart fluttered. Her traitorous, cursed, broken heart that he was fighting so hard to keep safe.

He kissed her mouth, her cheek, the spot where her shoulder was exposed through the collar of her shirt.

Her palms spread across the subtle dunes of his chest, his stomach, the hollows of his hips. He breathed as though her touch had hurt him, and all her blood went cold and then hot with expectancy.

It wasn't just his heart that drew her, Wil realized. It was all of him. Every tendon, every muscle, every loose curl that puddled around his head as he lay beneath her. She loved all of him, and she wanted him the way that he wanted his kingdom.

After, she lay still, considering the subtle ache that had pooled somewhere deep between her hips, the flutters of warmth that trailed up and down her chest in erratic lines, sharp and then soft.

Loom kissed her temple, nudging her, and she knew that he was asking if she was okay. He had done this several times throughout, pausing in motions that were otherwise deft, searching her eyes until she nodded up at him, her lashes lazily fluttering. Yes, she was telling him. Yes, she still wanted him. Yes, she was still here.

She leaned against him now, anticipating his arm wrapping around her side an instant before he moved.

Her body had changed in some subtle way that intrigued her. From the time she learned to fight, she had come to understand all the cogs that shifted and stirred when she moved, like a sort of machine. She had always relied on herself, but now there was someone who knew her the way that she knew herself. Someone she knew just as well.

She rolled her head against him, placing a loose, sleepy kiss against his chest.

They coasted into a light half-sleep, stirring and shifting to stay close to each other.

Wil saw dreams that were too flimsy to fool her. Things like castles and her mother's shanty songs. Through it all she felt Loom against her as steady as a rock in shifting tides.

It was the dawn that finally woke her for good. She sat up, craning her neck to see through the porthole. The water was placid, everything calm.

Pale light spread over their bodies, and she saw Loom clearly for the first time in hours. He lay on his back with one arm strewn over the edge of the bed, the sheets bunched over one of his thighs.

She settled back down beside him and traced her finger over the lines of his tattoos, where the ink ended and gave way to his chest.

She traced the heart impaled at his throat. He would bear this tattoo even if all the Southern Isles crumbled into the sea, and every time he saw it he would be reminded: He was the king whether he had been crowned or not. He was the king whether his kingdom stood or fell, because it was on his skin and in his blood.

His eyes moved behind their lids, and he shifted with a soft moan. When he opened his eyes, he smiled tiredly and tufted her hair between his fingers.

"Hey," he said.

"Hey." She swept the back of her hand across his forehead. "I didn't mean to wake you." This was a lie, she realized. She had been greedy for the way that he looked at her, and had been impatiently waiting to see his eyes again.

"How far are we from Arrod?" he asked.

"We should arrive within the hour," Wil said. She had been staring through the porthole as Loom slept, watching her kingdom slowly dawn on the horizon.

He turned his head to kiss her bicep. She felt lighter at his touch. Her legs moved against the sheets and she could have believed they were floating.

Loom had never been so beautiful as he was now, all the pretense he put on for the world stripped away. This was who he was when he was alone.

She loved him. She tested the words once again in her mind. She had expected that if she ever fell in love, it would be the way her father had loved his queen, or the way that Owen had loved Addney. But the love she shared with Loom was something entirely its own, and she wondered if love by its nature was always uncharted. It was certain, but not simple. Giving, but not selfless. A fluttering mast on a ship that often capsized.

"I'm glad you're cursed," Wil said.

"Really?" Loom mused, the soft hum of his voice meshing with the sound of the waves crashing. "Why's that?"

"The first time I saw you was in Brayshire," she said. "In the midst of all that chaos, you swept me off the ground. I looked at you and I thought: He's going to die. I've just killed him. Sometimes I imagine what it would have been like if I had. If you were just another thing I destroyed." It made her muscles rigid, just thinking about it. Another beautiful thing she would have taken from this world.

"Lucky me," Loom mused as she rested her head on his outstretched arm. "The first time I saw you, I thought you were a thief smuggling gemstones."

"I wish," Wil said. "And you're not too far off. I did a fair bit of thievery and smuggling in Arrod."

"I also knew you were trouble."

Wil smirked at him. "Bit of an understatement."

"You hated me," he said.

She studied his face. Heavy eyelashes, strong jaw, and that sad sort of kindness that always seemed to haunt him.

"I didn't hate you," she said. "In the days before and after we met, I was lost. The entire world felt like a stranger to me. I wasn't capable of feeling much of anything for anyone."

"Everything shadowed over," he guessed, and she nodded. Of course he would understand loss.

They both felt it now. Things hadn't gotten any better. No kingdoms had been saved. The dead were all still dead. And she was so worried about what she would find when she returned home. Unanswered questions swam in the sea all around them, but as vast as the world was, she wasn't alone in it. He was here.

Somehow, in the darkest time of her life, she happened upon the prince of an enemy kingdom and fell in love. "What are the chances that we ever would have found each other?"

"Chance," he echoed. "Chance and luck are meaningless. I

only care about what is, and what will be."

"What do you suppose will be?" she asked.

"I'll be king." He kissed one of her cheeks and then the other. "This war will end. Our kingdoms will come to an alliance. Your heart will stay in your chest, exactly where I like it."

She rolled her head back, breathing out a laugh as he kissed the scar over her heart. This was the first time she had ever shared her body with him, or with anyone, but it felt like the hundredth time. The thousandth. "Will that be a royal decree?"

"Yes, it will," he said. "Anyone who tries to take your heart loses theirs."

His sober tone made her wonder if he was kidding. "And what if I give my heart to someone else?" she said, just as soberly. "Or suppose I decide to keep it for myself."

He looked from her scar to her eyes and said, "As long as your heart is still beating in this world, I'll be happy."

He pressed his palm over the expanse between her hips, in the place where she could still feel him. A fluttery moan escaped her, as though he had anticipated it.

Soon, morning was going to break this spell under which they had fallen. Everything that existed yesterday was awaiting them beyond this room.

"I'm so afraid," she confessed. "That I'll be alone when all this is over."

"No," he said. Her gaze had flitted away, and Loom said, "Look at me, Wil."

Wil. The way he said her name was its own little song. It was a melody he had memorized and turned over in his head, admiring the way it sounded when she wasn't with him.

She raised her eyes to meet his. "You won't ever be alone," he said.

When Wil took his face in her hands and kissed him, she knew that she was only stalling for time. And when his body eclipsed hers once again, she almost could believe that time would stand still.

They lapsed into silence, as rich and comfortable as the bedsheets.

The sea swayed their bodies, and Wil thought about all the places this water reached. She thought about what would await her when she went home, and she thought about her family.

Her head rose and fell with Loom's chest as he breathed. He had been dozing for a while, but now he stirred awake. He kissed the crown of her head, and it set her ablaze. She closed her eyes, savoring it.

"Is it too much to ask what you're thinking?" he ventured. He would prefer silence rather than a lie, she knew.

She wrapped an arm around his stomach, squeezing herself closer. "My family," she said. "My mother."

He caught her hand and laced his fingers through hers.

"I wouldn't know how to describe my mother," Wil said. "She's this—mythical creature. I don't know half the things she's seen, but I can feel them anyway. Under her skin and even on it. When I was a little girl, she used to wrap me in her arms and it felt like the entire world was scooping me up. And the tighter she held me, the more I could taste that world. Smell it. Hear it."

"Like the ocean in a seashell," Loom offered.

"Yes," she said. "My brother feels safest when he's in his laboratory, at his cauldron and surrounded by things he can control. But I feel like everywhere is home. Everywhere and nowhere sometimes." She exhaled hard. "Look what that's done. I wasn't there to protect them."

With that, the spell was broken. All her fear and guilt came rushing back; the air was pierced by it.

Loom sensed it, and he brought their joined hands to his lips. His breath was hot against her fingers.

"This isn't your fault, Wil."

"But it is," she said. "Anything that happens because of my curse, I caused. I'm the reason Arrod doesn't have . . . an heir." Her voice hitched. Owen. An heir. As though that was all he'd ever been. "I'm the reason this war has happened."

"I don't understand you," Loom said. "When you do marvelous, brilliant things, you don't take the credit. But when anything goes wrong, you're first to take the blame." He put his hands under her arms, hoisting her so that she was lying on his chest and facing him. Her knees fitted around his hips. "I know quite a bit about wars, Your Royal Highness." There was a bit of a smile when he said that. "And this war is not your fault.

Its casualties are not on you. Sometimes you have the power to turn things to stone, and sometimes you are only human. In the face of this war, we are all only human."

She studied his face, looking for some sign that he was placating her. But he was in earnest. "You really think I'm human," she said.

"Of course I do." He saw the tears fill her eyes. "Hey. Come here."

She rested her forehead to his and broke, with a sob. Human. It was a word she had taken for granted before her curse came about, and now it was a luxury to hear.

His hands were on her skin. On her body, bare and exposed. There was nothing between them, not even pretense. She had shown him everything now. Every inch, more than anyone had ever seen, much less touched.

With her eyes closed, she felt the weight of him beneath her. The bumps of muscles in his stomach, pressed to hers. His arms and all their stories. His lips, full and warm and dry with winter air. She had never touched anyone in this way; she couldn't imagine being here with anyone else.

If their love now was only a curse, she would never know what love was.

As Northern Arrod drew closer, Wil thought she smelled smoke, though she couldn't be sure how much of it was her imagination. She wondered if bodies had been incinerated by the fires. She wondered if those ashes were in the air and if she was breathing them into her lungs.

None of these thoughts had been in her head just moments earlier. But now, standing on the ship's deck, the world had once again found her.

Loom brought her a mug of something hot and bitter. Some sort of tea that he claimed would help her stay awake, as though she needed any assistance with that.

He smoothed a lock of hair behind her ear, and his fingertips lingered on her skin. "Are you doing all right?" he asked. She knew that he wasn't asking her about Arrod.

Last night, he had been so certain, so confident. But now suddenly he was softer, even concerned.

She gave him a smile—something that seemed impossible in light of what they were about to face—and nodded. She forced herself to draw back from him. It felt like waking up too soon.

"How did he do this?" she asked.

Loom stood beside her and followed her gaze. "While we were securing the ship, Zay picked up some of the chatter in the port. They're saying that it was a bomb, but I know that's impossible. The Southern Isles don't have the resources for something of that magnitude. Whatever he did, it was marvelry."

"Pahn?" Wil asked.

"That's what I'm thinking," Loom said. He narrowed his eyes contemplatively, but said nothing more.

"Masalee thinks your father is doing this to bait me," Wil

said, guessing at his thoughts.

"My father thinks that people are so easily broken," he said. "First me, then Espel, now you. But he can't have any of us."

Wil feared that this wasn't true. She was not like Masalee, who persevered no matter what she lost. If Wil's family was gone, then all her attempts to save her kingdom would have been for nothing. Her grandfather would have won. The curse he cast upon the entire Heidle line would finally have destroyed them all.

*They aren't dead,* she tried to tell herself. *They can't be. I won't allow it.*

# TWENTY-FOUR

THE PORT CAPITAL WAS DESTROYED. Ships were sunken, or sinking. Wil could scarcely register the buildings, many with gaping holes as though some giant creature had come and shredded them with talons.

"This is the work of marvelry," Masalee said, her voice a strained whisper. "Pahn is here somewhere." She was still laboring to conceal their ship as they coasted alongside the city, seeking a place to drop their anchor. Wil barely heard any of it. She was too busy scanning the debris for bodies. For life. For anything.

The city was quiet and coated in ashes. Gas streetlamps flickered in the early morning light because no one had come to turn them off.

Masalee's step faltered, and Espel clung to her arm to keep

her upright. "You may as well let go," Espel told her. "It won't matter if our ship is in view. There's no one to see it."

"Pahn is here," Masalee said again. "He'll see it."

"Let him," Espel said. "We aren't here to cower and hide from him."

"We aren't hiding," Wil said. It was the first she had spoken since their arrival, and everyone turned to her. "Masalee, if you can conceal the ship, that would be for the best. We'll need a safe place to retreat and regroup."

"I don't think—" Espel began, and Wil cut her off.

"Just hear me out." Wil turned away from the Port Capital so that she could face Espel, who was standing between Masalee and Loom. "Most of Northern Arrod is wooded. We'll be able to move through the trees undetected as we head for the castle. That's where your father will expect us to go, right?" She looked to Masalee. "You'll stay here and conceal the ship. Zay will go belowdecks at the helm in case we need to make a fast exit."

Wil didn't linger to hear any objections. They could follow her plans or not. Either way, she couldn't stay on this ship and waste a moment more. They were close enough to the port now that she was able to jump over the ship's edge and land crouched on the cobblestones. Dust flew up around her from the impact. It coated her skin. None of it turned to crystal, because there was no life here. Nothing moving or breathing, save for the odd fortunate smattering of weeds.

This was not home. The thought hit her with clarity that shone like a beacon over a sea of frenzied other thoughts. There was nothing to fill these streets or buildings, not even ghosts. And yet she knew that there were bodies—living and dead— hiding somewhere beneath all this rubble and lurking in alleys. Those with sense would stay hidden, Wil knew. If their homes were destroyed, many would retreat to the sewers or into the thick of the forest, in the uninhabited wilderness no enemy kingdom would see fit to bomb.

Because the Port Capital and outlying cities were at sea level, most buildings within a mile of the water wouldn't have basements or bunkers. There was no protocol for this. Her father had planned and considered many attacks over the years, but he had never bothered to anticipate what would become of Arrod should it fall under attack. It had been an impossibility. Arrod had all the resources, all the wealth.

Wil didn't let herself succumb to the sickness that tried to weaken her knees. She didn't let herself collapse or even cry. She walked forward, because that was the only useful thing to do.

Loom caught up with her just as she reached the forest, and he touched her arm, gently staying her. "Hey," he said. "Are you sure you want to march right up to the castle? You know there's going to be a trap waiting."

"What do you suggest?" Wil asked. "If your father did this to bait me, then it worked. And if he did this to bait you, knowing you'd follow, then that worked."

"I'm not concerned with my father," Loom said. "This is Pahn's work."

Wil shrugged. "I know that." She shrugged out of his grasp and began moving forward. She didn't let herself feel anything in that moment. She knew that it would take only the slightest taste of fear or dread to stop her. If Loom was going to insist on reminding her of the risks, then she would leave him behind. It wouldn't take much to lose him in these woods.

"I don't want him to kill you." Loom kept pace beside her. "My father wants your curse, not you. He wants the power to turn things to stone."

"He can have it," Wil said.

"He would cut out your heart and have it sewn into his own chest—" Loom's words were cut short when Wil threw his back against a tree. The collar of his coat was bunched in her fist.

In response to her stony glare, he held his hands up in surrender.

"Zay told me that you broke through a door when you heard her screaming," Wil said, letting him go with a shove. "So I know you understand how this feels."

There were no words spoken after that. Espel never caught up with them; maybe she was planning to betray them, Wil thought. Maybe she was joining forces with her father and this had been part of the plan.

No. Wil didn't believe that, if only for what King Zinil had done to Masalee. In trying to take away the girl his daughter loved, King Zinil had lost his daughter forever. Wil knew little else about the Southern princess, but she knew that.

The castle was not a long walk from the Port Capital, and for all the hundreds of times Wil had made this trek home, she had never once imagined that the prince of her nation's enemy kingdom would be beside her for it.

Loom was silent. He had a way of making his energy scarce when he wanted to. She could barely even sense him moving.

In contrast, her own strides were heavy now. Twigs snapped under her boots. Leaves rustled and crunched.

It had snowed the night before, and a thin sheet of white covered everything.

More than half of Northern Arrod was forest. Beyond the Port Capital, there were cities clustered with miles of trees between them. Arrod was so big; it was the largest land mass in the world, and Wil didn't know how she would ever account for all of it. She didn't know what the rest of the kingdom looked like. If it was untouched, or if it was as demolished as the Port Capital. If Owen were here, he wouldn't be traveling in the direction of the castle. He would be in the Port Capital, digging up survivors and lining up the dead so their remains at least could be returned to their families. He would have men combing every city, every home. He would find a way to bring everyone across the Southern Arrod border, which was far enough inland that homes had basements where people could seek refuge.

But Wil was not the heir. She was not as noble as her brother. She was selfish. She cared only about her own family.

The castle appeared in the distance, and it was still standing. But there was no relief in this fact. The gates were torn from their hinges as though they'd been broken by enemy forces. The iron bars were bent. One gate lay useless on the ground while the other still clung by a single hinge, waving feebly like a hand reaching up for help.

Wil broke into a run. Around her, the castle's gardens were still intact. Flowers and hedges sleeping under the snow. Whoever had been here hadn't bothered to destroy useless things like the queen's beloved garden or some late-blooming pear and apple trees. Whoever had been here had made a clean path through the snow, right up the castle's steps. Wil stopped here.

The castle doors had appeared to be closed from a distance, but now she could see that one was ajar, revealing a sliver of the darkness inside.

She was breathing hard. The world was gray and dark and hollow.

The castle was so big. How had she never realized that before now? Tall enough to blot out the sky when she looked up. With dozens of rooms, walls that made everything echo. Passageways that existed within the walls, filled with staircases and sconces, where she and her brother used to play when they were small. It was a wonder they had never gotten lost. Wil felt certain that if she stepped inside this castle, she would never find her way back out of it.

"Wil?" Loom said from beside her.

She moved forward. Her steps were slow. Her legs felt heavy. If King Zinil and Pahn awaited her on the other side of this door, flanked by dozens of armed guards with swords and guns trained on her, she would welcome it. But what she feared was far worse.

The door creaked when she pushed it open. Sunlight filtered into the foyer through windows framed by snow. She didn't call out for her mother or Gerdie or even Baren. The castle had come under attack, and if they were able to flee, then they would have done so. If they were still here, they were dead.

For all her hurry to get here, Wil suddenly found herself incapable of moving at any degree of speed. Her boots were whisper soft against the stone floor. It seemed impossible that her chamber and all her things were at the top of the staircase before her. It seemed impossible that anyone had ever lived here.

She moved toward the servants' kitchen. Loom stayed beside her. He had drawn daggers now, bracing for an attack. One of them had to be on the offensive; Wil knew that her own shock was leaving her vulnerable.

She stopped at the door to Gerdie's lab. It was closed, though not locked. The red bulb, which indicated her brother was at work and not to be disturbed, was flickering erratically, casting a loud, pattering buzz like flies trapped under a glass.

"Don't follow me," Wil told Loom as she moved forward.

"Wil, I—"

"Don't follow me." She said it again, louder that time, and he backed off. Whatever awaited at the bottom of these stairs was for her and only her. Gerdie hated it when anyone else entered his lab. She pushed open the door and took the first step down. The basement's only window was coated in ash and scarcely let in any light. She unhooked the electric lantern mounted along the wall and switched it on. Its blue-white light formed a protective sphere around her as she moved. One step. Then the next.

She stopped on the final step, her boot hovering over the floor. But she didn't move. There was Gerdie, lying in a heap beside his metal table, on which some gummy pink liquid had spilled from its flask and pooled.

His monocle and leg braces were gone. His skin was ashen, his lips bruised blue. Blood congealed at his slashed throat.

His chest was also slashed, severing his shirt clean in half at a diagonal, all the buttons still neatly buttoned, his gray vest still fitted over his shoulders. The ruffles of his collar and sleeves were brown with old blood.

The entire world turned into a scream.

Loom bounded down the stairs, blade at the ready, and Wil realized that the scream had come from her. Loom tried to touch her and she threw his hand violently away and scrambled forward.

She knelt before her brother. This wasn't possible. This

wasn't real. But she could smell the blood. He was dead. She touched him and he didn't turn to stone.

As she pressed her palm to her brother's cold cheek, she realized that she was probing for some sign that this was one of his alchemized corpses. A trick. She hoped to feel leather. But what she felt was skin. The hard slope of a cheekbone. His jaw. Him.

She shook her head, arguing against words that hadn't been spoken. Pleading with something that had offered no bargain. "No." It was a strained, tearful word, though she was sure that she wasn't crying. "No."

Loom tried to haul her to her feet. Her knees buckled. Her grandfather drove his blade through Aleen's heart, cursing them all before they even existed. Her grandmother threw herself into the sea. But all of them had died along with Aleen that night. Wil, Owen, Gerdie, Baren, the king and queen. This was in their blood. This had all been planned. Her grandfather had wanted to destroy them. All because his wife had taken a lover.

Loom tugged at her again. She screamed. The world was a frenzy. It was a storm and she couldn't see through it. She couldn't walk or breathe or speak. Loom didn't let go of her. He made her walk up the stairs, dragging her much of the way, and once they had reached the servants' kitchen again, he grabbed her shoulders.

"We can't stay here," he said. "My father is coming for you."

"I don't care," Wil said. Her vision was wet and blurred.

"I care," Loom said.

"I have to find my mother," Wil said. Dazed, she moved for the door that led back into the foyer. She knew that if Gerdie was dead, her mother would be as well. But she didn't move upstairs for her mother's chamber. Instead, she found herself going in the direction of the throne room. Her footsteps thundered. Baren. She had the horrible thought that he had done this in a fit of delusion and that it hadn't been King Zinil at all.

But when she burst through the high arched doors of the throne room, that theory quickly ended. There was Baren, dead on his throne, bearing the same wounds as his brother.

# TWENTY-FIVE

WIL WAS GOING TO KILL King Zinil. This thought emerged through her shock. She clung to it through the fog of her stunned grief.

It was a hollow mantra that brought no solace, but it kept her standing, and that was all she could hope for.

Her head throbbed with that persistent ache she'd felt the last time she was in Northern Arrod. The kingdom was still cursed. When she grabbed at her mother's rosebushes, they didn't turn to stone.

"How is Arrod still cursed?" she whispered.

"What do you mean?" Loom said.

"Arrod was cursed when I returned. I thought Baren was the reason for it, but he's dead." She spoke this like simple fact, forcing away the enormity of it. She didn't know how long her strength would last before she fell apart, and she wouldn't squander it.

Loom stared at the rosebushes, considering this.

"We need to find Espel," he said.

Espel. The name had meant something to Wil several minutes ago, but now it was just another hollow sound in a world of hollow sounds. She turned to face the castle, offering it one final chance to appear as she remembered it.

But the castle, like all of Arrod, was gray and dead.

Loom had to pull on Wil to get her moving. She hated him for it.

"We have to find out if Southern Arrod is safe," she blurted. King Zinil knew to kill her family, but he had no reason to care about Addney, the late prince's widow, seemingly useless, since as a widow she had no claim to the throne.

As long as Addney was alive, there was something. There was hope.

"I'm sure it is," Loom said. "There's not much down there worth attacking, is there? All their power comes from Northern Arrod."

They were deep into the woods before Wil had the cognizance to realize she was walking back to the Port Capital. *Wake up,* she told herself. But nothing made sense. Everything was dead and useless and gray. Her entire family. Dead. The thought fell through her without taking root.

"You need to be present right now," Loom said. "This is

still your kingdom, and you're all it has left. Wil, look at me."

She didn't. She walked faster, her face pointed stubbornly forward.

"Wil!" He moved ahead of her, blocking her path. Softer, he said, "Wil. You're Arrod's queen."

He said them. The words she had been trying desperately not to hear. The words she had never in her life expected to be true. For an instant she imagined herself sitting on the throne, and in that instant she understood why her father had been so cold. He had not been heartless. He had been haunted.

"Queen," she laughed. It was a bitter, ugly sound. "I have no army. No people. No defense against an invasion. What sort of queen is that?"

"You have people," Loom said. "There are entire cities that likely haven't been hit. If you don't have an army, you assemble one."

A cursed princess turned queen, trying to save a cursed kingdom. She shoved him roughly out of her way.

She stopped walking. Something caught her attention, cradled in the roots of a towering oak tree. A circular piece of glass, framed by copper, with three metal loops meant to accommodate leather straps.

She dropped to her knees. Her hand hovered over it at first, afraid to touch it. And then she cradled it in both hands.

"What is it?" Loom asked.

"A monocle," Wil said. She held it up, as though this should have made sense to him. "It belongs to my brother. He's blind in his left eye without it." Not that it mattered much to Gerdie, unless he was in his lab, trying to decipher his own small, elegant handwriting.

"What's it doing out here?" Loom asked.

Wil stared at it. Her own distorted reflection stared back at her, trapped in a scrap of daylight. Gerdie could have been trying to flee, but then why would his body be all the way back at the castle? And without its straps, the monocle itself would be of little use to him. He wouldn't have left those behind.

He would, however, know that she frequented this path because it was the shortest distance between the castle and the Port Capital. Had he hoped to meet her here? Had he been alive after the initial attack and hoped for her to return? Was it a warning?

"It's a message," Wil said. "It has to be." She looked to Loom. "Gerdie has never done anything without a reason. He's never careless. He doesn't lose anything."

Loom was kind enough not to point out that she was still referring to her brother as though he were alive.

"Or it's a trap," Loom said. "My father could be trying to lure you."

Wil shook her head. "How would your father know to leave this where I'd find it? My brother knows all the paths I take. He knows. This means something."

She stood and began pacing through the trees, along her familiar path. Soon she could hear the river in the distance. This far from the rapids, the water was calm. She ran for the water and stopped at its edge.

Loom was humoring her, she knew. He might have even pitied her. But he did not know Gerdie's genius. When she stepped
onto a rock embedded into the mud beneath the water, Loom
said, "What are you doing?"

"Going across," she said. "There are wanderer camps
nearby. Maybe some are still here. Maybe he wanted me to go
to them."

Loom followed her, if only because he knew she couldn't
be stopped. In some bizarre twist of events, the prince from her
enemy kingdom was in Northern Arrod, protecting his enemy
queen.

Queen. Another hollow, meaningless word that fell through
her.

She made her footfalls lighter, trying once again to be
stealthy and silent as she moved in the direction of the wanderer
camp that had been here the night of Owen's party.

As she moved, she drew her dagger. She hated herself for
this small bit of instinct. Despite everything, she wanted to live.
She was willing to go on even if her family could not. It was
comforting and a betrayal at once, the way her body still geared
for a fight no matter what she had endured. Owen would be
proud to know she had retained the years of training he'd given
her.

The wanderer camp, if it was still here, was only a few
yards ahead.

Wil stopped, her senses on alert. The way that Loom

pressed his back to hers said he had heard it, too. Something moving, light as wind, through the trees.

Everything went still. There were no winter birds, Wil realized now. There had been no life in the kingdom at all. She was just about to say this when the blast hit.

Wil saw the smoke before she heard whatever had caused it. Her ears rang. Her vision filled with thick, heavy smoke. Loom was no longer pressed against her—was he calling for her? She could hear nothing but a shrill, keening whine.

Something grabbed her arm and she spun on her heel, her knife making contact with skin. But it was undeterred by her blade. Through the smoke she saw the blur of a rich blue robe, embroidered with gold thread. A robe? She tried to land a kick to her assailant, but whoever it was moved with a force she couldn't combat, and she hit the ground hard. Her back slammed against the jutting roots of a tree and she gasped to catch her breath.

Through the haze she saw him. Pahn. He stood over her, his boot to her stomach. Fire burned around them in patches, casting hard shadows on his face.

She couldn't move. It was as though invisible arms held her wrists and ankles. Instinctively, she tried to slip free, the way she would if it were a body holding her in place. But there was no escape.

The flames weren't giving off any heat. The smoke moved around Pahn, leaving him in a clearing.

This was marvelry. A paper-thin illusion, like the one Masalee threw over their ship.

"What do you want?" Wil spat. "My curse? Have it. Look around and see what it's brought me."

"Haven't you heard the news?" Pahn said. "You're the queen of Arrod."

Again, Wil heard those words and again she didn't believe them.

"You seem disappointed by the title," Pahn continued. "That's good. It won't be yours for very long." He raised his arms in a grand sweeping gesture toward the kingdom, and Wil felt the pressure on her wrists and ankles tighten. "All this is soon to become the property of King Zinil. Perhaps, if you beg, he'll let you keep Arrod's name. The same won't be true for your life."

A figure blurred through the smoke, and just as Pahn turned his head, Espel's dagger tore through the air and struck him in the throat.

No blood came from the wound. The pressure that had been holding Wil in place dissipated, and Pahn disappeared into the smoke.

Espel reached out a hand and tugged Wil to her feet. "We have to get you back to the ship," Espel said. "Masalee can hide us there. Pahn will be back for you."

"Where's Loom?" Wil said. The smoke and flames were beginning to disappear.

The forest was empty.

# TWENTY-SIX

LOOM AWOKE TO THE SOUND of rushing water.

He opened his eyes and clutched at his throbbing head, certain his hand would come back covered in blood. There was no blood.

"This is where it happened," Pahn said. Loom sat bolt upright at the sound of his voice. Pahn stood at the edge of the river, through which water sped and churned and spat. He nodded ahead to a slab of rock that acted as a sort of makeshift bridge. "According to the gossip in Arrod's streets, at least. This is where Prince Owen of the Royal House of Heidle was rumored to have drowned trying to save his little sister. We know that story isn't entirely true, though, is it? Still, maybe this is his final resting place."

Loom, guarded, rose to his feet, untrusting. He looked to

the water, and he imagined what the world would be if Wil had truly drowned here. If her curse had died and been buried like a secret beneath the water. He wouldn't know to mourn her, and yet still something told him that he would. He would feel her absence in the world. Maybe he had always felt it. All those moments spent desperate and longing without a destination for his restless heart, without reprieve, had really just been her absence.

"She's going to make a terrible queen," Pahn said. "You know that."

Did he know that? The Wil he knew was fierce and brave. Impulsive, but compassionate. She was overzealous, but deliberate. Brutal, but kind. She could not observe pain without taking a small bit of that pain and folding it into her own heart, making it a part of herself.

Wil may have been the last in a long line of spares, but no. She would not make a terrible queen.

"Where is she?" Loom asked. A horrible feeling came over him now. He imagined Pahn subduing her. Pahn throwing her into the rapids. Her lungs filling up with water.

"She's hiding somewhere, I'm sure," Pahn said. "Further proof that she would make a miserable queen."

"If you thought she would make a miserable queen," Loom growled, "why did you kill her family?"

Pahn blinked, as though this question surprised him.

"I'm not the one who killed them. Your father's men did that."

"Where is my father?" Loom demanded. "Why isn't he here to face what he's done?"

"King Zinil is safe in his palace," Pahn said. "I was sent to retrieve you."

"Retrieve me?" Loom echoed. Why would his father send for his banished, traitor son?

"You are standing on what will soon be the property of the Royal House of Raisius, of which you will once again be the heir," Pahn explained.

The words sounded so strange that Loom could not react, even to balk at them.

"Make no mistake," Pahn said. "No matter what happens here, this kingdom will become Southern property. What I'm offering you is a chance at redemption. A way back into your father's good graces."

"My father has no good graces," Loom said.

"Your father is a man of business. Bring him what he wants, and you'll be reinstated as heir. This is your only chance to be a part of your kingdom once again. Wouldn't you like to return home without your own palace acting as a poison?"

"I'm sure you're about to offer this to me at a reasonable price," Loom said dryly.

"The price is the girl's heart," Pahn said. "Carve it from her chest and bring it to me."

Loom's own heart jolted with pain, as though Pahn's words alone could stab him.

Wil had been right. King Zinil wanted her cursed heart

so that he could have her powers. The plan had been for Wil's brother to alchemize a ruse, but Wil's brother lay dead on the cold floor of a castle basement now.

Pahn was searching Loom's face for a reaction, but Loom offered none.

"I'll meet you here tonight, under the light of the full moon," Pahn said. "Bring her to me then." He smiled. It was a broad, ugly smile. "I know you think you love this girl. That's how cursed hearts work. But if you expect to be worthy of your kingdom, you must love it above all else. That is real love."

Though he was in no position to pity anyone just then, Loom pitied Pahn. All his life, Pahn had been a towering presence in his life. As a child, Loom had thought Pahn to be the most powerful man in the world. Perhaps he even was. But that power had left him empty. He lived to serve his own power, to grow greater and stronger and destroy all who stood in his path. The word "love" sounded gray and meaningless on his tongue. Pahn would never know what it was to love a kingdom, or another living soul.

Loom could use this to his own advantage, he realized. A man who didn't understand love would believe that a banished prince would betray anyone to further his own needs. Pahn would believe that Loom would bring him Wil's heart.

Loom steeled himself.

"We have a deal," he said.

Wil knew that her time in Arrod would be short. Already her muscles were taking on the familiar ache she'd felt the last time she lingered too long in her cursed kingdom, unable to turn things to stone.

But she would not allow her mind to grow foggy. She would not allow herself to collapse into grief. She was at odds with her mind now, trying to convince herself that she hadn't found her brothers dead in their castle, and that her mother was not surely nearby.

She would not go to that awful place of grief again.

She clutched her brother's monocle. Her hands were shaking. Winds, where the hells was Loom?

"He'll come back," Masalee said, as though she had been reading Wil's thoughts. She unwound the blanket from her own shoulders and draped it over Wil's.

They were standing on the deck of the ship, masked by the illusion of water that kept them hidden. Wil wasn't sure how Masalee was able to hold fast to her marvelry. She looked weary for it. Her warm, tawny skin had paled and sweat beaded her brow, but she still stood tall.

Wil stared at the Port Capital. It was silent. Dead.

"This doesn't make sense," she said, her voice hoarse. "Where is everyone?" She had a horrible thought that some great force had swallowed the people of Arrod alive, and that whatever had taken them had taken Loom as well.

Arrod had many cities, but they were spread out between

densely packed wilderness that went on for miles and miles. Two-thirds of the kingdom was uninhabited, except by wanderers and cargo trains. Was it possible the entire kingdom had gone into hiding? Who would guide everyone? Certainly it couldn't have been Baren, lost as he was in his own tormented mind. When she saw him last, he had scarcely seemed to notice there was a kingdom under his rule at all.

Zay and Espel had gone to look for Loom, and Wil felt useless being left behind.

She turned to Masalee, hopeful. "Could this all be an illusion?" she asked. "Could Arrod and my family be safe underneath this, while Pahn tries to break me with a lie?"

Masalee's expression was stoic as ever, but there was kindness to it sometimes, if one knew to look for it. "There's no marveler energy," she said. "If this were an illusion, I'd feel it here." She pressed her palm to the center of her chest. "But this just feels like stillness and death."

Wil had learned that Masalee was a girl of few words, but when she spoke, it was always the truth.

Still, it did not seem real.

When something moved through the rubble, Wil jolted to attention. Loom emerged through the lingering ashes in the city air, and Wil scrambled down the side of the ship and ran to meet him.

He was the only real thing in the kingdom just then. She threw her arms around him. "Where have you been?"

His arms coiled around her; his hand pressed her head to his chest, and for just a moment, Wil felt as she had the night before. When all of the world would wait, and they were together and whole and safe.

When he drew away, she felt the cold air rush between them. He was holding her shoulders now, and his grip tightened. His eyes were eager. "Your brother's formula for alchemizing a body," he said. "Do you remember what it was?"

"It wasn't a formula exactly," Wil said. "More like a process that came together one piece at a time."

"Whatever you'd like to call it, then," Loom said. "Can you do it?"

"I don't know." Her words came out fast and uncertain. "I was always terrible at alchemy, but I helped him sometimes. I think—I think I could try to mimic his process."

"That's all I can ask," Loom said. "We need to get to his cauldron now. There isn't any time to waste."

# TWENTY-SEVEN

WIL COULD NOT RECONCILE THE strange castle that stood before her, standing tall against a gray winter sky. This was not the home she had always known, nor was it a piece of the world she had always known. It was nothing. It was a shell. A shell whose hallways and rooms vaguely resembled a place she had once frequented.

When she reached the basement steps, Loom at one side, Espel and Zay at the other, she was expecting her brother's body to be gone. She expected—she realized now—him to have gotten up and left, the way that living things did.

But he was still there, forever slumped, blood frozen to his wounds, incapable of ever waking.

Her vision tunneled. Her mind turned blank, like the thin coating of snow that concealed the kingdom just enough to make it appear empty.

Zay was the first to move toward him. Loom followed suit, moving one arm behind Gerdie's back and another under his bent knees to lift him.

"No," Wil cried, surprising herself. Her voice slapped loudly against the stone walls. She rushed forward and fell to her knees between her brother and Loom.

"Wil," he said gently. "We have to move him."

She was shaking her head, even though she couldn't understand why. Her vision blurred with tears she had not summoned, much less expected. She heard her own voice creaking out a mantra of "No, no, no."

Zay stepped beside her and put an arm around her shoulders, gently drawing her away, until both of them faced the ribbon of light stealing in through the window.

Wil slumped. "You can't move him." Her words were almost indecipherable through her sobs. "This is his lab. It's all he has."

"Shh" was all Zay said as she folded her arms around her.

Wil did not understand completely that she was crying, or that it was her body—not the earth—that was shaking. Someone with her voice was screaming, and the sound was muffled and scared.

She had the thought that if Zay let go of her, she would fall into whatever gaping hole had swallowed her family, had swallowed her entire kingdom.

"Don't hurt him" was all Wil could think to say.

"He won't." Zay kissed the crown of her head, and Wil

didn't know know if that small bit of affection came from pity or genuine friendship. "I promise, he won't."

"There's a garden surrounded by hedges shaped like an oval," Wil said.

"There's no time to bury him," Zay said.

Wil nodded. "I know."

Loom said nothing, but Wil heard his footsteps moving up the stairs. His stride, so often anticipated, felt strange to her now. This was her brother's sacred space. These were his things, labeled and neatly stored, awaiting the purposes that had been promised to them, and with him gone, anyone seemed like a stranger here.

What would become of his things? That was all she could think.

She was still sobbing when Loom returned, but Zay helped her to her feet. Through the sheen of her tears, the room was still familiar to her. She knew what all the bottles meant. She had collected most of the powders required to mix them. But even so, without her brother here, none of these pieces seemed capable of life.

She cleared her throat, wiped her sleeve across her eyes. She retrieved the rag that had been thrown onto the floor in the struggle and used it to sop up the pink liquid that had congealed on the metal table. It was an anti-rusting agent used when forging metals. Nothing of value.

Loom and Zay hovered at a distance, letting her get her

bearings. She consulted the heavy leather journal by the table's edge, turning through pages of handwritten notes until she found the formula her brother had used to make Addney's corpse. None of his recipes were labeled. There was only a list of ingredients and vague instructions, but Wil remembered. She remembered the afternoon they'd spent extracting limbs from the cauldron steam until, bit by bit, they had a body.

"Okay," she finally said. Her voice was deceptively confident. Her head still felt muddled and hazy. "If you're both willing to do exactly as I say, I think we can make this work."

Once the task was set in motion, Wil lost herself in it. The first attempt to make a hand failed; the leather scorched and broke into pieces. Five attempts and a dozen several silk scarves later, the first limb emerged from the cauldron victorious.

There was an explosion when she attempted to make the torso. Bits of leather and ink splattered like gore on the table and the rusty overhead lamp. It smelled of burnt cloth and copper, and Wil closed her eyes and grasped the table edge as she composed herself. It was the smell that nearly did her in—the memory of how these small mishaps had wafted up the stairs a thousand times before.

"Wil." Loom didn't dare to touch her. He was being as patient as he could, Wil knew.

Wordlessly she reread her brother's notes and tried again. The measurements weren't exact, and she was left guessing what some of the odd squiggles on the page meant. She began again. Another string of failed attempts was her reward. And then, just as she was beginning to worry about their shortage of leather, a torso emerged, eerie without its head attached.

Wil didn't have the wherewithal to be disgusted. She felt nothing but determination, and she wondered if it would always be this way. She wondered if Gerdie's death had been the final thing to break her, after everything else she'd lost. She couldn't mourn both her brothers.

Wil had always believed that she and Gerdie—as the youngest spares—would outlive their family. That someday, a hundred years into the distance, they would still have each other when everything else was gone.

*Later,* she told herself. She would sort it out later. She repeated the word over and over in her head, until she was able to carry on.

By the time Wil extracted the last limb, they were losing daylight. Loom retrieved the lantern and drew the shutters on the window to hide the light.

Zay sat on the floor, carefully painting details onto fingernails and veins. She had a steady hand even as she worked in haste. Her neat, practiced attention to detail was indicative of a girl who had endured hours of formal handwriting lessons.

The alchemized head produced several rounds of failures, but at last it emerged from the cauldron, ashen and sleeping and still.

Wil's stomach lurched. Disgust was the first feeling that had managed to reach her since she'd taken on this task. The head had long hair, fashioned from the silk threads of an old robe and some dark brown dye. The hair floated and tangled as it filled up with air.

Wil nearly dropped the thing. Beside her, Loom didn't falter, but he averted his eyes.

When all the pieces were stitched together, the sight at last proved too much for Loom, who paced up the staircase as Wil and Zay began sewing the eyelashes in place.

"It looks dead," Wil fretted, gnawing on her lip.

"Masalee will have to work her magic, I guess," Zay said.

Wil stared at the corpse. She couldn't be sure it looked like her. If Gerdie were here, it would have turned out perfectly. And again Wil caught herself believing that her brother was elsewhere in the castle. She shook her head, forced herself to her feet, forced herself to wake up.

"There isn't much time before the sun sets," Wil said.

"Doesn't look much like you," Espel said, as the alchemized corpse was laid out on the deck of the ship and unrolled from the burlap that had been concealing it.

"I can fix it," Masalee offered.

As Masalee set to work enchanting the thing, Wil wondered why she and Espel were doing so much to help them. If Loom was reinstated as heir, it would do nothing to help Espel. Espel must have believed there was something to gain by earning

Loom's good graces, even if she herself expected to be queen.

Loom was pacing the length of the ship. His shoulders were raised, his strides feather silent but broad.

Wil ran to catch up with him. He flinched when she touched his arm, lost as he'd been in his thoughts.

"We don't have to do this, you know." She spoke quietly so that the others wouldn't hear her.

"What alternative would you propose?" he replied, his tone sour.

"We could face Pahn," she said. "Kill him ourselves."

"It would be nearly impossible," Loom said. "I've seen men try to kill him. If he thinks there's a risk, he creates an illusion of himself. That's what he'll do tonight. He'll be expecting us to try something foolish."

"Killing him wouldn't be foolish," Wil said. She wanted him dead. For what he had done to Loom, but now more than ever for what he had done to her family.

"He's going to die," Loom said. "But not tonight."

Wil pressed her back against the ship's railing. "What are you planning?"

"First, I'm going to kill my father," he said. "For what he's done to both our kingdoms. And then I'm going to kill Pahn. I'll need Masalee's help, so it's important that we keep Espel on our side." He glanced across the ship to his sister, who knelt beside Masalee at the alchemized corpse. "As much as I'd like to believe she sees our father for what he truly is, and as much as

I'd like to believe she's on my side, I still don't know."

"I don't think she's on anyone's side but her own," Wil said.

Loom's gaze was trained on his sister for a moment longer, and then he looked to Wil. He swept one finger through her hair, curling a lock of it around his knuckle.

"Wil, if this doesn't work, I want you to know—"

She pressed her fingertips to his mouth to shush him. "This is going to work," she said. "Trust me."

He turned, and his arms coiled around her and his hands knotted together at the small of her back.

"I was taught to speak and write a dozen languages," he said. "But there isn't a word for what you mean to me."

She swept her hand through his hair and she kissed him. His lips were warm and soft. He was filled with life and with some brilliant promise that there could be life beyond this nightmare. Wil clung to that bit of hope. She needed it, or she would crumble to ash like everything else in this kingdom.

His arms tightened around her. For just one moment, they ignored the dread of what awaited them. They ignored the kingdoms that were falling apart.

They ignored their fear, and the path that would take them to Pahn, and the possibility that they would not live to see the morning sun—if the sun ever again rose over the Northern Isles at all.

"I'm sorry," he said. "I'm sorry for all this. If I hadn't brought you with me that day in Brayshire, Pahn wouldn't have known about your power and you wouldn't be in danger."

"And where would you be?" Wil said. "Living in a broken castle with a view of a kingdom you couldn't touch?"

His expression was so broken.

Wil didn't like it. It felt too much like a good-bye.

"I'll tell you what," she said. "If we survive this and you become king, you owe me a spot on your council. But if we all die and our kingdoms are annihilated by war, I'll admit that I was wrong."

"That seems fair." He bowed his head to place a gentle, lingering kiss over her brow.

Wil felt his body release the slightest tremor. That was it. That was all the grief he could afford. The rest of it had to be folded and tucked inside of him, because there was too much at stake for the two of them to fall apart now.

He said the only thing left for him to say, as he buried his face in the curve of her neck and her arms coiled around him. "I love you. I need you to know this, Wil. I love you."

# TWENTY-EIGHT

WIL COULD BARELY LOOK AT the alchemized corpse once Masalee had animated it. The thing's eyelashes fluttered and Wil flinched. But it didn't wake up because it didn't truly have anything inside of it. It didn't look at her.

Loom drew a breath and released it slowly, and then he slid his arms under the thing's shoulders and behind its knees, easing it into his arms as he stood. As though instinctively, the thing slumped against him. Its head canted back, mouth open, skin ashen.

Loom looked as though he'd be sick. And then his gaze hardened and he moved forward.

Zay was the only one to stay behind, unwilling to leave Ada alone or lead him into harm's way.

The plan was as simple as it was dangerous: Loom and

Espel would present the alchemized offering to Pahn. Wil had done her best to alchemize a realistic heart, using the heart of a pig, which Gerdie had been storing in a jar for gods-only-know what purpose. Masalee and Wil would hide at a distance, watching from the trees.

Halfway along the river, they stopped. Loom traded a glance with Wil. Just a look. Masalee and Espel did the same. No good-byes were spoken.

Loom and Espel headed the charge after that, while Wil and Masalee diverted into the trees.

For all the time Masalee had spent controlling Wil's heart, Wil felt bonded to her now. She could feel her pain, her anxiousness, her longing.

But Wil didn't try to console her with platitudes. The most she could offer now was a bit of distraction, to ease the fear that rose over both of them like a wave.

"Can you teach me how to control my own heart?" Wil asked her. "With marvelry, the way that you were able to do it?"

"You aren't a marveler," Masalee said.

"But it can be learned," Wil said. "Can't it?"

"Marvelry is in you or it isn't," Masalee said. "The best vocalists in the world could teach you to sing, but if your voice is sour, there's no lesson that can help you."

Wil trudged on in crestfallen silence. If she were truly a queen, she would put this kingdom above herself. And the only way to break the curse would be to stop the heart that held it.

Masalee must have pitied her, because she said, "Perhaps there's another way. Marvelry isn't the only element of a curse. Your mother, for instance. She isn't a marveler, is she?"

"No," Wil said. Her mother had such a powerful, deft presence, and she was so strong, even addled as she was by her compulsions. But she wasn't a marveler; her magic was purely in her own spirit.

"She's not a marveler, and yet she gave birth to a daughter who was cursed by marvelry," Masalee said, and she was trying to be reassuring. "So maybe there's a solution somewhere."

Wil considered it. She knew that Masalee was showing her kindness with this small bit of possibility, but Masalee also wasn't the sort to give empty platitudes. There was hope yet.

Maybe Pahn's bargain with Loom wasn't as cruel as she wanted to believe. The ruler of a nation didn't cower behind trees or try to save their own interest with smoke and mirrors and alchemy. The ruler of a nation would fall on their sword.

But she was never meant to rule a nation. She would never deserve it; not the way that Owen had, and not the way his child would.

Loom knew that Pahn was nearby. He could sense it. It was the same slight, inexplicable pull that had led him to Wil. He'd first seen her from a distance, her long hair blurring over her arm as she fought the marauder in the market square. She was all muscle and motion. He couldn't see her face, couldn't know who she was or what she could ever possibly mean to him. But still he had gone to her with anticipation, moths to flame, flowers to sun.

This thing in his arms afforded him no such thoughts. He had made it this far into the trees without looking at it, but now as he stopped to catch his breath, he found himself staring down at its sleeping face.

It looked like Wil. Too much, and even knowing it was all an illusion created for Pahn's sake, he felt Wil dying in his arms. He felt certain that soon it would be her heart that he tore from her chest, and then she would be gone forever. And it wouldn't matter if his kingdom survived or if it all collapsed into the sea and pulled him down with it, because her life was too high a price to pay.

"Hold it together," Espel said, and he realized that his breathing had become labored. "You aren't just doing this for yourself," she said. "I don't care what happens to this bleeding kingdom. Truly, I don't. But our home will be lost to us forever if you fail, and I won't let that happen."

Espel. Tethered to their falling kingdom as surely as he was. What would become of them if they could never return home?

He wouldn't let anything happen to his sister, even if he couldn't be sure she'd return the sentiment. Under their father's command, Espel had not even been granted a childhood. For fifteen years she'd lived trapped in the mold their father created for her, and it was long past time for her to be set free. She was owed that much. Her freedom had been stolen from her moments after she was born, when she lay on their mother's chest, her body rising and falling with the force of their mother's final breath.

"I know" was all he could say.

He could no longer hear Wil and Masalee behind him, and he knew that Wil had the same idea to stay out of range. Everything would fall apart if Pahn saw her. The real, living her, heart still beating.

She was safe, he reminded himself, despite the prodding sense that this body in his arms belonged to her. This hideously cruel likeness of the girl who one day earlier had been warm and alive and safe in his arms.

The closer they walked to the waterfall, the more the feeling of dread churned in his stomach. He had done the one thing he'd vowed never to do. He had made a deal with a marveler. And he was going to betray that deal.

The alchemized corpse shifted in his arms, and he flinched, nearly dropping it. Espel cut him a sharp glare. "If he sees either of us panic, this will fall apart," she hissed.

She was right. Though she hadn't been victim to one of Pahn's curses, she knew them every bit as well as Loom. She had seen what he was capable of.

They reached the point in the river where the rapids turned violent. Water jumped and spat. There was a clearing here, which the moon filled with its white light, like an electric lantern's glow.

Loom laid the alchemized corpse on the dusting of snow.

It was heavy, but it wasn't the weight that had burdened him.

Pahn, pristine and prim as ever, emerged from the darkness that surrounded the clearing. He was as elegant as he was conniving—tall and lean, dressed in a long blue robe with gold embroidery. His long beard and ponytail were fine and white, coming to a point at their ends.

His eyes went to the alchemized corpse, and then quizzically back to Loom. Was that understanding on his face? Did he know what this was? Loom stood stoic, betraying nothing.

If Pahn anticipated their plan, it was over. They would all be dead before this night ever saw its end. Loom hadn't allowed himself to think about that—really think about it—until this moment. A wave of grief rose through him. Zay and Espel and Wil and even Masalee, blanketed by the sea, never waking as they drowned. All of them just fresh souls to haunt the Ancient Sea.

With that came a small voice of reason. Maybe it came from Wil, too far behind him now for him to hear. This was one of Pahn's tricks, the voice told him.

He should have told Wil not to come, he thought. He should have had her wait on the ship so that she at least could be spared if this all went wrong. But even as he thought it, he knew Wil wouldn't have listened. It wouldn't matter how he tried to convince her. She was too stubborn and she loved her kingdom too much.

The energy became louder and it lanced through his head

like an iron spike. He came upon a clearing filled with that strange light. The air was humid, heavy. Steam rose from the ground, swirling around Pahn's feet as he moved closer.

That noise—Loom's head throbbed. He couldn't think. Everything blurred and he felt as though he were floating outside himself. He looked to the thing on the ground and for a fleeting moment he saw two Wils, ashen and blinking and turning their heads. He blinked and his vision cleared.

Beside him, Espel stood at attention, wearing the glazed, guarded expression that had frightened her instructors when she was a child. Espel was the master of her own features; she knew how to use her youth and her high, melodic voice to her benefit. And she knew how to be fierce and powerful and intimidating in a blink.

Loom wondered if Espel had inherited this gift from their mother. He wondered if this was why their father favored her so much, or if Espel was so wholly unique, so mysteriously her own creature, that she had fascinated their father the way she fascinated all who encountered her.

Pahn, for his part, was unfazed by the pair of them. "The prodigal progeny are working together," he said. "I never thought I'd see the day." He nodded toward the alchemized corpse. "And you've brought the girl. Still alive, I hope. I'll need that heart beating."

"She's alive," Loom said. "I gave her a sleep serum. I didn't want her to feel any pain."

"The pain wouldn't last for very long," Pahn said. He knelt beside the alchemized corpse and cupped its cheek in his hand. The thing recoiled from his touch. It must have had something of Wil's in there after all, Loom thought. Some ghost of her instincts.

"I'm glad you came to see reason on your own," Pahn said.

Loom felt as though he were dreaming now. He could barely hang on to the words being spoken, and still Pahn spoke, his voice loud and echoing in the small space. "Your father is no marveler, but he can be very prophetic," Pahn said. "He knew on the day you were born that you would go on to betray him. He didn't know how, but he could sense it."

Loom stared down at the thing. He stared at Wil's face. At Wil's body rising and falling with breaths that weren't really breaths.

He wished Pahn would stop speaking. There was something about his voice that made Loom feel ill and sleepy and strange. His blood felt thick. "I counseled him for years," Pahn said. "Did you know that? I told him to raise you and your sister as enemies. I told him that if you grew to care for one another, you would conspire against him and be his undoing."

"You . . ." Loom's voice came out as a whisper. He pressed his palm to his forehead, trying to block out that persistent shrill sound. "You what?"

Through the haze of his mind, he saw Espel as a child, back when she was still helpless, when her eyes were wide and innocent and her cheeks were streaked with tears because their instructor had just hit her. She had looked at him for just a moment, and he'd seen the pleading on her face. He knew that he was supposed to protect her.

But he couldn't. At six years old, he knew there was no safety in coddling. There was safety only in one's own strength.

Espel learned this quickly. There were whole weeks in which they never saw each other at all, and came together only as rivals in combat. She grew up hard and she grew up invincible, cold, brilliant. And she was a stranger to him.

He shook his head now, trying to fight the haze that was drowning him.

It was Pahn's fault. All these years. Pahn was the reason he and his sister were brought up as enemies.

Pahn advanced, and Espel moved between them, shielding her brother. She said nothing. She didn't draw a weapon. But her stance was rigid.

"It seems destiny can't be avoided," Pahn said. "Both of you came together anyway. Your father was right." Pahn took Loom's chin, and his gentle grasp turned into a bruising vise. "You both betrayed him, one after the other. When Espel joined forces with you, he knew you would be back. I didn't have to tell him that. He decided that if both of his children were traitors, neither of you should inherit the kingdom. He'd just as soon have it burn down to nothing."

"Our father is already burning the kingdom down to

nothing," Espel said. "We have never tried to steal our legacy. We're trying to save it." She was staring him down. "What do you get out of this?"

Pahn laughed. "You know, that's a question your brother never thought to ask. If it were my decision, you would still be the heir." He went on, "I will stay here and rule all of Arrod. That's my reward."

Loom felt his fingers tightening around something, and when he looked down, he was holding his own dagger with no memory of having unsheathed it.

"Enough stalling. I'll ask you once to be sure," Pahn said. He looked into Loom's eyes, and Loom saw just how dark they were, like the ocean at night. "Are you willing to stop this girl's heart in exchange for your kingdom?"

"Yes," Loom said, and the word felt wrong, even though it was a lie. His own heart began to race. His body felt cold, slick with sweat. The thing laid out before him looked too real, too much like her.

"Then it's done," Pahn said. "Give me her heart."

Espel turned to her brother. She put her hands on his shoulders and moved closer. "Are you sure that you want to do this?" Her brow was drawn in . . . something—concern? He couldn't be sure whether she was being sincere or whether this was an act for Pahn's sake. His vision swam for a moment. His head felt light, his body heavy and sluggish.

"A deal's a deal," he said.

He knelt beside the alchemized corpse. Gingerly, he undid the buttons of the tunic the thing was wearing, exposing its left breast, the ripples in its skin that looked like ribs.

Here was where he could tell the thing apart from Wil. Though it had her cursed birthmark, that was where the similarities ended. This was not her body. He knew Wil. After their night together, he'd awakened jarred by some terrible dream only to find her sprawled on the mattress beside him. He'd watched her in the dim light of the lantern, enraptured by the way she stretched and sighed and breathed. He'd memorized the shape of her. He'd leaned over her and planted a soft, lingering kiss between her breasts. In her sleep she'd raked her fingers through his hair.

And knowing that this thing was not Wil gave him a new strength.

He plunged the knife into its skin.

The thing shuddered, and its mouth opened as though to cry out.

For a moment, Loom succumbed to the haze that surrounded his mind. Welcomed it, even. In what felt like a blink, he had reached into the thing's chest, and now he held its heart, rich with blood. He felt it still beating. And though he tried not to, he found himself looking at the thing. At the gaping hole where its heart had once been. The torn, ruined skin, the blood already darkening to black. The eyes half open and staring back at him. *How could you,* the eyes were saying.

It wasn't Wil. It wasn't her.

The heart felt fleshy and soft and slick, and his stomach lurched. He wouldn't get sick. He wouldn't.

He thrust the heart at Pahn in his cupped hands. "It's done," he said, through gritted teeth.

"One heart for an entire kingdom," Pahn said. "It's more than a fair deal."

He took the heart into his hands, and he slowly turned it, admiring the thing. It was gruesomely convincing. Wil had touted her brother to be the genius when it came to alchemy, but she'd moved with skill and grace, even love. She had given life to the sodden heart of a long-dead thing, a heart that had been stored in a jar.

Pahn held the heart, bleeding, in his hands. Loom tried to focus, but his vision was stabbed by flashes of white; he couldn't concentrate. Blood rushed in his ears. He staggered, and Espel caught him by the arm.

"That girl of yours is quite the marveler," Pahn told Espel. "I was tasked with training her, but her gift is one that can't be taught. Truly profound. I hope she'll return to the palace with you."

At the mention of Masalee, Espel's jaw tightened. But she did not betray a drop of her murderous rage.

"I almost didn't find your ship, it was so well hidden," Pahn continued. "Return to it now. You'll find that it's tethered to mine by an impenetrable energy. We set a course for Cannolay tonight."

From her vantage point, Wil watched Pahn hold the disembodied heart. A purple glowing energy surrounded it. The heart's beating was more forceful, audible even from where she stood.

"We have to get to the ship before we're seen," Masalee whispered.

Wil hesitated. She had not allowed herself to think of what would come after Loom had deceived Pahn. It would take several days to return to Cannolay, and during that time, Arrod would be vulnerable, without a leader, without anyone to attempt to pick up the pieces. There were survivors hiding deep in the villages away from the Port Capital. What would become of them?

Her hand was in her pocket, she realized, and she had been worrying the monocle against her palm.

"I can't," she blurted, realizing it only as she said it. "My kingdom needs me."

Her kingdom. Somehow, Arrod was at the mercy of a cursed spare whose strength would soon dwindle like a snuffed flame the longer she went without turning life into stone.

"You won't be gone forever," Masalee said.

She shook her head. "I can't." Footsteps were drawing closer. Loom and Espel were making their way back to the ship. They had left the alchemized corpse at the water's edge—the ruined remains of a short-lived queen.

"Tell Loom I'm sorry," Wil said. But she knew he would

understand. They each had their own kingdoms to protect.

She didn't know what sort of queen she could be until the new heir was born; all she had was a broken castle filled with bodies to bury. But she was going to try. She had to try.

# TWENTY-NINE

LOOM STOPPED WALKING BEFORE THE Port Capital was in sight. His heart throbbed in his ears. The earth was quaking. The stars shook in their sky.

Espel was beside him, and she looked calm. How could she be calm when the world was falling apart?

She narrowed her eyes. "Pahn has done something to you," she said.

He shook his head. "Where's Wil?"

"She'll be headed back to the ship. If she's smart, she's hiding."

"No," Loom said. He was certain that Wil had not gone ahead. He was certain that he could feel her, as surely as he had felt Pahn's energy by the water's edge. She was not going toward the ship. She was going toward the castle.

He turned on his heel and ran back into the thick of the woods. Espel chased after him, muttering curses.

She was talking, and Loom got the sense that she was trying to make him see reason. But her words were too far away, too soft, too nonsensical for him to comprehend. All that mattered was Wil. She was just ahead. He had to find her.

Once she had passed through the castle gate, Wil began to feel the old familiar ache in her muscles. The kingdom was cursed and dying and taking her down with it. No greenery crystallized under her touch, though the current moved desperately through her blood, pushing at the insides of her fingers and palms.

How would she rebuild this? She had the thought that she would die alone in that dark and empty castle, guarding its doors with her corpse.

Loom would be gone by now, off to save his own kingdom. He was the only hope that she had left. Once he had claimed his throne, perhaps he would afford some aid to hers. He would save the kingdom that had once been his enemy. There would be something left for Addney and Owen's child to claim.

Wil should have gone with him. She knew that. But Arrod was her first love, the place that held her entire life's memories contained, like the little globes Owen would bring back from his journeys.

When she heard footsteps charging toward her, she spun, unbelieving. She had expected one of Pahn's silent men coming to finish her off, but instead it was Loom, Espel on his heels.

His eyes were strange and cold. His steps, normally elegant and deft, were heavy. Even angry.

"Loom?"

She could almost believe that she was imagining him.

As he barged through the ruined gates, Wil recoiled. She took a cautious step backward and reached for her dagger, only to remember that it was gone. It had been left on the alchemized corpse.

Her breath hitched. At last she identified what was so strange about Loom. There was an energy radiating from his body that was alien to him. It was marvelry. It was Pahn.

"Wil," he said. His voice made her uncertain. He spoke her name the same way he always had. For a moment he was so familiar that she wanted to fall into him. She wanted to leave everything and return to his kingdom. She could almost believe, with that one word he'd spoken, that everything would be okay.

He put his hands on her shoulders. One hand moved to the side of her neck, and then to her cheek, cupping her face.

*This isn't Loom.* The thought woke her from the trance into which she had briefly fallen.

"I made a deal," he said. It was his voice, but not. Wil thought he was going to say more, but he moved the hand that had been touching her face. His grasp on her shoulder tightened, and he drew the dagger from his sheath and plunged it into her heart.

Wil didn't feel the blade cut through her. She didn't feel her fingers clutching at his wrist, wrestling him until her own dagger slipped through their bloody hands and fell to the dirt.

This wasn't Loom. This wasn't him. Pahn's energy turned repugnant. Her vision clouded with it, obscuring the stars and the moon, making Loom's face hazy.

Espel screamed. It wasn't the helpless shriek of a girl horrified by what she had just seen, but the purposeful call of someone coming to action. She was calling for Masalee, the only one among them who was strong enough to combat Pahn's energy.

Wil felt the earth rise up to meet her. She tasted blood, felt it filling up her lungs.

The air smelled like the dirt after a long rain.

Wil had hated that smell for as long as she could remember, ever since the year that Gray Fever came to steal her brother away.

She felt Masalee beside her, and she understood, too, that she was dying.

Masalee said something, but when Wil looked at her, she saw Gerdie instead, kneeling over her and sweeping her brow the way she had done for him when he was ill. She knew that he was not truly here; his face was blurred and missing details, as faces often were in dreams. He said something about the story of the singing wolf, a bedtime fable their mother used to tell them.

It was one of Gerdie's favorites, and so Wil had pretended to love it as much as he did, so that their mother would tell it to them at bedtime.

It had always been vivid in her imagination. A giant gray wolf whose howl caused the first bite of winter. The snowflakes were fragments of its song. Only now, when she thought of it, the sky was dark and it smelled of rain. The snow was black and crumbling like soot. The song was a scream.

Time was bleeding into the wind and the wind was carrying it away. She tried to stop it. She tried to make the world go still, but the wind didn't listen. It never did.

Gerdie's face became Masalee's again, and Wil wanted to tell Masalee to drag her inside the castle. To close the doors and cover the windows so that death wouldn't find her. But it was too late. Death had already come. Wil saw it; it was a shadow standing over her, bearing Loom's shape.

# THIRTY

THE MOON BROKE FREE OF the clouds, and the world became sharper in its glow.

Loom was staring up at it when he awoke from his trance. Espel's knee pinned his stomach in place, her hands pressing his wrists into the ground. He would always be astonished by his sister's strength, but especially now, because when he looked up at her face, he did not see the ruthless monster their father had raised. He saw pity. He saw what looked, for just an instant, like love.

"What have you done, you idiot," she whispered.

The kingdom swelled with the loud breath of a winter breeze. All the trees and leaves shook. Thin lines of snow twirled across the ground.

When the wind passed, Loom became acutely aware of the

silence. He felt Wil's stillness, several yards off to his right. He knew, even before he turned his head, that the sound of her breathing had stopped. Without it, the world felt impossibly quiet.

His own breath hitched. He tried to throw Espel off him, but her grip only tightened.

"What have you done to her?" he hissed. He tried again to throw her, and that's when he saw the blood on his hand. The streaks from where it had dripped down to his wrist and stopped.

Espel didn't answer him, but she eased her grip, waiting for him to understand.

The memory was far and faded, like the stories the palace servants used to tell about his childhood, until what he truly remembered was tangled up with and indistinguishable from what he had been told.

"No." He pushed Espel away. She didn't try to stop him as he staggered on his hands and knees to where Masalee knelt at Wil's side. Wil's tunic had been torn open, and the wound lay exposed. Smeared blood buried the mark of her curse in violent depths of red.

Masalee's eyes were closed, her breaths shallow and quick, her brow drawn in strain. One hand was pressed over the wound, which had stopped bleeding and turned into a gaping pit as black as the night had been before the clouds dissolved. The other hand was to Wil's forehead.

Wil was still breathing, Loom realized.

His hands were shaking, but the persistent numbness that had plagued him earlier was gone now, replaced by a vicious clarity that would not allow him reprieve from what he had done. "Wil, stay with me." His voice cracked. "Please stay with me."

Her eyes opened at that. Her eyes, dark and deep, and where he always felt himself drowning.

She shook with a feeble cough, and a line of blood slid from the corner of her mouth. Her teeth were coated in red. No. No, Loom refused to accept this. This meant death. It meant that the blade had severed something vital and she was going to drown in her blood.

Pahn knew. He had to know. Anyone else who ever came at Wil with a blade would be dead before they could so much as take their aim. But for Loom, she had hesitated. She had ignored her instincts because she trusted him.

He remembered, now, the wet sound of the blade tearing into her flesh. He remembered her eyes going wide with shock, and then immediately dulling. He remembered the hilt in his fist and the sound of the dagger hitting the grass.

Masalee had since drawn a vial from the belt and poured it over the wound to clean away some of the blood and have a better look. It was Espel's belt, Loom noticed for the first time.

"You can fix her," Loom choked out.

"You tore her arteries," Masalee said. Her tone was practical and even.

Wil rolled her head toward the sound of Masalee's voice, and Loom wondered if she was still conscious in there, or if the spirits of the Ancient Sea had swum all the way to Northern waters to lure her under with their whispers.

"Marvelry isn't a magic show," Masalee said. "I can't bring back the dead."

The dead. Loom's world was going dark around him.

Loom became aware of Espel sitting behind him. For once in her life, not presenting him with some sort of challenge. He thought he felt her hand touch his arm and then withdraw.

"It isn't your fault," Masalee told him. "You were in a trance. It nearly knocked me over, it was so strong."

Wil's eyes were closed now. He had done this to her, and not just with the dagger. This had been set in motion the moment he made a deal with a marveler.

Pahn arrived as though Loom's thought had summoned him, in a swish of dust-light snow and silken robes.

"This is much more preferable to a congealed pig's heart," Pahn said. "But you haven't completed our deal. I need that heart cut from her chest while it's still beating."

Loom rose to his feet, but before he could lunge, Espel moved before him and stared at Pahn. "We both know that my brother is reckless and shortsighted," she said. "And you knew that this deal was never going to be made. What is it you truly want?"

"I truly want the girl's heart," Pahn said. He canted his

head to look at Loom. "I will have it, and you will be the one to bring it to me."

Fog was pervading Loom's mind again. His body was light, caught in a dream. He didn't feel his knees bend as he crouched. He didn't feel his hand fumble in the frozen grass and grasp the dagger hilt.

Espel threw him onto his back, hard. The air left his lungs and he curled onto his side, heaving, straining to get his breath. *Wake up,* he pleaded with himself.

With a weary sigh, Pahn unsheathed his dagger. "I had hoped to return you to your father alive," he said to Espel. He lunged for her, but she dropped into a somersault, missing his blade by a hair.

She jumped to her feet behind him and raised her dagger, but before she could throw it, he twirled in a flourish of silk and sliced her forearm. The pain was no deterrent, not to Espel, who knew how to get lost in her fury. She dodged his next swipe, her blood splashing a dotted line into the snow. Her dagger flew at his chest, but he evaded it, and the weapon disappeared into the darkness behind him.

Something crawled across her skin, something small and biting. She rubbed at her leg, her arms. Hundreds of spiders had invaded her clothes and were pouring out through her sleeves and collar.

It was an illusion. She knew this, even as their bites made her swell and bleed. She ignored the burning little stabs of their fangs even as her throat and eyes began to swell shut from the venom. *This is an illusion,* she told herself over and over again. Ifpac mountain spiders were indigenous to the Eastern regions; one bite would kill a man thrice her size. Hundreds would leave him a bloated and purpled corpse.

When her next dagger landed in Pahn's shoulder, he laughed. "You were always the best your kingdom had to offer," he said. "A fighter from the day you were born, excelling where the world's finest soldiers have faltered."

She wanted to claw the skin from her bones.

"And this battle has been a true pleasure," Pahn said, "but I need that heart still beating, and our time for games is over."

His arms were still at his sides, but his sword swept forward and slashed her ankles, tearing the tendons. She fell with a scream, not of pain, but of rage. Masalee rushed to her, and Espel shoved her away. "Stay with Wil," she commanded. This was what Pahn had anticipated. He had trained Masalee from a child, and he knew how to toy with her heart. He knew how to tear her from the side of a dying Northern queen.

Too late, Masalee realized it too. Pahn had advanced on Wil. He knelt over her. His hands glowed with the same throbbing purple energy he'd used to handle the false heart by the river. If all else failed, then he would reach into Wil's chest with his bare hands and take her heart for himself.

Masalee charged, but she was too late. She wouldn't reach Pahn in time to stop him.

Something else would reach him, though. A cloaked figure moved through the castle gardens. A blade gleamed in the figure's hands. No—it was not gleaming in the moonlight. It was glowing, with a dark energy to match Pahn's. Before Pahn could turn, the blade tore through his back, pinioning his heart to his ribs as the blade broke through his chest.

The figure removed his hood, revealing a medley of golden curls. He set his boot on Pahn's shoulder, pushing him as he withdrew his sword. Pahn crumpled, already dead.

Loom rose to his hands and knees. Pahn's marvelry had filled his head, and the sudden release of it left him dazed.

He must still be dreaming, he thought, because it was impossible that this figure standing over him now was real. He had seen this man just hours earlier, slumped dead on his throne. He blinked, but King Baren of the Northern Isles stood before him, as alive as he had ever been.

And then he turned for the open gates and was gone.

# THIRTY-ONE

IN THE DREAM, WIL WAS watching Aleen from someplace high.

Aleen was floating along the calm shallows of the river, her arms fanning at her sides. Her blue skirt and white petticoat rippled and tumbled and swam.

"I wanted to live to be a hundred," she said, and Wil knew she was talking to her. "I wanted to see how far electricity would go. If eventually the entire world would be filled up with wires and lights that outshone the stars." She was beginning to sink. Water crept up to her cheeks and touched her lips when she said, "If I'd lived, my brother wouldn't have met his queen. It's because of my death that he fled the kingdom, and that's when he found her. If I'd lived, he would have stayed in Arrod and there would have been someone else eventually, I suppose, but he wouldn't have loved her. He wouldn't have had you, or your brothers. You wouldn't all have my curse."

Wil felt her body turn heavy. She dropped to earth and she knelt at the water's edge. She reached out a hand to Aleen, but Aleen didn't take it.

"How do I undo the curse?" Wil said. "There must be some way."

"I can't help you," Aleen said. "No one can." The river pulled her under and she let herself drown.

# THIRTY-TWO

ESPEL AND ZAY CARRIED WIL inside the castle on a stretcher that had been hastily fashioned from a blanket and tree branches. Masalee moved alongside them, fixed by concentration.

Loom had never seen Wil so fragile. Having been trained to duel to the death under his father's watchful eye, Loom knew the look of someone who was about to die. The ashen skin. The strangled rattle of breath. And he knew what it was to have caused it.

He knew this sickening knot forming in his stomach as well. And, for once, he couldn't push it away. Dark dread was filling him. If Wil died here tonight, he knew the world would end around him.

"There must be bedchambers upstairs," Espel said.

"No," Masalee said. Her voice was strained. Her collar and

under her sleeves were dark with sweat, despite the cold. "She's already been moved too much. She's going to die if we carry her all around this castle."

"There's a fireplace in there," Zay said, peering down the hall into the open doorway of the servants' kitchen.

Loom kept distance between himself and everyone, watching as Wil's stretcher was laid before the fireplace on the floor in the servants' kitchen. Just carrying her this far had been a risk; she wouldn't have survived being carried to a bed.

As Ada slept curled in a blanket by the hearth, Zay was the one to stoke the fire. She drew her thread and carefully stitched Wil's wound while Masalee labored to keep Wil's heart beating and to drain the blood from her lungs.

She wasn't going to survive the night. Loom knew this. Pahn was dead and he had dragged Wil down with him. There would be no kingdoms left to save. There would be no end to this war.

It was his fault. How many times had he warned Wil about making a deal with a marveler? And here he had done that very thing, risking her life as the cost.

He knew better than to go to her. He couldn't stop himself from imagining her body wrapped in that blanket rather than stretched out atop it. He had killed her. Soon she would be gone.

A memory he didn't know that he had, of his mother slowly dying as servants tended to the infant crying elsewhere in the room. He'd been hiding under his mother's dressing table, where no one could bother to notice him in the frenzy. More than the unfocused image of his dying mother, he remembered the powerlessness he had felt. The surety that she was slipping away and there was nothing to be done.

He was so lost in his nightmare that he didn't hear Espel coming up beside him until she spoke.

"She's going to be all right," she said. "Masalee is a skilled healer. She's in good hands."

Of course Masalee was skilled. Their father had been so paranoid about an assassination that he had spared no expense to protect himself. As Espel's guard, Masalee was trained to use her marvelry both to kill and to heal. It was a precaution meant to save Espel's life should she ever find herself impaled on an enemy's blade. But why would she focus her efforts on Wil, a girl who meant nothing to her?

He shouldn't have been thinking this; he should only have been grateful. But still he couldn't help asking, "Why did Masalee try to bring her back?"

"Because she hates suffering," Espel said. "She's never been able to bear it."

"She could have fooled me," Loom said.

"That's the idea, isn't it?" Espel said.

Loom was beginning to understand what had drawn Masalee and his sister together. Even in a palace where love was a weapon and happiness was forbidden, his sister had managed to find both of those things. He very much wanted to know this Espel who had been hidden behind their father's precious monster.

"This isn't your fault," Espel said.

He looked at his sister, for the first time noticing the blood that stained her tunic, her trousers. She was leaning against the door frame as though standing upright was too painful. Whatever injuries she'd sustained in her fight with Pahn, she hadn't allowed Masalee to squander her precious energy healing them.

For once, they weren't rivals. There was no suspicion or pretense. She was being earnest. She understood nearly losing someone she loved.

"It *is* my fault," he said, and his voice was hollow. "When I said I would trade Wil's heart for my kingdom, I sealed her fate."

"You didn't seal her fate," Espel said. "Or she would be dead."

"Our father always knew exactly what to take away from us," Loom said. "He knew I didn't have what it took to be heir."

"You have never been what our father thinks an heir should be," Espel agreed. "I've always envied you for that."

Envy was not a sentiment to which Espel had ever admitted. Under different circumstances, Loom would have cherished the small victory of having anything his sister wanted. But his eyes hadn't left Wil, and as her life hung uncertainly in the firelight, so did his own.

Wil's heart stopped at dawn, just as the cool blue light of a winter morning stole in through the window to touch her. Loom felt it, even before Masalee's concentrated expression gave way to exhaustion. She had done all that she could. She'd kept Wil alive longer than the most skilled medic would have been able to do, but all those painful hours had prolonged a predetermined outcome.

"No," Loom said. The word had become his mantra by now. For the last hour of Wil's life, he'd sat at her feet, afraid to touch her or leave her side, but now he was crawling over her and taking her face in his hands. He could feel the heat from her cheeks. The bright pink of her fevered lips was already beginning to fade. He couldn't breathe. The world shook, or maybe it was him.

"No." It was a cry, and then it was a whisper. "No."

"I tried," Masalee was saying, as she collapsed against Espel's shoulder. She looked so defeated. "I tried to keep her heart beating. I tried."

"Wil." Loom said her name with insistence, as though that would wake her. Death was not her destiny. This enigmatic creature who had tumbled into his life, all fight and sweat and blood, was destined to outlive them all. Still holding her face, he leaned close. His lips were shaking when he touched them to hers. "I'm sorry," he whispered. "I'm sorry for all of it." And he was. He was sorry that he had ever spotted her in Brayshire, trading gemstones for coins. He was sorry that he learned of her power and tried to use it to save his kingdom. He would give everything back—every argument, every kiss, all the hollows within himself that had been filled by her warmth—if it would mean that she was still out in the world somewhere. That she was alive. That she was safe, even if it meant they never found each other.

Wil's chest rose with a breath, and Loom drew back, startled. But it was not the true breath of a living girl; Masalee had resumed her efforts with renewed fervor.

Zay was at Loom's side now; she wrapped her arms around his shoulders and drew him back. When he broke with a sob, she began to rock him back and forth, the way they had done for each other when they were children. He tried to look at Wil. Maybe there would be life in her face again. Maybe she would come back. But Zay took his face in her hands and she forced him to look at her instead.

She was the only one who still looked the same. Everyone else looked evil and wrong.

"I couldn't stop it," he blurted.

"Shh." She put an arm around him. She was all gentleness. He was too weak to protest. "I know you couldn't, *ansoh*. I know."

Zay went on shushing him, not bothering with platitudes. She didn't let go of him, and Loom thought that if she did, he might somehow disappear entirely.

"I take it back." Loom was still muttering to Wil. "I take it all back. I don't want my kingdom if you're the price."

A gasp commanded his attention. He went rigid with fear and with that wretchedly cruel thing called hope.

Wil shuddered. Blood burst from her mouth when she coughed. A terrible moan came out of her, anguished and barely human.

Loom was watching Wil, only Wil. She twisted with pain. Her brow furrowed and she tried, as ever, to fight her way back.

"Get your sleep serum," Masalee commanded Espel through gritted teeth. "Put her out or the pain will throw her into shock and we'll lose her again."

Wil's fists unclenched when the serum passed her lips. She sank into unconsciousness. But she was breathing. Loom saw the rise and fall of her bloody and torn chest. He heard the rattle of blood in her lungs.

Masalee was sweating now. Dark stains bloomed from under the arms of her robe. Wisps of hair clung to her face. It wasn't just Wil's heart she was coaxing life into, but her lungs as well.

"What did you do?" Espel asked. "How did you bring her back?"

"I don't think that was me," Masalee said, breathing hard. "Loom was the one who stopped her heart so that he could be heir, and you heard what he said. He gave it up."

Daylight filled the room now, relentlessly bright. There was the sound of birds, faraway at first and then rising in a crescendo of scattered song.

Loom was scarcely aware of any of this as he took Wil's

hand in both of his. He could feel her pulse thrumming in her fingertips, strong and forceful now. He was afraid to clutch her hand any tighter. He was afraid to speak and break whatever force had brought her back.

Wil's teeth were gritted. Her legs moved against the floor, as though it were at all possible for her to get up.

"Stop fighting," Loom said. He brought his face close to hers and he felt her breath against his lips. "Rest," he said. "For once in your life, you have to rest."

The Wil he knew was returning, though, and she didn't know how to be still. "Loom?" Her eyes opened, cloudy, far away. He could see the frustration knotting her brow as she tried to focus on him. As she tried to wake up.

"I'm here," he said. "I'm not going anywhere."

Sweat washed across her face; her fever was starting to break. She was still so fragile, gasping when she tried to move. Loom was fearful that death would be back to claim her. He had the sense that death hadn't truly left the room.

"What are . . . you doing?" Wil managed to cough out when he buried his face in her hair.

"You once told me that death smells like the dirt after a long rain," he said.

There was a smear of blood on one side of her mouth, and when he brushed it away, she tried to smile. "Do I smell like death?"

"No," he said. "Just dirt."

Her laugh turned into a cough.

Masalee stood abruptly. She clutched at the hilt of her sword, which brought Espel to her side. "What is it?" Espel asked.

"Something is coming," Masalee said. "Could be a threat."

"Pahn?" Espel asked. "When I tried to kill him earlier, all I hit was an illusion. Could that have happened a second time?"

Masalee shook her head. "Pahn is dead, unless he's concealing his energy so well that I can't feel it. This is something else."

Wil struggled in her delirium; her eyes had closed and she was beginning to fade. "Baren," she murmured.

"King Baren?" Espel said. "He's dead, isn't he?"

"That's who the cloaked figure was," Loom said. "He killed Pahn and then he disappeared, as though he'd never been there at all."

"You might have mentioned that," Espel snapped. "Our kingdoms are at war; he could be on his way to kill us."

She was right, Loom knew, but looking back on it now, he hadn't possessed the cognizance. He had been dazed, still, by Pahn's spell, and focused only on Wil. And he had been the only one to see Baren, besides. Espel had been fading in and out of consciousness as she bled onto the snow, and Masalee was tending to Wil. Zay had still been on the ship.

"We should go back to the ship before he finds us," Zay said as she knelt to scoop a still-sleeping Ada up from the floor.

"Wil shouldn't be moved," Masalee said. "She's too weak. She wouldn't make it that far."

"I'm not leaving," Loom said. "If he comes, I'll fight him." A plan was beginning to form in his mind. Wil was alive and the world made sense again. Things had a purpose. "Zay, you fire up the ship. It'll be safer for Ada there, and if we need to make a fast exit, we'll be ready."

"I'll conceal it for as long as I can," Masalee said, and it astonished Loom that she was still standing after all she'd done the night before.

Zay brought herself close to Loom. "Don't do anything foolish," she said.

He smiled. "I can't promise to meet such an outrageous demand."

All night, Wil had dreamed that she was trapped in the lens of her brother's monocle. Aleen was screaming from within the darkness of an old train tunnel, and Wil couldn't find her. She couldn't find anyone, and she had no voice. The snow had melted, turning the ground into mud, and the mud rooted her in place.

When the light of day reached her eyelids and turned the darkness the color of flesh, at last she found her voice. She screamed, not for Aleen, but for Baren. He was the one who had trapped her here, she knew. He was coming back to finish her off.

Sound hardly left her mouth at all. The voice that answered her was not Baren's. Loom's presence filled the dream up with light, until the tunnel broke away and the dream shattered.

Loom. He knelt over her now. His eyes were bleary and bloodshot. For a moment, Wil didn't understand where she was, and then the servants' kitchen came into view. Behind Loom's shoulder hung rows of copper pots and wooden spoons. A fire was crackling beside her, and she shivered in spite of it; the warmth didn't seep through her skin, and when she tried to move, her limbs were sluggish and heavy.

"Welcome back," he said.

"Are we still dreaming?" she asked. It was the only explanation that made sense. She recognized the servants' kitchen around them; she couldn't remember returning here.

"No." The word came out eager. He hadn't expected to ever hear her voice again, and he was grateful now for the sound of it. Even her rattling breaths were their own sort of blessing. "No, we're both awake. What's the last thing you remember?"

He waited for her face to change with understanding. She remembered all of it now. Her hand went to her hip, where her dagger was missing, because Loom had used it to tear a hole through her chest.

"You were different." Her voice was scratchy. Her throat burned with the taste of blood. "Your eyes were all black."

She tried to push herself upright. Pain lanced her and she gasped.

"I'm going to fix this," Loom said, as he eased her back against the floor. "All of it. I promise."

The promise was too lofty for any of them just then. Wrestling with the marvelry that Masalee used against Wil so many times had given Wil a sense for it. She felt the presence of it now, coming through the trees. But the sky didn't darken, even as the unease became so palpable that Loom and Espel and Masalee felt it too.

"Help me up," Wil said.

"You can't—" Loom began, but she interrupted.

"If my brother is coming to kill me again, I won't die lying down."

"Hells," he swore, but as Wil struggled to sit upright, he guided her with his arm under her back. She clutched his shoulder. Blood leaked from the stitches of her wound, adding a fresh bloom to the red stains on her tunic. Her lips were blue, her skin drained of color, and her shallow gasps for air echoed against the stones.

Her vision briefly darkened, but when it cleared, she realized just how bright the light was as it stole through the kitchen window. There was none of the cursed gloom she had come to expect; Arrod was familiar again.

It was then Wil noticed the trail of blood that led to her. There would have been no sense hiding now even if she wanted to. Baren was going to find her. Perhaps he would tell her how he had managed to claw his way back from the dead before he attempted to finish her off.

But it was not Baren's frantic voice that filled the great room. "Wil? Wil!"

Wil knew that she was delirious. She could see the blood she had lost; it was staining the floor and her clothes. She could feel her strength waning. But she was sure that the voice calling out to her was Gerdie's.

She fought to stay awake. She had to know that she wasn't dreaming and that this was real.

The door opened. Espel and Masalee drew their weapons. "Stop," Wil said, or tried to say. "Don't hurt him."

Over their heads Wil saw him. He wasn't wearing his monocle—he had left that for her to find, but he was alive. He was here.

Loom's grip on Wil's arm tightened protectively. He didn't trust what he was seeing, and who could blame him? Wil didn't understand it herself. But her brother had broken death's rules countless times, and Wil had never cared much how he managed to do it.

Gerdie saw that the trail of blood ended where she stood.

"You're alive," she managed to gasp out. Not only was Gerdie alive, the entire kingdom was alive. She heard the faraway trill of the clock towers over distant churches, and winter insects and birds chirping and singing and flying through the trees.

Every muscle of her body screamed for reprieve, but she refused to sink into darkness just yet.

Gerdie ran to her. He knelt before her, and the braces on his legs creaked loudly the way they always did when it was cold.

She leaned back against the table leg for support, and her head lolled against her shoulder. "You're alive," she said again. "And we aren't dreaming."

"Why did you come here?" He pressed the back of his hand to her forehead; it was an old habit from all the times she'd returned to the castle broken in some way or other. Maybe he forgot the risk. The kingdom must still have been cursed, Wil thought, because he was unharmed from her touch. Or her heart was just too weak to muster up any adrenaline.

"I heard about the attack." Her speech was slurred. She blinked through her exhaustion, frustrated. "I thought you were dead. I saw—" Her eyes narrowed. "I saw your body. You were dead. Cold."

"It wasn't real," he said.

"Yes it was," Wil insisted, fully aware that she was arguing with her brother about whether or not he was alive. It was an absurd argument, and she was grateful he was here to listen to it. "It wasn't alchemy. I know your handiwork. I know all the chemicals that could be combined to smell like blood. It was real."

"It was Baren," Gerdie said.

Wil's eyes were closing. She felt her heart rate slowing. It had to be Masalee, putting her out because she was stubbornly refusing to rest. But how could she rest when Gerdie had come back from the dead?

"Is Baren still alive?" she whispered.

"Yes."

"Mother?" she asked.

She couldn't stay awake to hear the answer.

# THIRTY-THREE

LOOM HAD ONCE TOLD WIL that she looked like royalty.

She had been barefoot at the time, her callused heels crusted with sand, her boots hanging over one shoulder by their laces. They were standing in the grand foyer of his broken castle, and she had been furious with him, he remembered. Her fury was especially beautiful, because anything Wil felt, she felt with her whole body—her jaw, her fingers that had clutched the banister, the tension in her lean biceps. And her eyes. Her dark, wide eyes that took the world in and tore it apart in turn.

As she stormed up the stairs, her footsteps carrying in the wide, empty space, he wondered how she couldn't see it. Didn't she know she commanded more than just his heart? Didn't she know that the world was always hers where she stood?

Now that they were in Northern Arrod, Loom saw Wil in

her own castle, and he understood why she did not want to be identified as royalty. She fit into a castle as easily as she fit into a fight with a marauder in a town square. Royalty was just a skin she wore from time to time as a means of survival.

He was the one to carry her this time. She was unconscious and ashen. Her head hung over his arm, and he moved slowly so he wouldn't jar her injury.

If Wil's brother hadn't told Loom which chamber belonged to her, at a glance Loom never would have guessed it.

There was a large four-poster bed netted with white lace, and a massive iron chandelier that looked to be an ancient candelabra that had been updated to outfit electricity in candle-shaped fixtures.

He eased her onto the mattress. She moved instinctively for the center, as though even in sleep her body recognized where she was.

Her hair was matted now with blood and dirt and sweat, but it fanned against the flannel pillowcase in a phantom attempt at elegance. In this room, she would always be a princess, and, for the first time, a stranger to him.

Masalee didn't have to work as hard now to keep Wil alive; Wil was beginning to take control of that task for herself. If not for the sleep serum, she would be awake. Even now, she was fighting it. Her brow furrowed; her fingers curled and uncurled.

If they had been alone, he would have climbed beside her and laid his head on her chest. He was so tired and so defeated by his own relief. He wanted to sleep to the sound of her breathing and feel the breeze of it in his hair.

But they weren't alone, and Loom suspected he wouldn't be able to rest yet, or for a long time.

Wil's brother stood in the doorway with his arms folded, watching them. He looked nothing at all like Wil; his eyes were a bright, persistent blue. His hair was as light as Wil's was dark, and his tall, broad frame stood in contrast to Wil's slight but muscular build.

But Loom saw the bond that existed between the siblings nonetheless. He saw the worry Gerdie tried to mask. Like his sister, Gerdie was ever on guard, anticipating a perpetual storm. The guns and knives sheathed along his hips and thighs all bore the same patterns as Wil's.

This was Wil's family. And this castle, unfitting as it might have seemed, was her home. Wil was not entirely lost in the world, as he had thought when he first met her. She belonged somewhere. There was someone to miss her when she was gone.

Loom stood away from the edge of the bed to face Wil's brother. Espel stood at a distance; she had been studying the boy just as closely.

"Who did this to her?" Gerdie asked. There was nothing murderous in his tone, but his eerie calm spoke to a very patient sort of rage. And here is where he differed from Wil, who was impulsive when she wanted revenge.

Loom opened his mouth to speak. He was going to tell the

truth, all of it, and face whatever consequences they brought.

But Espel was faster. "A marveler by the name of Pahn," she said. Recognition flashed in Gerdie's eyes. He knew that name, but he said nothing as Espel continued. "My father is King Zinil." She took a confident step forward, making a show not of pride but of fearlessness. She knew that this boy would see her as an enemy, and she wanted to make clear that she was unafraid of him. "He couldn't leave his kingdom, so he sent Pahn to attack your kingdom. He's the most powerful marveler the world has to offer. Was," she amended. "Before your king killed him."

"Baren is my brother, not my king," Gerdie amended, and then shook his head to dismiss whatever else he'd been prepared to say about it.

"We thought you were dead," Loom ventured. "We thought—" His voice, like his thoughts, tapered off into silence. His mind was still fogged by the lingering aftermath of being under Pahn's spell, and he hadn't slept. So much had happened that it seemed he had been on this continent for a thousand years. Was it only two nights ago that he was on a ship headed to this kindgom, with its princess in his arms?

"How can I be certain you won't kill me?" Gerdie asked. "Being that we're enemies."

"We aren't your enemies," Espel said, and Loom was grateful to have her on his side for this. Espel was clever and quick even when she was nursing her wounds and on her second day without sleep. "We came here with Wil, and we came here to help."

It took Espel less than an hour to explain their banishment and Wil's initial plan to dupe King Zinil with an alchemized corpse. The time was kept by the grandfather clock on Wil's chamber wall. When it broke into a trill at the top of the hour, it startled Loom from a lull he didn't realize he had fallen into.

Espel didn't betray her own fatigue, but he knew that she felt it. She had to. Despite all evidence she meticulously presented to the contrary, she was human.

After answering all possible questions Gerdie could have had for them, she ended with a question of her own: "Is the rest of your family still alive? King Baren?"

Gerdie had remained stoic throughout everything, his eyes occasionally flitting to Wil, who was still lost in her serum-induced sleep as Masalee kept vigil.

Though this was the only question any of them had asked him, he didn't answer it. "You must be tired," he said. "Let me show you to a place where you can rest."

Once again, Wil struggled her way to the surface of her nightmares and broke through them.

"Wil?" Gerdie's voice was there to greet her when she awoke. Her eyes opened, and she saw him on a chair at her bedside, his face alight with relief.

"Hey," she croaked.

"Hells." He bowed his head. "You have to stop scaring me. It's becoming a pattern."

"I've been told I am very hard to kill," she said drowsily. "It seems you are, too." She tried to push herself upright, but a fresh stab of pain to her chest stopped her. She closed her eyes, not because of the pain, but because she wanted to hide from his answer to what she was about to ask him. "Gerdie, where is Mother?"

In a flash, she imagined her mother cold and dead, just like her brothers had been—at least, as they had appeared.

"Mother is safe." He lowered his voice. "She's in Southern Arrod with Addney."

Wil blinked. "How did you convince her to flee?"

"We got word that a retaliatory attack would be hitting us. Turns out Baren actually had the foresight to employ proper spies. We all went into hiding. She went to protect the future heir just in case soldiers invaded the southern half of the kingdom. I stayed behind to make sure Baren didn't let this place burn to the ground."

"But it did burn," Wil said. With the memory of the Port Capital, she felt overwhelmingly useless. This was her kingdom and she had set out to save it after robbing it of its heir, and she couldn't even sit up in her bed. "Everything is ruined. Everyone is dead."

"Most got out alive," Gerdie said, though he seemed to know how empty those words were. Just as in Cannolay, one life claimed by war was one life too many.

"Where is everyone?" Wil asked. "I didn't see any survivors. I didn't even see any bodies."

Gerdie hesitated, and she grabbed his hand in both of hers, clutching it until her knuckles turned white. "Where?" she demanded.

"Baren's soldiers led them through the woods in the darkness. They didn't even use lantern light. Baren—he did something to the trees. Cast an illusion so that it would hide the people passing through the forest. If they're lucky, they've made it to Southern Arrod by now."

"Luck" was not a word Gerdie had ever used, and it made Wil uneasy. He was not dealing out certainties, because he knew they would be lies.

"You were right," he said. "Baren was dabbling in marvelry. More than dabbling. It turns out he has a real gift for it. I guess it's in our family's blood, though I'm not sure where. We sure as the hells don't have any."

"You're rambling." It was an accusation. Gerdie only rambled when he was either lost in the channels of his own thoughts, or he was stalling for time.

Gerdie drew a long, heavy breath. "The bodies were an illusion. Pure marvelry."

"It was so real," Wil said. "I *touched* you. I—"

"He's stronger than I would have thought possible," Gerdie said. "Then again, a year ago I wouldn't have thought it was possible for you to turn an entire garden into diamonds."

"Where is he?" she asked.

"He's . . ." Again Gerdie hesitated. His shoulders rose and then sank in defeat. "He's made some sort of a deal with that old woman in the train tunnel."

Wil's blood went cold. That old woman was dead. She saw their mother kill her. But maybe it hadn't been her. Espel had stabbed Pahn and he'd disappeared into wisps. Could the old woman have cast a similar illusion?

"Is that where he is?" Wil felt the desperation all the way to her bones. "That woman is dangerous, Gerdie."

"Baren is more dangerous," he countered. "He's been practicing this ability for years, Wil. Right under our noses."

"It wasn't under our noses," Wil said. "We all took care to avoid him." She laughed ruefully. It made her chest hurt. "All these years, I thought I was the invisible spare." She considered. She remembered Loom stabbing her, immersed as he was in Pahn's spell. She remembered the blade feeling as though it were on fire when it tore through her. And then very little after that.

"Baren saved me," she said. The words came out slowly, a puzzle she was trying to solve. "I remember Pahn kneeling beside me. I remember that my body had gone numb from the pain. I couldn't move. He would have finished me off, but Baren . . ." She trailed off. She turned the memory over in her mind, but it never changed. "Baren killed him. To protect me." She had been staring at her chandelier as she processed this, but now she looked to her brother. "Why would he do that?"

Gerdie's face had gone ashen. He hadn't known the details of her latest brush with death. He made a quick recovery and said, "I don't know. I was surprised enough that he protected me when the attack began. I was certain he'd leave me to fend for myself, but he made sure we both got out before Pahn came for us."

"Pahn came alone," Wil said. "He was so certain he could kill you."

"He did kill us." Gerdie shrugged. "The illusion of us, at least."

Wil felt sick. Her mind would never be free from that horrible image of Gerdie dead on the floor of his laboratory. He had been alone. That was the worst part. She hadn't been there to protect him.

"I found your monocle," she said. Her voice sounded weak. "In the snow."

She reached under the blankets and dug into her pocket. The motion sent waves of pain to her chest.

Gerdie held the lens up for inspection. "You smudged the hells out of it."

She laughed, and the laugh broke with a cough. "Sorry."

"Baren was the one who said you'd be back. Something about your curse and all of us being meant to die. It's hard to suss out what was madness and what was true."

"He isn't mad," Wil said. "He never was." Her eyelids felt heavy; she tried to stay conscious, but her body was through listening to her. "I need to tell you a story. Shake me if I fall asleep in the middle of it."

She told him about Aleen. She told him that this curse was kept alive in her heart, but that it had spread out to all of them. First it took Owen, and then it took all of Arrod.

She was scarcely awake by the end of it. Frustrated, she fought against her own exhaustion.

Gerdie was frowning, but it wasn't for Aleen. It was for her. "You were never a curse to me, Wil," he said.

"Yes." Her eyes closed, and she forced them open again. "I'm the reason all this has happened."

"Our grandfather is the reason this happened," Gerdie said, with the familiar practicality he employed when he was certain he was right. "You aren't the cause." He smiled, and the sight flooded her with so much relief and happiness; hours earlier, she had been certain she would never see him again, and here he was, alive; and faring better than she was. "You're the reason I was able to forge so many weapons in my cauldron," he continued, "and Owen was able to learn the Port Capital gossip. You've done more to help our kingdom than a dozen of Papa's best soldiers."

Wil didn't believe those words, but for now she let them wash over her and she pretended that she did. She wouldn't have been able to go on otherwise.

"Papa knew, all this time, and he never breathed a word," Gerdie went on.

Wil closed her eyes, not from exhaustion, but to try and

shut out the image of her father's face. It didn't work. She could see him so clearly just then, in more detail than any oil portrait or sepia photograph could render. She could see all the subtle ways she looked like him, hidden though those details were.

"I can't pretend I ever understood Papa," she said, her voice tight. She meant to say more, but tears threatened, and she knew that if she spoke another word, she wouldn't have the strength to stop them. What she had meant to say was this: She hoped her father had loved her. She hoped he knew that she had loved him, in her own broken sort of way. He had not shown her much kindness, and though she competed with her brothers for his approval, she hadn't been kind either. She had lied to and cheated him, and often thought the worst.

But she had loved him.

Gerdie dabbed at her sweaty brow with his sleeve. He seemed to know what she was thinking, and Wil was so grateful to him. Grateful that someone in this world had always understood her, even when she was a tangled mess beyond sorting.

"We have to find Baren," she said, when she was able to speak. "If he's with that woman, he's in danger."

Baren had tried to kill her more than once since learning of her curse. The recollection didn't leave her feeling sentimental about having him back. But he had also saved her life when Pahn tried to end it once and for all, and she had to find out why. Maybe there was some good in him after all. Maybe he truly did care about the people of Northern Arrod when he arranged for them to flee the kingdom.

"Rest now," Gerdie said.

She shook her head against the pillow. "There's no time."

"We won't be able to leave until nightfall anyway," Gerdie said. "It'll be safer to move in darkness. We'll be less vulnerable to an attack."

Wil wanted to argue. Her kingdom was falling to pieces all around her and she should have been the one to save it, because this was all her fault. But Baren was the one laboring over it now. Baren was acting as king, and surely the world had gone mad.

"You nearly died." A hint of pleading stole into Gerdie's tone. Her stubbornness had often frustrated him, just as his did for her.

"Yesterday I thought *you* were dead," she said. Her eyes closed, though. Exhaustion and pain were at odds, and she was tempted to sleep if only to dull the aching in her chest.

"Now that we're even, let's make a pact to live for another eighty years," Gerdie said.

"A hundred," she said.

"Deal."

# THIRTY-FOUR

As she slept, Wil felt the energy of marvelry coursing through her chest and she knew that Masalee was nearby. This time, she wasn't trying to control Wil's heart, but heal it.

From the depths of her sleep, Wil could hear Masalee's voice, faint as the whispers of the Ancient Sea. The words were in a language she couldn't understand. It might have been one of the Eastern tongues spoken in Masalee's childhood.

Her voice was soft and cool and gentle.

Sometimes Wil felt water being spooned between her lips. She felt Loom nearby, watching her. Worrying.

And then, eventually, she felt Baren. This was the thing to startle her awake. She pushed herself upright, gasping. Pain twisted in her chest as though her heart were barbed with thorns.

Gerdie had been sitting at her desk poring over sheets of

paper, but now he rushed to her. "Hey. What is it?" He was trying to ease her back against the pillows, but she fought him off.

"Something is coming for us," she said.

"She's been dreaming," Masalee said. She was sitting at Wil's bedside, where she had likely been for hours. Night was beginning to fall outside. The sky was heavy with the thick darkness of a Northern winter.

Wil shook her head. She ignored the spots of brightness in her vision. "No," she said. "I heard voices."

Masalee and Gerdie went still to listen, until the only sound was the ticking of the grandfather clock, which had grown aggressively loud with each tick.

Wil slid out of bed. Her legs wobbled, but she didn't fall as she made her way to her window. Frost glazed the twin panes of shuttered glass, freezing them together, and she had to hit the seam between the panes with the heel of her hand to loose them enough to open.

Night had not finished falling yet, and there was enough light left for her to make out the outlines of figures moving toward the castle. Dozens of them. Gerdie and Masalee were on either side of her now, crowding the windowsill.

"We have to move," Gerdie said. "We're being invaded."

"Wait." Wil heard one of the men shouting orders. He spoke in Northern Arrod's accent. "They aren't enemy soldiers," she said. "I don't think King Zinil sent any of his men, did he? He only sent Pahn."

"Are those our soldiers?" Gerdie asked, bewildered. And

then he shouted down to them, "Who's out there?"

Wordlessly, Masalee wrapped a blanket around Wil's shoulders. Wil was grateful for this. She hadn't noticed the bitter wind dusting snow into her chamber. She hadn't noticed that her fingers were numb from the cold.

The figures had stopped charging forward. They stood assembled at the gate now. Only one of them moved forward, tilting his head to stare up at the window. "Your Highness," he shouted. "We've returned to protect our royal family."

"That's one of Papa's soldiers," Wil whispered to her brother. They had been gone after Baren took over. Dead, she had assumed, or banished somehow.

"You're certain?" he asked.

"Yes," she said. "You don't evade soldiers every day of your life without learning a few of their voices."

"Stay where you are," Gerdie shouted to the men.

He moved for the door and Wil followed after him. "Wait," he said. He drew two of his daggers and one of his guns, fitting them into Wil's empty sheaths and holster. "Really, Wil, is it too much to ask that you not lose the weapons I give you?"

"It's been a long couple of days," she said. Though she felt rested now, she was still filthy. She could smell the blood and the sweat souring her skin.

"Where are Loom and Espel?" she asked, as they moved down the hall. She tried to keep up with her brother's pace, pretending every step wasn't its own contained hell of agony.

"Guest chambers," Gerdie said, though his tone was grudging. He had never been especially fond of strangers, much less the children of the king who had attacked his home. But he hadn't complained, and he hadn't sent them away, though he could have. Wil trusted them, and that meant something to him.

Loom and Espel had heard the shouting and they met them in the grand foyer. Loom regarded Wil with uncertainty and guilt; she hated to see him like this. Just as her memories of what happened the night before had returned to her slowly, so had his. She could see that much on his face. He remembered being unable to control his hand. He remembered plunging the dagger into her chest. And now he was faced with what he had done.

Wil hadn't seen her reflection, but she could guess at how she looked. She wanted to tell Loom that she had endured worse, but it wasn't true. For all the attempts that had been made on her life—resulting in cracked ribs, broken bones, and endless blossoms of bruises—the worst had been sustained by the boy who loved her.

No. It hadn't been Loom, she reminded herself. It was Pahn. Pahn, who lay dead in the castle garden where he'd been slain, his body still, his robes fluttering in the illusion of breathing.

Wil had grabbed the lantern that hung on a hook inside the servants' kitchen, and now she held it up. The sharp blue glow highlighted Pahn's corpse. He was on his back, gaping at the stars. It had taken a marveler to kill a marveler. King Zinil surely hadn't anticipated that.

*It isn't a trick,* she tried to console herself, though it wasn't working. *He's truly dead.*

She followed her brother to the group of soldiers standing at the gate. When she came to stand at Gerdie's side, the foremost soldier dropped to a kneel. In a wave, the others followed.

"Your highnesses," the foremost soldier said. "We've come to serve you."

Wil recognized him. On the night she discovered her curse, she and Gerdie had returned to the castle, battle weary and limping, and this soldier had been the one to greet them.

"Where have you been?" Wil asked, though she was a fine one to ask such a question, seeing as she'd been gone for nearly the entirety of Baren's reign.

The man rose to his feet, giving her another cordial bow of his head. He showed the same respect he had always offered to the princess of Northern Arrod, and Wil, for her part, looked as bedraggled as ever.

"King Baren sent us to the outlying cities when he became king. He was certain that an attack was coming, and he wanted soldiers at all corners of the kingdom."

Wil and Gerdie exchanged a look. They had never known Baren to strategize. As king especially, he had been frenzied. Erratic. Sleepless. Did he have a plan all along?

"We've been sent to escort you to him," the man went on.

This could have been a trap, Wil thought. But it didn't seem likely. Her father's soldiers had been loyal to the throne; many had served her family long before she or her brothers were born.

Still, she kept her guard up. She switched off her lantern so that its glow would not give away their location—though it didn't seem that enemy soldiers were coming.

"How are you?" Loom whispered. His sudden closeness startled her; she hadn't felt his presence or heard his approach.

"Best I've ever been," she said. "I'm thinking of running. Care to race me?"

She'd meant to make him laugh, but his silence said that she had only made him feel that much more guilty.

"You're limping," he said.

"I'm all right."

"You're going to pull your stitches," he said. "That's if you don't collapse first. It would be easier if I carried you."

She glared. "Like a baby?"

"No. On my back."

She scowled.

"I promise you will look very gallant," Loom went on. Wil didn't reward him with a laugh, though she wanted to.

It irritated her that he was right. But each step dizzied her. Against the darkness of night, her vision roiled with flashes of metallic brightness, and she knew that her blood pressure was dropping. Her stubbornness wouldn't be productive, and there wasn't the luxury of time.

She conceded to his invitation, climbing onto his back and

coiling her legs around his hips, her arms around his neck. She was surprised at what a relief this was. His hair was thick and heavy with sweat and grease, his skin had the bitter smell of blood, so heady she could taste it. But he was familiar to her. So warm and safe. She placed her head to the back of his neck and closed her eyes. It was dark. No one would notice if she rested. Just for a little while.

Later, she would never admit to falling asleep, jostled by his deft and quick steps. She didn't mean to. She shouldn't have. But for a few fleeting moments, the entire kingdom just . . . fell away.

"I love you," she whispered, half dreaming. He kissed her arm that was draped over his shoulder.

But the time to rest was short-lived. Soon they arrived at the mouth of the abandoned train tunnel. Wil could not sense her brother's marvelry as she had once been able to. She couldn't even sense Loom's cursed heart beating beside her own. This last thing caused a panic that she pushed to the back of her mind.

There was no buzz in the air; there was no glow. Baren had made himself wholly invisible to the outside world.

Wil slid to her feet. Winds, she was exhausted. But as before, she was determined to face Baren standing. Masalee was nearby, casting gentle, healing threads through Wil's blood. It did little for the pain, but it gave her the strength to keep going.

One of the soldiers lit a lantern and headed the charge into the tunnel, but Wil said, "Stop."

The soldier turned to face her.

"Your Highness?"

"He's our brother. We should be the ones to speak to him." Wil looked to Gerdie, who hesitated for a beat, then nodded.

Wil and Gerdie took a step forward. When Loom moved to follow, Wil stayed him. She brought herself close to him and said in a low voice, "We should go alone."

She could see that he was uneasy, but he didn't try to protest. "I'll be right here," he said. "In case anything goes wrong."

She laughed without any humor. "What could possibly go right?"

She lit her lantern and turned for the tunnel, Gerdie at her side. "Do you have any idea what we should expect?" she asked.

"None whatsoever." At least he was honest.

Wil felt the energy before she saw it. A faint glow identical to the one she had seen the first time she encountered the marveler woman. It was a pulsing, nauseating hum.

It didn't have the effect on her that it had when she met the old woman for the first time, and now Wil thought it strange that her fatigue only came from her physical wounds; she didn't feel the strain of the kingdom's curse countering her own.

She saw Baren, and if the way Gerdie grabbed her wrist was any indication, he had seen him, too. Baren knelt in the dirt, at the heart of the purple glow, which flashed with thin, webbed flashes of brightness, like lightning in a bottle. His head was down, his golden hair covering his expression.

Slowly, he tilted his face up to meet them. His eyes were eerily bright, not the shade of blue he shared with his mother and brothers, but more electric, like the street lanterns Wil had seen dotting the Eastern cityscape.

His mouth curled into a sneer, revealing his teeth.

Gerdie drew his weapon. It was Owen's long sword, slim and light, and so all the more deadly. But Gerdie didn't raise it against his brother. Not yet. Instead, he extended his arm, shielding Wil. Baren's gaze was undoubtedly fixed on her, and she was no match for him now. She might not have been a match for him even at her best, she realized. He had grown stronger.

Baren had always been a bumbling child. Never quick or clever. It wasn't his shortcomings that made him mean; it was their father's disdain. What use did their father have for a spare who could scarcely shoot an arrow at a target? If he had not been born the son of a king, Baren would have been a softer sort of boy. He would have found his talents. Wil wasn't sure what made her think this now, standing here. She had never thought it before. But in Baren's merciless stare, she saw more in her second-eldest brother than she ever had in nearly sixteen years of living down the hall from him. Baren had not been allowed to pick up an instrument, or a paintbrush, or a book; he was deprived of the frivolous and yet essential element of pleasure, all his life. Instead, he was given swords and arrows and chains; his wrists were slapped by impatient instructors when he couldn't properly wield them. He was always a failure, because he was only allowed to attempt things at which he would fail.

And in this same moment that seemed to contain a lifetime, Wil thought of her own lessons on comportment and sewing and plaiting her hair. If those frivolous things had been all she was ever taught, it would have been a miserable childhood of glaring in jealousy as her brothers pursued their weapons training and their world history lessons.

Baren—was he telling her this? It was all so clear.

"Baren." She spoke in the same tone she would afford a feral wolf whose den she had just encountered. "Did you kill Papa for what he did to you?"

Baren rose to his feet. Gerdie readjusted his grip on the sword hilt. Wil put her hand over Gerdie's, staying his hand as she stepped in front of his sword. It would only provoke Baren's anger. No one had ever protected him.

She stepped forward. "Answer me." Her tone was gentle. She wouldn't have hated him for the truth; she believed that. "Papa wasn't a perfect man, Baren. I know that. He was often cruel."

"If he was cruel, it was your fault," Baren said. "You did this to our family."

This was a sentiment Wil had forced herself to face since the night of Owen's death, and especially after she learned the truth of what had happened to Aleen. It was her fault the kingdom had lost its heir. Her fault her father had been so tormented by the love he felt for his children that he hid it even from himself. She had said this to Gerdie and her mother, to Loom, and countless times to herself. She should have said it to Baren also. She should have been able to agree.

But what she said was, "I was just a baby, Baren."

"You were evil before you were out of the womb," he seethed. "You should never have been born."

"And then what?" Wil countered. "If I had never been born, someone else eventually would have been. Is it so inconceivable that a queen might love someone just a little bit more than her king?"

"Our mother had three other children, and she doesn't love any of us more," Baren said. "Just you."

"I know," Wil said. She took a step closer, and Baren bristled, as though he were the one afraid of her. For a blink he looked truly terrified of his little sister, who was bloodied, and small by comparison. Her mother had always favored her; Wil knew that. She also knew that she was no more worthy of love than her brothers. Being born a girl had been the only thing to set her apart.

Her mother had wanted a daughter the way that some people wanted diamonds and gold—all the things Wil had been cursed to create with a touch. And wanting anything so much was an irrational thing. Wil would never understand it. Perhaps her mother had expected her daughter to be a piece of herself that she could keep and admire, like a jeweled comb. Like a song.

"But I'm not your enemy," Wil said. "You know that or you would have let Pahn kill me."

Baren laughed, and it came out like there were two voices in his throat. It was not a human sound. "You think I did that to spare you? I killed Pahn to stop him from bringing your ugly, cursed heart to our enemy king. I don't want our kingdom destroyed."

Wil heard Gerdie breathing behind her. The damp had cast a rattle to his lungs. She heard, too, his sword tip dragging against the dirt, a subtle reminder that he was still holding it.

"I believe you," Wil said. "But you have to let go of the curse you've placed over it."

"The curse was to keep you out." Baren's voice was strange. It no longer sounded like him. He stood tall and his shadow grew behind him. With a cry that no living thing should make, he charged at her.

Wil was thrown to the ground before she knew what happened. She pushed herself upright, quickly scanning her body. No new wounds.

Gerdie stood where she had been a moment ago, his sword poised to strike. He'd pushed her out of the way, and though Wil knew this was a sensible thing for him to do given the state of her, she was furious.

She struggled upright just in time to see Baren throw the sword from Gerdie's grasp. Tendrils of the strange purple-pink smoke coiled Gerdie's wrists like cuffs, shackling him to the dirt.

Gerdie gritted his teeth, and when he struggled, the restraints tightened. But the object of this was not to hurt him,

Wil realized; it was to keep him out of the way.

Baren was not himself. Wil knew his outrage; just as she stole the lion's share of their mother's love, she bore the burden of Baren's hatred. And this was not the same brother who had taunted her, who had smashed her things and poured ink over her calligraphy and dangled her from her bedroom window.

This was something far darker than that. He ran at her, and she saw the old marveler woman's eyes where his should have been. It was the old marveler woman's voice, not Baren's, that screamed as his body charged at her.

"Wil!" Gerdie cried, but he couldn't reach her. That was for the best. This was not his battle.

Wil drew her gun and fired a shot right into Baren's chest. But the bullet tore through him as though he were air.

Baren grabbed her arms, his grip so tight that she was lifted from the ground. These were not his eyes. This was not him. And for a moment, the cavern disappeared. Wil saw her grandmother screaming over Aleen's body. She saw her grandmother fleeing the castle in the dead of night and throwing herself into the sea. She saw her grandmother's body wash up along the jagged rocks on the city's outskirts. She saw the body convulse and cough up water, and grapple for hand- and footholds.

Her grandmother had not killed herself in despair. She had meant to, but she'd lived. It was pure chance that had saved her, but in that moment, awakening on the rocks, Wil's grandmother had believed herself invincible. She stood, blood running down her shredded palms and knees, and she looked toward the Port Capital in the distance. She wasn't thinking of the son who still lived, but of the daughter she had lost. Of her traitorous husband; while she was underwater, any love she had left for him turned black and rotted inside her.

There was nothing left for her here. When she boarded a ship that evening, she was not the queen of Arrod. She was not the mother of two children, or the wife of a king. She was nothing and no one, and it was a relief.

In her world travels, she would go on to discover marvelry. She would discover that she still wanted revenge. Even before her granddaughter was born, she sensed the time was drawing near. The moment Wil's heart came alive in the womb, her grandmother felt the curse, as she'd come to feel a great many of the world's little tragedies.

And the once-queen of Arrod wanted to have her revenge now, though her body had been irreparably destroyed when Wil's mother killed it. She was inside Baren. Baren. The most vulnerable of all the royal children. The one who was so desperate to belong, so alone in his hatred of his cursed sibling, had been the easiest to manipulate.

"How long have you had this hold on him?" Wil spat. Her chest ached so much that she thought her wound must surely have torn open. "Since he was a child?"

Baren laughed. Again, it was not his laugh.

Through Baren's mouth, the old marveler woman answered,

"Since the day you were born."

Wil felt her mind starting to fog. Not with delirium or even with pain, but something that resembled wisps of cauldron smoke. She saw Baren on the day she was born. He had been a pretty, elegant child with large eyes and a willowy stance. His expression was sour, though, his eyes brimming with tears.

He was running away. No one in the castle truly loved him. There was no place for him there. No place for him anywhere.

He ran until he'd gotten lost in the forest, and only when he realized that he no longer knew where he was did he stop.

The old woman, trapped in Baren's body, let out a scream that awoke Wil from her trance. She was pinned against the dirt wall of the tunnel now. The lantern had fallen from her grasp and shattered, leaving only the purple glow. It waned and then flared with brightness. "Once you're gone, the curse will be broken," the old woman's voice and Baren's spoke in unison.

Gerdie was shouting, but Wil couldn't hear what he was saying. Her ears filled with the rush of blood. All the strength was draining from her heart, down her limbs and through her skin like blood through a wound. Her lungs constricted. She struggled but found she could scarcely move. The old woman in Baren's body was draining the life out of her.

With what was left of her strength, Wil screamed. She screamed until her voice sounded very far away and faded.

Everything went dark and silent. The wisps of bright smoke

were gone, and Wil would have believed she was dead if not for the drip of water falling into a puddle somewhere.

Heat swelled behind her rib cage, right where her heart lay, still beating. The heat turned into a fire, and the fire flooded her veins and she came alive again with a scream as she released it.

Light filled the space again, but it was not a marveler's unnatural light. It was the lanterns of a dozen soldiers running toward her. They skidded to a halt when they saw the hold she had on Baren.

Only it wasn't Baren at all. Wil saw the eyes of the old woman—her grandmother—in her brother's face. "I may be a curse," Wil said through gritted teeth as she struggled to maintain whatever force had filled her with the surge of power she felt now, "but I will never cower in the shadows as you have."

She was struggling with her own curse, Wil realized. All those weeks of fighting Masalee for control over it had given her a new strength. She could draw upon her curse, like a current in her blood. She could mold it, twist it, summon it to her fingertips and call it back.

In addition to her own curse, she felt another tide shifting. Just as she fought, Baren fought, until the curse he had placed on the entire kingdom shattered and broke. Wil felt it fall away.

Baren's body went rigid. His eyes—the old woman's eyes—rolled back.

All Wil's strength went out, and she let go and fell to her

hands and knees, gasping. It was a wonder, she thought, that she could prop herself up at all. She felt as though her muscles had melted and her insides had gone hollow. She coughed and spat a trickle of blood into the dirt. Soldiers were coming for her now. One had already reached Gerdie, who was no longer shackled and was pulling himself to his feet.

Baren lay several yards ahead—had she thrown him? She crawled to his body, which was limp and facing skyward. For an awful instant she thought that she had killed him, but then she heard the rattle of his breath.

Someone knelt beside her and put an arm around her back. Loom. She couldn't feel his presence as she had so often been able to, but she knew the feel of his touch, the smell of him, the rhythm of his labored breathing when he was frightened. He took her face in his hands and turned her to look at him. "Are you all right?"

Dazed, she nodded. "I think she's dead now."

"Who's dead?" Loom asked.

"My grandmother." The words felt so strange to say. She'd never had a grandmother, but at the same time she'd always had one, waiting in the wings for the opportunity to kill her.

Loom didn't press her for more answers. He cared only that she was still alive. "Can you stand?"

She nodded. "I think so."

Two soldiers lifted the unconscious heap of Baren's body. Just as Wil felt drained, Baren also looked as though everything had been scraped out of him, leaving him hollow.

"Be careful with him," she said.

Wil didn't allow Loom to carry her back to the castle. She walked, and he patiently kept up with her slow pace, even as she swayed and stumbled.

Gerdie flanked her other side. Soldiers carrying Baren had moved ahead of them, and Gerdie's eyes were filled with the light of their distant lanterns.

"What happened to you?" he asked Wil. "What was that?"

"Maybe there's a little bit of marvelry in me after all," she guessed. "It's in our blood."

Gerdie thought about this. Normally he would have argued against such a thing, but given that he had seen marvelry for himself in recent history, he could not scientifically dismiss it. Rather, he would have to learn how it worked so that he could gain an understanding. That was how his genius worked, and one of Wil's favorite things about him.

"Could marvelry be how I survived Gray Fever all those times?" he wondered aloud.

"Maybe." Wil shrugged. "Or maybe it's just that you're strong."

# THIRTY-FIVE

FOR THE FIRST TIME SINCE her return to the castle, Wil drew a bath. The water was hot and coated in a pearlescent sheen of bubbles. She smeared her chest wound with a waterproof salve and then submerged herself, working the lather through her hair and under her nails. And then she rested her head on a folded towel on the tub's edge and closed her eyes.

She must have fallen asleep like that, because a knock at the door startled her. The water was turning cold, and she kicked her leg, trying to stir up the last of the warmth.

"Wil?" Loom's voice was muffled by the heavy oak door. "Just checking that you're still alive."

She laughed. The sharp intake of breath hurt. Now that the chaos had subsided—at least for now—she was beginning to notice things like pain again. And she was in a great deal of it.

"Come in and see for yourself," she said.

Loom opened the door just enough to step inside and then close it behind him. His hair was damp and had left wet spots on the shoulders of his borrowed shirt. It was gray, with a ruffled collar and sleeves. He'd probably found it in one of the infinite guest bedrooms that occupied the halls. Wil had often wondered if her mother had been prepared to have a hundred sons and fill all the castle rooms if she hadn't been given a daughter on her fourth try.

Loom knelt by the tub. He brushed his thumb along her jaw and tugged gently at a clump of her wet hair.

"Are you all right?" she asked him. He looked haggard. His eyes were sunken with exhaustion, and swollen.

He laughed. "Am I all right? Asks the girl who's been stabbed in the chest by her own dagger."

She waved her arm, coaxing up a splash of soapy water. "It'll take more than that to kill me. Pahn should have tried a bit harder. Some dynamite, perhaps, or fire."

Her teasing brought no light to Loom's grim expression. "You *were* dead," he told her.

"Well, I'm alive now," she said.

"Because of me, you almost—"

She pressed three fingers to his mouth to shush him. She sat up in the water, and her chest felt cold when it touched the air. "Help me up," she said.

He held her arms to steady her as she stepped out of the tub, and then he grabbed the towel she'd draped over the stool by the dressing table. As he fitted the towel around her shoulders, he couldn't help staring at the wound his own hand had inflicted. It was still raw and ugly, her skin held taut by Zay's even stitching of black surgical twine, and it shone with salve.

Loom's fingertips hovered over it, not quite touching. Instead, he touched her bare hip, drawing her a step nearer. She sucked in a breath.

"Did I hurt you?" he asked.

"No." She put her hand over his so that he wouldn't draw it away. She shrugged the towel from her shoulders and it puddled at her feet. "It just feels different is all."

"Different?" Loom's other hand went to her waist, and then across her stomach. It was exactly where he had touched her after their night together. It had made her tremulous and excited then, but now it made her feel safe and at peace, not just with Loom but with the entire world around him. She felt truly seen by someone who did not want her for her curse or her kingdom or because she had been born a girl. Someone who just wanted *her*.

She leaned forward and rested her head to his chest.

Moments earlier, she had wanted nothing more than for this night to end. Now she didn't mind if it went on a little longer.

It took her longer than usual to dress. Raising her arms aggravated her wound. In the end, she conceded to sitting on the stool and letting Loom help her. She had selected black trousers from her wardrobe, and a bright blue tunic with red birds printed all over it like dots. It was hand-dyed, purchased from a wanderer's cart last summer, which seemed a lifetime ago now.

After, Loom brushed the tangles from her wet hair and began pulling it into a braid that wrapped around her head. Wil watched him in the mirror. "You're good at that."

"I used to do it for Zay," he said. "In the thick of the summer, it's hot as all the hells and the last thing anyone wants is hair sticking to their sweaty skin when they're trying to sleep."

Zay's name didn't flood Wil with the jealousy it once had. There were times, on the ship, when she'd resented Loom and Zay's intimacy, not only for what it was, but because it would never go away. If they each lived a hundred more years, they would fill those years with more secrets and more memories.

This was still true, but it didn't seem so menacing now. She wanted Loom to have love in his life. He'd been deprived of it for so long. He looked different to her now, as though she had been looking at him through a fog all this time and had finally emerged. He was beautiful—she'd always thought so, even when he infuriated her—with dark eyes that contained all the kindness and heartbreak and knowledge in the world. His hands were thick and veiny, but long and elegant too. Wil could see the tendons move under his skin as he worked.

He pinned the tail of her braid into her hair, hiding it.

"I know I'm not as familiar as you are with Northern

fashion," he said, "but you don't look like you're dressed for bed."

"I'm going to check on Baren," she said, wincing as she stood. "Before I think about sleep, I need to make sure he's not been possessed by any more of our ancestors."

Loom followed her to the door of Baren's chamber, which was being guarded by two ever-loyal soldiers. For all her father's faults, he had picked fine men and women to guard his kingdom.

When Wil turned the knob, Loom knew not to follow her. He stepped back and let her go in alone.

The antechamber was cold and dark. It was the sort of deep chill that only existed when a place had been very cold and without light for a long time. The chamber itself was a little warmer. Someone had lit a fire at the hearth. Two more soldiers stood at the foot of the bed, where Baren lay thrashing fitfully. Another soldier—an appointed medic—sat beside him. Her hair was gold with bits of red. She was dabbing at his face with a damp cloth.

"He'll be fine, I believe," she said. "Just a light fever."

Wil wasn't sure that Baren had ever been ill in his life. Growing up, she'd taken great lengths to avoid her second-eldest brother. If she didn't encounter him for several days at a time, she'd count herself lucky and not question why. She thought she knew her brother quite well: cruel Baren; hateful Baren; sneaky Baren, always finding his way into shadows and beyond thresholds with an ear for all the castle's whispers. But now she realized just how much of a stranger he was to her. How much of what she'd believed of him had been filled in by her own fabricated image.

She had thought Baren weak and even stupid, but he had turned out to be his own sort of genius. Wil thought she was the castle spy, but Baren had found a way to make himself even more invisible still: he made himself hated. When he was gone, no one looked for him. No one questioned him when he returned. And all that time, he was meeting with a marveler in an abandoned train tunnel, on a path no one ever followed, slowly accumulating enough power to become a formidable marveler himself.

"Leave us," Baren croaked, and opened his eyes. At first, Wil thought he was talking to her, but it was the soldier who stood, bowed low, and moved for the door.

Baren watched her go, and then his gazed fixed on Wil. She was standing at the foot of his bed now.

Once the door to the antechamber had closed, he sat upright and propped himself against the headboard. There were heavy blue and purple rings around his eyes, and he was so pale she could see the veins in his cheeks. His expression was sour, but then it turned curious. "What do you want?"

"I came to see how you are," Wil said, surprised to realize this was the truth. When Baren didn't answer, she went on. "I know what our grandmother did to you. I saw her lure you in when you were just a child."

"You don't know a thing about it," he snapped. "She knew what you were. Everyone else thought I was crazy to hate you as I did, but she knew. She predicted everything: that you would kill Owen, that I would become king, that you would be back to bring destruction."

It was true. All of it. Wil steeled herself against the enormity of it. But was all of it her fault? Her curse was the reason Owen was dead. That was what set everything into motion, but where had Baren been between then and now?

"Baren," she said, and her fists clenched at her sides. "How did Papa die?"

Baren's cold gaze turned soft for just a moment—just a beat as long as a flicker in the firelight—and then it hardened again. "He got sick."

"How?" Wil pressed. "He'd never been sick."

Baren averted his eyes. He clenched his teeth so hard that his jawbone jutted.

"You should know," he finally murmured. "It was a poison you smuggled in."

That didn't narrow it down. She had brought in dozens of chemicals for Gerdie or her father, any number of them lethal.

"Tallim," he clarified. "Mixed with mint, it's rendered flavorless. I put it in his tea."

"Why?" she gasped.

"Because," he snarled. "I didn't know he had exiled you, but I knew he still suspected you were alive." Baren turned his head toward her again, and Wil could see that he was forcing himself to look at her. "I overheard him talking to one of his soldiers. He didn't tell the soldier the truth of what happened. He said that Mother had lost her wits with grief and convinced herself that you may have hit your head when you fell into the water and developed amnesia, and that he should go out and look for you. But it was a lie. Mother said no such thing. Mother believed you were dead. Papa had just changed his mind."

Wil staggered a step back. Her father had wanted her to come home. She thought of his words on the night of her banishment: *I should have killed you long ago, and I still can't bring myself to do it.* He had known of her curse, and yet still he'd looked at her and seen his daughter. Perhaps he had even seen Aleen, the child whose face Wil had all but stolen for her own, and he couldn't bear to end another life too soon.

"He wanted me," she said, still breathless.

"He would have let you destroy everything," Baren spat. "Everyone does, when it comes to you. No one has ever had the nerve to kill you for this kingdom."

"This kingdom is still standing," Wil cried. "If it was in any danger of falling, it's because of you. You killed the king."

"You killed the heir," he snapped. "Sending you away was the best thing Papa could have done for this kingdom and he knew it. I could almost respect him for that, but his heart softened for you. You had him under your curse just like everyone else in this bloody kingdom except for me."

She paced closer to his bedside now, and he winced when her shadow touched him. "We could have worked together, Baren."

He laughed.

"It's true," she said, and her voice went quiet. "You've been spying on me from the moment I was born, so you must know that I have done everything I could for our kingdom."

"Don't act so pious," Baren said. "You hid things from Papa. You think I don't know that? You and Owen and Gerdie, all of you whispering and conspiring against him."

Wil controlled her temper. Her brother wasn't wrong, but she still wanted to damn him. He knew so little about his own siblings because he had poisoned himself against them. But it wasn't his fault.

"Our grandmother," she said. "You let her into your head, and she controlled you. You thought you were saving the kingdom, but, Baren, she was going to use you to destroy it. She wanted all of us dead. You must see that."

"You're wrong," Baren said, but his voice had turned distracted. "She wanted to protect this place from you."

"I am not the only cursed thing in our family," Wil said. "Suppose you'd killed me, and then what? Somewhere in the future generations of Heidles, there would be another queen who loved someone more than her husband and it would begin all over again. Think about it. Our grandmother was trying to break the cycle. She convinced you to provoke a war with the

Southern Isles so that we'd all be killed."

"No," Baren said, but he didn't sound certain.

"You were a child," Wil went on. "The day I was born, you ran from home. Our grandmother sensed that I'd arrived. She felt my curse, and she knew it even then. But she sensed you, too, didn't she? An angry, impressionable little boy she could manipulate. She used you."

"You don't know anything about it," Baren said.

"But I do," she said. "I caught a glimpse of it in the cavern. She manipulated you. How many times did she try to convince you to kill me? And when you couldn't do it, she used you to provoke this war so our entire kingdom would be destroyed."

"I could have killed you," Baren spat out. "I could have killed you in your crib and there would have been no one to stop me."

"Then why didn't you?" The edge left Wil's tone because she was asking in earnest.

He looked away from her, and his silence was its own answer. He couldn't do it. Wil remembered when she was too small to fight, before Owen had taught her how to wield a blade; Baren grabbed her under the arms and dangled her from her bedroom window as she screamed and squirmed, Gerdie furiously kicking at him. He could have dropped her, but he never did.

Maybe there was something more than hatred in his heart for her, buried deep.

"Get out," he said. It was a growl, but when Wil didn't move, the next time it was a scream. "Get out of my sight!"

Two soldiers burst into the room, but Wil had no reason to linger. There was nothing more to say.

# THIRTY-SIX

IT WOULD HAVE BEEN WISE, Wil thought, to sleep aboard the ship. But she didn't fear Baren's wrath as she once had. Whether she was in Baren's good graces or not, he had not officially banished her from the kingdom, and she was still a member of the royal family. For that reason, guards also kept watch at her chamber door.

When Wil changed into her nightgown and slid into her bed, Loom came and lay beside her.

They were quiet in the light of her dimmed chandelier. His arm was draped across her stomach, and as she playfully danced her fingers between his, she tried to work out what was so different about him. He smelled a bit of the herbal soaps that were common in Arrod, rather than the more floral and fragrant soaps ground from plants indigenous to the Southern Isles, but everything else was the same. He exhaled a hard breath through his nostrils and it rustled her hair.

"We should sleep," he said.

"I don't quite remember sleep," Wil said. "How does it go again?"

He laughed, and she burrowed closer.

"We should set sail in the morning, don't you think?" Wil said. "With Pahn dead, your father will be more vulnerable. Now is the perfect time for you to strike."

"Espel and I talked it through while you were in the bath," he said. "We've decided that this is something we should do without help from the North."

Wil shifted, canting her head to look at him. "Without me, you mean? I don't understand. You've been wanting my help from the day we met."

"I wanted you for your power," he said. "And last night I saw what that sort of greed can do. It almost killed you."

Wil considered this for a moment. "You're not the same as Pahn," she said. "Or your father."

"No," Loom agreed. "But if I use you for my own gain, then there's no difference." He sat up, gently breaking his hand out of her grasp. "The Southern Isles is my kingdom. If I want it to be saved, then I should be the one to save it. Espel feels the same. Whichever one of us ends up on the throne will have earned it."

Wil found herself wanting to argue. Months earlier, when

they first met, helping Loom had been the last thing she'd wanted. Rather, she'd wanted to toss him into the sea and steal his ship for demanding her aid, and again for the awful things he had said about her family.

So why, now, was she so eager to change his mind? The answer was simple, and for the very same reason, she was going to let him go. Because she loved him.

She sat up to face him, and then she leaned forward and placed a soft, lingering kiss on his closed lips. His hand cradled the back of her head.

"Be careful," she whispered.

The castle would never be what it had been when Owen and their father were still alive. Gerdie knew that. He also knew that Wil's return would be short-lived. Without the rigid rules of their upbringing to hold her in place, she was like a fish that had found its way out of the fisherman's net. Her instinct was to swim and swim, until the yawning black of the sea had swallowed her up.

There was a time when Wil's wanderlust exasperated Gerdie. Now, though, he didn't care if his sister sailed the world's every sea. He didn't care if she jettisoned herself into space and swam among the stars, so long as she was not pinned beneath the rapids as he had once been told.

In the summer, the castle would meet even more changes. Addney would be back, carrying the new heir in her arms.

Baren didn't know this yet, and Gerdie could almost pity him for that. It was late when Gerdie arrived at his brother's chamber door, but he knew that Baren would be awake.

"Just tell him to come in," Baren muttered to the servant who announced Gerdie's arrival.

"I've brought something to help you sleep," Gerdie said.

Baren was sitting up in his bed, staring into the fire. Had he been sitting like this all night?

"It won't work," Baren muttered. His eyes were heavy.

Gerdie drew up a chair and sat by his brother's bed. He placed a vial on the nightstand; its candied green color warmed in the firelight. "Come now. Don't underestimate me," Gerdie said. "I'm quite familiar with insomnia. I get it from Mother."

Baren eyed him warily. "Isn't it just?" he said at last. "Owen and our sister inherit our mother's flights of fancy, while you and I inherit the demons."

Gerdie laughed at that. He never expected to have anything in common with Baren, but he supposed that was true.

Baren lifted the vial, inspecting its contents. "You could be trying to poison me."

"Only one way to find out."

Baren set the vial down again. He went back to staring at the fire. "She used to speak to me through the flames," he said at last. "Our grandmother."

Gerdie betrayed nothing even as his stomach flipped anxiously. He had spent his whole life evading Baren, and now suddenly he found himself eager to know more about him. He didn't say a word. He scarcely breathed. He didn't know what small thing might break this fragile line of trust that Baren had cast.

"It began in the days after our sister was born," Baren said. "It was mid-October, and it was quite cold. The fire burned through the night as I slept, and I used to . . . see things. I saw our entire castle in flames. I saw Mother dying in such horrible ways. I saw the tides rising up and flooding the Port Capital. And I knew she was to blame for all of it. I knew she was cursed."

Gerdie fought to stay silent. The Wil he knew had been very different. When he was ill, she climbed onto the bed, beside him, and read from his notes so he wouldn't fall behind in his experiments, or told him stories. And when he was well, she chased him through servants' passages in the walls, or goaded him to sneak sweets from the kitchen. The Wil he knew had been stubborn, infuriating, and kind.

At last, when Baren was silent, Gerdie said, "We were all cursed." It was a big concession for him, a boy who would have insisted curses were a fairy tale only a few months ago.

Baren's eyes turned on his brother and he said, "I see that now. She killed Owen, and I killed our father. I let myself be used as a pawn." He lowered his head, and for the barest moment he looked like a child. "I don't know what was real. I suspect it will take me a long time to sort it all out."

"I could help you," Gerdie ventured, cautiously. "I'm good at solving things, you know."

"Not everything," Baren said.

"A few things are still a work in progress," Gerdie admitted.

"Why would you want to help me?" Baren said. "We've hated each other all our lives. I've killed our father." Something in him broke after he said that. His jaw tightened, and Gerdie saw his fists clutching the blankets.

All of them, cursed by the horrible thing their grandfather had done. All of them broken. Not just Wil.

"Because I want to save our family," Gerdie said. "What's left of it."

# THIRTY-SEVEN

As THE SUN ROSE OVER the Port Capital, Wil stood at the port to watch everyone depart. Loom was the last to climb aboard, and before he did, he took her hands.

She didn't tell him to be careful, or even that she loved him. It felt like tempting fate. And though Loom had not been raised by a superstitious wanderer, as Wil had, he seemed to share the sentiment.

"I suppose with your brother still acting as king, an alliance between our kingdoms is asking too much."

"You'll have your alliance," Wil said.

He laughed, but when it became evident she wasn't making a joke, he said, "What makes you so certain?"

"Do you trust me?" she asked.

"I do."

She tugged at the lapels of his coat. "You worry about claiming your throne, and let me worry about an alliance."

And there was quite a bit to contend with, she was coming to remember. Northern Arrod had the coffers to repair the damage done; it would be unwise to rely on ally kingdoms now. And there was the matter of Baren yet, and whether or not it was safe to return citizens to Northern Arrod while he was still on the throne.

She stayed at the edge of the Port Capital until the ship was well out of sight. In its place came the sun, warm with harvest shades of red and gold. It warmed the winterscape, Wil thought. But it didn't console her. Already she was beginning to worry about Loom, whose curse turned his own palace into a poison, and whose sister was as elusive as she had the potential to be duplicitous.

Gerdie came up alongside her, and he was silent for a moment before he dragged her back into the reality they both had to face for their kingdom.

"How are you feeling?" he asked.

"Hm?" She looked at him. "Fine. The stitches are surprisingly sturdy and—"

"Not that," Gerdie interrupted. "You haven't turned anything to stone since your return. Don't you feel ill?"

From the time Wil arrived home, she'd had little time to consider how she felt at all. But Gerdie had reminded her. She paced to the edge of the port and brushed away a dusting of snow. The grass beneath it didn't change. Little surprise there; the kingdom's curse would cancel out her own. But as she stood and looked around, Arrod no longer seemed cursed. Its sky was blue, patterned with gray winter clouds, but still bright. The buildings were tattered and abandoned, but they didn't seem dreary and dead, but rather patiently awaiting repairs.

Had Baren lifted the curse? Or had she, when she'd driven their grandmother's spirit away? But if the curse had been lifted, then why wasn't the grass turning to stone?

Her concentrated expression was beginning to worry her brother. "What is it?"

"Usually, if I can't use my curse, there's a horrible pressing feeling like there's an animal trapped in my blood that wants to burst free. But it isn't there now."

"Could your curse be gone?" Gerdie presented this theory so simply, as though it wouldn't change her world entirely and forever.

"How?" She tugged at the collar of her shirt and stared down at her chest. Her mark was still there, overlapped now by her latest wound, which formed a gruesome X.

Beneath the bruises and scars, her body still looked the same. But she didn't feel the same.

# THIRTY-EIGHT

ESPEL DIDN'T TRY TO KILL Loom even once on the journey home, which was promising.

On the journey, they began to formulate a new plan, one which took Pahn's death into account. Without Pahn, their father was reduced to a man and his soldiers.

"All the soldiers will turn on him if he loses power," Masalee assured as they sat huddled in the kitchen the morning of their departure. "He hasn't taken care of any of them. Half of them have children who are starving or dying of Gray Fever."

"My father won't turn," Zay said. She knew her father's loyalty to the king better than anyone; he had been willing to cut off her head to maintain the king's favor. She let out a loud sigh into Ada's hair. "You may have to kill him, if it comes to it. He won't swear loyalty to either of you."

She had just given them permission to kill her father. Loom put a hand on her shoulder, but she ignored his attempt at comfort. She was steely when she was sad, cold when she was determined.

"You still won't be able to set foot inside the palace," Espel said. "We'll have to lure our father away from it. To the mountains would be best."

"How?" Loom pressed. "What makes you think he would follow us up a desolate mountainside after banishing us?"

"There is no need to get short with me," Espel said pertly. "We had a perfectly stable plan thanks to Wil, and you're the one who left her behind."

"I'm not risking her life again," he growled. "This is our mess to sort out. She'll be busy sorting out her own."

Espel rolled her eyes, but there was something playful about the gesture. She wasn't at all disdainful, and for once Masalee's presence was not entirely to thank for it. For just a second, she and Loom were allies. Siblings, even.

"We could scare him out," Zay said, and looked to Masalee. "You could create an illusion that the palace is on fire. Generate heat and smoke and things."

"Lure him out like we're smoking out a bee's nest," Espel emphatically agreed. "Yes. You steer the soldiers toward the city and guide our father through the west-most balcony of his chamber. He'll be forced to jump the railing and seek refuge in the mountainside. We'll be waiting for him there."

Masalee smiled, happy to be useful. Then she said to Loom, "I can't break your curse, but there may be a way out of it."

"Cutting out my heart?" Loom asked dryly.

"Your curse was an order given by the king," Masalee said. "If he's no longer king, the order no longer stands."

"That isn't true," Loom countered. "It was meant to keep me away long after his death, to ensure I'd never be able to claim the throne."

"He intended for Espel to inherit the kingdom, which means she inherits it. It's hers to command."

Espel stiffened her posture, unable to hide her smugness. Loom could gather that she had already known this.

"Well, I won't do it," Espel finally blurted. "If you're the one to kill our father, you've earned your place as heir. If I am, you can take a position on my council if you want it and come and go as you please."

She held out her hand, and Loom took it. A firm shake sealed their deal, but coming to trust one another was a different matter entirely.

The last night of the journey was quiet. Loom muttered and tossed in his sleep; Espel heard him as she passed his cabin on the way to her own. He would be dreaming of his Northern princess again. Loom was never one to accept the present; rather, he would dwell on the most torturous bits from his past over and again, reliving not just that memory, but all the possible ways it could have been made worse. Espel knew how he wondered about their mother, though she hadn't lived long enough to give either of her children any memories of the fond or terrible sort.

It was a waste of time. The past was a dark sea filled with lessons to be learned, but it was no place to linger. One could drown doing that.

Espel turned into her own cabin and closed the door behind her.

Masalee was there, standing against the wall beside the door frame. This had been her favored spot in the palace, ever ready to strike intruders who came for her future queen. Masalee had been waiting in the dark, the only light coming from a lantern that hung over the dressing table. It was the old-fashioned sort, with an orange flickering bulb that mimicked candlelight.

Espel didn't turn to look at her, but the way she moved for the dressing table was its own invitation.

The Northern patterns on this ship were quite different than what she was used to, but now that she had been inside Arrod's castle she realized that every bit of Northern architecture was meant to mimic it. The exposed oak beams made even newer things, such as this ship, feel ancient and enchanted.

The dressing table wasn't much—just a mirror framed by oak that had been carved in the shape of antlers, and a glossy wooden table bolted to the wall.

Espel stared at her reflection, her light brown face and

shining silver tunic floating in the dim of the room behind her. She reached behind her head, working at the elaborate loops of her hair until it shook loose and fell all around her shoulders like a confession. She laid the gleaming pins on the table before her in a neat row. This small gesture was the only thing to betray her just then; she always sorted and counted things when she was worried.

Masalee came up behind her and crouched until her chin was on Espel's shoulder. Her arms coiled around Espel's chest, and Espel could have floated away, she felt so light.

"You are the most beautiful thing in this life," Masalee said, and Espel tried to ruin the moment with a dry laugh and a wrinkle of her nose. She had never felt worthy of love, and yet Masalee seemed to be in endless supply of it.

Still, the laugh faded from Espel's lips. Her dark eyes became serious and thoughtful as she stared at their reflections. This time tomorrow, they would be invading her own kingdom under the cover of nightfall. It wasn't that she feared death, but it was a possibility. Loom could betray her, or her father could prove stronger than she expected.

"What is it?" Masalee asked. "What are you thinking?"

"How much I enjoy staring at your face," Espel said. "And what a shame it would be if I was no longer able to."

Masalee's eyes narrowed thoughtfully. "You think you're going to die?" This had never been among Espel's small supply of fears.

"I think it's good to be prepared for all outcomes."

"You aren't going to die," Masalee said with no obstinacy. "You forget I'm still your guard."

"This isn't your fight," Espel said, sharp. She was still addressing their reflections in the mirror. "You're not to do anything. Not a thing at all, do you understand?"

Masalee's gaze turned fixed. Her jaw tightened, the same way it had in the palace when Espel made a show of barking commands at her in the presence of others. Anyone who did not know Espel had thought her a monster; they had pitied Masalee for being tethered to her side. They could never know that Espel's cruelty was the only tool she had to protect the girl she loved.

Now there was no one to see them. There was no reason to put on an act, and yet Espel caught herself being hard and vicious and cold. Once again, she had meant to protect Masalee.

The way that Masalee's arms tightened around Espel said that she understood. This was not anger. This was fear. There was no one else in this world to hold her when she was afraid.

"This is my fight," Espel said. "If I expect to rule my kingdom, I have to be the one to fight for it."

Masalee considered for a moment, and then she sat beside Espel on the bench, and instinctively their bodies turned to face each other. They held each other's hands.

"If Loom betrays you and tries to kill you, then you destroy him," Masalee said. "But you don't be the one to turn the fight dirty." She took Espel's face in her hands, and then she pressed her palm against Espel's heart; it fluttered, but not at all due to marvelry. "Fight with all the honor you've always had," Masa-lee said.

Espel pushed forward and kissed her, if only to stop this talk of death and of honor. This time tomorrow, she would step up to claim her throne, mortality be damned. Tonight she only wanted to be here, in the middle of the Ancient Sea, her entire world only as big as the sphere of lantern light. Just two girls and their hearts, and all the words webbed between them that never needed to be said.

# THIRTY-NINE

THE KINGDOM FELT STRANGE WHEN it was empty.

Guards lined the stone wall that surrounded the castle, and for a long time, Wil sat perched on the wall's edge, watching them. All her life she had evaded guards to do her father's and her brother's bidding. But it hadn't been entirely for them. She would take any excuse to leave the castle.

At dawn's first, she had scaled the wall and stolen away to the Port Capital, but there were no smuggled chemicals to bargain for. Rather, she had seen the skeletal beams of buildings Baren had already ordered to be rebuilt. He was using the family's coffers to restore them.

A train would be arriving soon with Northern Arrod citizens returning to sweep away the ashes of their homes and start anew.

Her mother wouldn't return. Not until summer, when the new heir was born. Owen's child was the only secret that had been kept from Baren. He seemed to know every other secret that existed in Arrod.

She climbed down the inside of the wall and walked back to the castle. A guard at either door stepped aside to grant her entry.

The castle's electricity was still unstable, and the castle was frigid even with fires burning at every hearth. There was a chill that lingered. Almost like a curse.

She made her way to the throne room, where she knew her brother would be sitting upon the throne he had murdered their father to obtain. Her anger with Baren was rivaled by her pity, and she was at odds with herself.

Perhaps her father would have chosen neither anger nor pity. Perhaps, in his way, he would have been proud that Baren had inherited his ruthlessness after all.

She hadn't spoken to Baren since the night he confessed what he had done. He had screamed for her to leave his sight, and she'd kept away. His temper was a fragile thing, and now that he was king, with a wave of his arm he could order her death and there would be no shortage of guards to carry it out.

She approached with caution, and to her surprise, the guards held open the doors for her. Had her brother been expecting her?

He dismissed the guards when he saw her, and once the

doors had been closed, they were left alone in the grand space, surrounded by murals of wars their kingdom had won in centuries past.

"You look well," Wil said, before the silence could grow unbearable. It was true. He wasn't sallow as he'd been the other night; his eyes were bright and alert, no longer glazed by fever. There was still a distracted look about him, as though he were still trying to make sense of everything. She couldn't fault him for that.

"And you're still here," he said.

"There's no place else for me to go."

"There's an entire world out there," Baren said. "Isn't that what you were always going on about? You wanted to be out there, exploring."

"I didn't think you paid much attention to my wants," Wil said. She didn't reach for her dagger, but she braced herself. If Baren tried to kill her, she would be ready.

"You didn't think I paid attention?" Baren snapped. "I've been looking forward to it from the day you were born. There are several other kingdoms and infinite seas for you to go out and curse. Just this one kingdom is all I want to protect—from war, and from you."

"I've never wanted to destroy this kingdom," Wil said through gritted teeth. Then, remembering herself, she worked to control her anger. This dance with Baren was a fragile one. "Northern Arrod is my home, and it will always be my home no matter how many times I leave it, and no matter how far I travel. I want it to thrive too."

Baren shook his head. Gold waves moved across his forehead. He looked so regal up on the throne, with their mother's pretty eyes and their father's strong chin. To one who didn't know better, he looked as though he belonged there.

"What you want doesn't matter," he said. "A slug can want to be a butterfly, but it's still a slug."

Wil clenched her fists.

"I believe you when you say you love Arrod," he went on. "But you were born to destroy it. It was predetermined, the moment your ugly little heart formed in the womb and threw its first beat. So if you truly love this place, as you say, then you should go and never come back."

"And leave it to you?" Wil asked bitterly. "You—" She stopped herself. *You killed our father.* That's what she was going to say. Those were the words that burned in her chest. He had killed their father. And maybe killing their father hadn't broken the kingdom, but it had certainly broken their mother's heart. It had broken what was left of their family.

And she had killed Owen. Anything her brother had done, she had done in equal measure. This hadn't begun with Baren. This began that night by the rapids.

No. This began long before any of that, when their grandfather plunged a knife into Aleen's chest.

"My curse is gone" is what Wil said when she at last decided to speak. "I haven't turned anything to stone since the night my heart stopped."

Baren leaned back on the throne, basking in his position of power. And then he laughed. It was a hollow, haunted sound. "You are not a girl with a curse," he said. "You are a curse, who just also happens to be a girl."

"You're wrong," Wil said.

"You think that I don't know what you are," Baren said. "You think that because I never ran giggling through the gardens with you and Gerhard, because you never whispered your little secrets to me, that I don't know what you are. But I do. I saw the midwife tear you from between our mother's legs and the lake of blood you brought with you. Perhaps the only reason you didn't kill our mother when you were born was so that she could see what she had created and suffer for it. You haven't turned anything to stone since your heart stopped? You will again. Knowing you, it will happen just in time to destroy something else."

Owen's child. That was the first thought Wil had. What if Baren was right? What if her curse lay dormant and it would be back the moment Owen's child was laid in her arms?

Her blood went cold. She felt sick. Not only for fear of what she might do, but fear that Baren was right. She was the true threat, not him.

"You should go," Baren said. "Go. I won't have you followed or killed if you can give me your word that you won't be back to darken another doorway of this castle while I'm king."

"Why?" Wil's voice came out breathless. "Why would you allow me to live now after you've already tried to kill me?"

He stared at her. His expression was stony, and he pursed his lips, as though there was something he hesitated to say.

Wil imagined that he was going to say it was because she was his sister, and that meant something to him.

"Because I wish to have an alliance with Gerhard," Baren said. "His genius isn't lost on me, and the kingdom needs him. There's no one in this world who has his mind for weapons and for strategy. He's promised to serve on my council if I spare your life."

Gerdie had bargained for her life.

*You were never a curse to me.* That was what he said after she told him the story of Aleen, and he had meant it.

"All right," Wil said. "I swear that I will never return to Arrod so long as you're king."

It was a promise she would be able to keep.

After she'd left the throne room, Gerdie found her as she was ascending the stairs for her chamber.

"You spoke with Baren," he guessed, falling into pace beside her.

She turned the crystal knob and pushed open her door. "I did."

"When do you leave?" He followed her into the room and closed the door behind them.

"Tonight. Baren was generous enough to give me my pick of the family ships." She threw open the doors to her wardrobe and stared at the ghosts of all the girls she'd been before, hanging in a neat row.

She was silent as she considered them. Blouses that had been tailored to fit her, dresses her father brought back from his diplomatic excursions, tunics she'd worn into the Port Capital. They were all disguises, and now she didn't know what to take with her. She didn't know what sort of girl she was supposed to be.

"Returning to your Southern prince?" Gerdie tried to sound lighthearted, but his tone didn't lessen the enormity of their unspoken good-bye.

"No. He doesn't want me to interfere with his fight for the throne," she said. "I'll find him in the summer, when the new heir is born and I have an alliance to offer him. I don't know where I'll go for now. East, maybe."

Gerdie laid a hand on her shoulder and she shrugged out of his grasp. "Don't," she said. "I don't know when my curse will come back."

"It isn't coming back," Gerdie said. "Your curse died with you, when your heart stopped."

She tugged at the collar of her tunic and looked at the bandages wrapped around her chest. The mark of her curse stuck out from the edge of the white gauze, faded and shining.

The curse was in her heart, and even if that heart had briefly stopped, it was still in her chest now. Masalee had been the one to save her life, and she had used marvelry to do it. Maybe some of that marvelry was still inside her now. Maybe it had changed things.

She wouldn't let herself hope that her curse was gone. "Baren said that my curse will probably return just in time to kill someone else," she said. "What if he's right? I couldn't bear that." Not again. She thought she was hiding her heartbreak, but when she looked at Gerdie, she saw it mirrored back in his own eyes. Of course she should have known better; for better or worse, her brother knew her.

As ever, he didn't offer meaningless platitudes. He didn't tell her that Owen's death was not her fault, or promise that she would never again pose a threat to their family. Instead, he offered her the only thing he had to give. "I'll help you," he said. "There's an explanation for all this, and I'm going to find it."

Wil smiled. It was a weary, sad smile, and she felt like her mother when she gave it.

"I'll be all right," she said. "You have to stay here—wasn't that the deal you made with Baren? And with Mother gone until the summer, somebody needs to make sure he doesn't go mad with power."

"That doesn't mean I can't help," he said. "I have several of the things you crystallized. I'm not done analyzing them."

Wil didn't doubt her brother's genius. If there were a solution to this curse at all, he would find it. But perhaps there was no solution. Perhaps it would return, exactly as it had been, or in some new way, and she would have to adapt. But she would. She would not allow this curse to harm her family further.

"Make sure the baby takes Addney's surname," Wil said. "She can't give birth to a Heidle."

Gerdie blinked. "Why?"

"Because the curse will live on so long as a Heidle is on the throne," she said. "It's time for the Heidle reign to end, and a new one to begin. This curse will die with me."

# FORTY

Loom's ship arrived at the Southern Isles under the cover of darkness the following night, without pretense. It was a bold gesture: a Northern ship entering its enemy waters, bearing the banished prince and princess.

Masalee would be unable to summon the marvelry to hide the ship this time; all of her energy would be going into the palace fire. But the blaze would be so great that no one would notice their arrival.

Zay was the one to anchor them along the mountainside, in the shadows where the moonlight didn't touch the water. Fastened to her hip, Ada was staring excitedly at the palace. "Think he remembers it?" Loom asked.

"He was only an infant," Zay said. "He probably just thinks the lights are pretty."

"They're about to get a lot prettier," Masalee said, and a moment later, the palace was surrounded by a ring of flame.

Zay brought herself close to Loom, so that only he would hear her whisper. "I'll leave Ada with Rala where he'll be safe. I'll meet you in the mountains."

"It'll be the trail where we used to hide from our tutors," he said. "Stay safe." Ada had begun poking at his chin, and Loom smirked at him. "You be safe too."

"Don't get yourself killed," Zay said, by way of good-bye.

The illusion of fire had consumed the palace by the time Espel and Loom scaled the ship's ladder. Loom stumbled as he jumped to the rocks, and Espel grabbed his arm to steady him.

Even here, the sickening heaviness of his curse reached him.

"Are you hurt?" Espel asked.

"No." He made himself charge forward. The ship behind them was dark and they didn't bring any lanterns, but Loom knew all of Cannolay's mountains with his eyes closed.

The air was breezy but hot, the sky cloudless and pregnant with stars. How he had missed his home, especially after all those weeks of chilled air and frozen fingers and chapped cheeks. He didn't know how Wil could bear it. But she had been especially lovely against the snowy trees. Her cheeks were bright pink, as though the frost pinched extra life into her face, her dark eyes filled up with every shade of brown.

He thought of her, and of winter snow in winter trees, the entire trek up the mountain path. Thinking of her could cure anything that poisoned him, even the hateful energy of Pahn's curse.

Espel kept pace beside him, and he got the sense that he was moving too slowly and that she stayed beside him in the interest of fairness.

"I won't kill you," she said. "Not unless you try to kill me."

"Glad to know we share that sentiment," he panted. And then he repeated the terms of their new plan, "We're on our own when we see Father. No helping or turning our blades on each other. Whoever kills him takes the throne."

"I remember," she said. "Agreed."

They were walking parallel now to the top floor of the palace, and the smoke from the flames billowed out to greet them. It was only an illusion, but that didn't lessen the potency of the smoke and the heat. But while the fire wilted Loom, Espel thrived. Her posture was rigid, her eyes bright as they filled with the reflection of flames. And though she was more than a head shorter than he was, she had a way of making herself very big, as powerful and immovable as the mountains of their home.

"There," she whispered, clutching at his wrist. A figure moved through the firelight and smoke, stumbling and coughing.

Loom drew his sword.

In a beat, Espel was no longer beside him. He thought he heard her moving through the brush. The smoke was too thick now, but he refused to panic.

With a roar, the flames shifted, forming a broad ring around the clearing of rocks and large-leafed shrubs that were undeterred by the heat—they were made to thrive on it. Now, at last, Loom saw Espel on the other side of the clearing, their father at the center. They were dripping with sweat, all three of them. And when the king saw his children, he realized what this was. His back straightened. He saw Loom first and laughed, but then he turned and saw the murder in Espel's eyes. It wasn't her rage that undid him. He had been fanning the flames of Espel's rage for the better part of fifteen years. He had always taken credit for what she had become, prided himself for having created such a marvelous and unbreakable child.

But she had never fixed that rage on him. And he saw it now. He saw what he had feared from the moment he'd first looked at her. On her first day, Espel had taken away the woman he'd loved. He had feared that she would grow up to take his life as well. The thing he had created was no longer under his command, and Loom saw the moment the king realized it.

King Zinil drew his sword. He charged at Espel, but she jumped back into the flames, disappearing in their light.

Loom seized the opportunity and lunged, and his father regained his senses just in time to turn for him. Their swords clattered. Espel swooped down from overhead—she must have scaled a tree, Loom thought—and her dagger tore open the king's bicep.

The king spared Loom no mercy, attempting several lethal blows and howling in frustration when Loom evaded them. But for Espel, the king's moves were purely evasive. This went on for as long as the king could manage, and then he knew that Espel's stamina would far outlast his own. If he didn't kill her, she would kill him.

When the king raised his sword, there was a wicked flash of light in his daughter's eyes. She didn't sneer, as she so often did in battles. She waited for the blow, bracing her dagger. She knew everything about swords, and still she preferred her daggers.

She stood still, her shadow jumping erratically around her. Her grip tightened just slightly, and Loom began to understand what she was doing. She had worn this sort of expression when she was a child and her instructor had just slapped her, and she had realized all at once that nobody was going to come and hold and coddle and love her. Just that one time, she had been helpless. She was far from helpless now, but as her eyes stayed fixed on her father coming at her with his weapon drawn, Loom saw the falter in the king's step. The king surely saw it too. The child he'd starved of any sort of warmth or love.

That small falter in his step was what Espel had anticipated, and it was all she needed. With one quick motion and with her first cry of the entire battle, she slashed the king's throat.

The king was on his feet for a moment longer, staring at her. His lips moved and he might have damned her, or said that he was sorry. Whatever he would have said, they would never know. Blood burst from his mouth and he collapsed.

As he lay on his back, the flames died away. Masalee, hiding wherever she was, must have seen. The smoke dissolved for the illusion it was, and as the king lay staring at the stars, his children came to stand at either side of him.

Espel was breathing hard, Loom realized now that he was close enough to hear her. Her jaw was clenched and her eyes were glassy with tears.

She twirled her dagger so that the hilt faced Loom. "Take the final blow if you want it," she said, surprising him. "He stole your kingdom. You should have it."

Loom had been prepared for every outcome of this battle. He had been prepared for his father to kill him, or, more likely, for Espel to. But he had not expected her to offer him the kingdom that she wanted every bit as much as he did.

He reached out his hand, but stopped. As a child he had failed his sister many times. They had failed each other, growing up as enemies in the same palace, the same blood in their veins.

What Espel said was true: this kingdom did belong to him. He had been born to it. But what had Espel been born to?

He saw Espel as a child, her eyes filling with tears after their father cut the flower from her hair. The way she crumpled, years later, when the blade sliced through Masalee's chest. From the time Espel was small, there had been no laughter in her eyes, no humanity on display at all, because she learned that any piece of herself she showed would be cut away. All those years gone. Her entire childhood lost.

Espel had never been afforded a true moment. She had always been exactly what their father demanded, and now Loom saw that he wasn't the only one who had wanted to save his sister. She wanted to save herself.

Loom lowered his hand to his side. So long as Espel had been the one to deal the final blow, she had won. She had earned it.

Their father had taken a kingdom from his son, but he had taken something more valuable from his daughter.

They stood over the king until his eyes went black and empty and his chest went still, and there in the quiet and dark of the mountains, Espel became queen.


Zay found Loom after sunrise, when the first embers of the sun held their torches to the stars, taking their light.

He was sitting on a jagged cliff that overlooked his bed-chamber. Though he hadn't been there in years, it still smelled like home, like incense and the fragrant soaps from his wash-room.

Or maybe it was just his memory.

Zay dropped beside him, gracefully folding her legs and then handing him a flask filled with cold water.

"I don't want you to get dehydrated," she said. "It's hot as the hells."

"Thanks," he managed. Only when the water touched his lips did he realize how thirsty he'd been all night. "I suppose you've met your new queen."

"Nearly scared me to death when she told me what happened," Zay said. "I thought there was no way it could be true. I thought she must have killed you and tossed you into the Ancient Sea."

Loom turned his head to her and smirked. "For all else I've thought of Espel, I've never doubted she loves our home. I really believe she'll fight for it."

Zay considered this, squinting to get a better look at the city in the distance. "Hm," she finally said. "I don't know if I've mentioned this, but I've never cared much for your sister."

That made Loom laugh, and Zay smiled, pleased with herself for coaxing it out of him; he'd been so serious for so long. "But," she went on, "unlike your father, she understands that it takes more than a ruler to rule a kingdom. She'll need your help just as much as you need hers."

"I'm sorry you'll never be queen," Loom said.

"I think Masalee will make a better queen consort to Espel than I would have been to you," Zay said. "Royal life never appealed to me."

Loom's expression had turned grim again, and she bumped his shoulder. "This is still our kingdom," she said. "And now we can form an alliance with Northern Arrod and start to heal from this war."

Loom shook his head. "I'm not asking anything more from Wil."

"Who says you'd have to ask?" Zay said. "The two of you have been planning an alliance for weeks."

"She should be far away from me," Loom said. "After all I've caused her."

Zay rested her cheek on his shoulder. "Well, my dearest one," she said, "I'm certain Wil would take offense at your telling her where to go."

"If she has any sense, she'll never speak to me again."

"Sense has never been a strong suit for either of you," Zay said. She laughed, and when he didn't laugh with her, she wrapped an arm around his back. "Don't sulk. There's still far too much to do."

"An alliance requires her brother being dethroned," Loom said.

"Right. Wasn't that already decided?"

"Not exactly," Loom said. "Wil was hoping for something else. She said there was something she couldn't tell me yet."

"You'll find a way," Zay said. "It doesn't matter whether or not you're king. This kingdom still needs you."

Nothing was at all how he had planned, or hoped. But Zay was still the North Star unmoving in his sky. She always had been.

"I suppose, since I'm not going to be king, there's no useful reason to stay married to me," he said, musing.

Zay laughed. "Of all times, you want to talk about this now?"

"Maybe I'm being optimistic, but I think Espel and I can come to an amicable place," Loom said. "She isn't going to execute you for setting foot in the palace."

Zay had begun patting his back absently, trying to soothe his anxieties. "Ours has only ever been a marriage in name," she said. "It won't change anything. Maybe it is time."

He sat upright, gently breaking out of her embrace. "It does feel strange to think about."

"Yeah." She slid her joined hands between her knees. "Growing up knowing we would be married was the one constant in my life. It's been fun."

"Banishment curses aside," Loom said.

She snorted, and with an amused smile still on her lips, she said, "You know that you and Ada are my world, don't you? I'd do anything for you, and that won't ever change."

"Same, *ansuh*," he said.

"But sailing off in different directions once in a while would be good for us," Zay said.

Perhaps no one else in the world would catch the full meaning of those words, but Loom knew Zay. They were both staring at the Northern ship bobbing gently on the water's surface. The world felt impossibly fragile in that moment. One stilled breath, one failed beat of one cursed heart, and everything would end.

But Zay, in all her wisdom, was confident that there would be no endings. Only beginnings. And she was letting him go.

They were letting each other go.

# FORTY-ONE

Wɪʟ ʜᴀᴅ ꜱᴘᴇɴᴛ ᴍᴏɴᴛʜꜱ ɪɴ relative seclusion, in the woods that surrounded Brayshire. As predicted, her curse returned shortly after her arrival. But it had changed. Just as she had changed after being brought back from death, her curse had also changed. Rather than rushing out of her all at once, it began as a warm buzz in her veins.

For weeks, Wil concentrated on that buzz, until she saw it in her mind's eye as a glowing line moving through her. After much concentration, she could draw it to her fingertips or push it back into the depths of her blood. She could turn leaves into gold when she was thinking of her faraway prince, grass into emerald, wild blossoms into sapphire and amber and diamond.

After a month of this, she grew increasingly confident in her ability to control her curse. And it became less of a curse and more of a weapon, just as she had learned to wield a sword or shoot an arrow.

Her ship appeared on Cannolay's horizon four months into Espel's reign. From Wil's vantage point on the water, the mountain palace stood tall and shimmering as ever. What she could see of the city was bustling, and she even thought she could hear music reaching out across the Ancient Sea. The city was quite alive, and she felt the weight on her chest dissolving.

And then she saw him.

Loom emerged from the port entrance of the palace, his red satin tunic waving on a sudden gust of warm air. It was June, and the Southern air was thick and humid; already Wil could feel it weighing her limbs. But Loom was unbothered by the heat and had begun running toward the dock. Her breath caught in her throat.

She would have to tell him that her curse was gone. She hadn't been able to turn anything to stone in the months since she'd seen him; even the phantom urge in her muscles was long gone. Gerdie's theory was that her birth curse was meant to plague her all her life. But her heart had stopped that night, and however briefly, her life had ended. Her heart was rather ordinary now.

But her ordinary heart still went wild when it saw Loom. There was no curse to tether them, and yet she raced to the railing and clutched at it. She had to restrain herself from diving into the sea and swimming the distance between them.

He had been in the palace. Not skirting dangerously close to its perimeter, but actually inside of it. His curse had been broken. Did this mean he was finally king?

She had gone too long without speaking to him. Too many months spent repairing her own kingdom and wondering if he had even survived whatever showdown he'd had with his father, much less emerged the victor.

He was already climbing the ladder of her ship before she'd finished docking, and just as she'd opened her mouth to laugh at his urgency, he caught that laughter on his tongue with a kiss.

Her arms coiled around his neck and she smiled against his mouth. All her thousand questions died away. She forgot to ask if he was king. She forgot to ask if Cannolay was as well as it looked. She forgot to tell him how much she had missed him.

When at last they drew apart, Loom said, "I wasn't expecting you to come back."

"You weren't?" Now she noticed his troubled expression.

"I didn't think I would ever see you again," he said. "After everything—"

"Of course you were going to see me. I promised you an alliance, remember?" She straightened. "I'm here on official business to inform you that Arrod has a new queen."

"A queen?" Loom's voice trailed. He looked as perplexed as she had ever seen him. "You?"

She shook her head, laughing. "Not me," she said. "Addney, Owen's widow, gave birth to her just last week. We're all still getting to know her, but I think she'll make an excellent queen."

"So that's what you weren't telling me," Loom said.

"I hope you can understand. I had a responsibility to my brother. To my kingdom. Addney has taken the throne as regent until her daughter is of age."

He traced his thumb around the slope of her cheek, under her eye. He had been worrying about ending this war and striking an alliance for months, but now that Wil was here, all he wanted to do was look at her.

In a moment, Wil would ask him about his throne. She would tell him that her curse had been temporarily broken, and while it had been gone, she could be certain every bit of what she felt for him was real. In a moment, there would be bridges to build and kingdoms to aid and an entire world left to see. But for now, she closed her eyes as he kissed her.

It was an eager, honest kiss, and it bridged two kingdoms.

# EPILOGUE

THE NEW QUEEN OF ARROD was born on the first day of June, on a day so hot the sun was singing in its cerulean sky.

It wasn't a glamorous birth. Addney had labored for three days in a cottage in Southern Arrod, with the queen regent and an elderly nanny with kind eyes to help her.

So began the journey back to the castle, in a wanderer's caravan among bottles that sang against each other as the cart moved. Raya, hours old, didn't sleep for the entire voyage. It was as though she knew she was on her way to claim her throne.

One day, when she grew into a wise and lovely girl with light brown skin and her father's defiant kindness, she would learn all the ugly shadows of her family's story. She would know of a curse that had been broken when a dagger caused her aunt's heart to stop beating, only to return in a new way. She would want to hear every word of these stories, so that she might carry them in her chest because they belonged to her as much as the bright spots in her world.

For now, though, she would only know pretty things. The prisms of light on her father's chamber walls when the sunlight hit his abandoned treasures. Stories and songs. Soldiers who came one at a time to bow before her bassinet and all its white ribbons. She would know an uncle who always smelled of magic and smoke. She would know an aunt who left for long stretches of time and always came back with stories on her tongue and a Southern prince wound around her arm as though he were tethered to her heart.

In the years to come, Raya would evade her mentors and climb the castle walls when she knew her aunt's ship was due to arrive.

She would run to greet her at the Port Capital with wild-flowers in her pockets. She would beg her to turn them into stone.

# ACKNOWLEDGMENTS

Thanks as always to my family for all of their love and for believing in me; you're all the best.

A big huge basket of flower-lined thanks to Aprilynne Pike, who's been on this journey with me since before I wrote the first page. Huge thanks are also due to Beth Revis, who made me actually sit down and write it, and who always knows what to say.

Thank you to everyone who has been willing to hear my ideas over the years and offer their feedback: Harry Lam, who knows All The Things. Jodi Meadows, who has been such a source of encouragement. C. J. Redwine, my gem of a friend, for picking up the pieces and gluing me back together so many times. Thank you to Randi Oomens, who's been on this journey with Wil since nearly the beginning. Thank you to Sona

Charaipotra, Natasha Razi, and Tara Sim for your continued hard work and brilliance. Enormous and cake-filled thanks to Sabaa Tahir, whose skill for commiserating is unrivaled. Huge thanks to Laini Taylor, for all of the love and magic she brings.

Thanks to my cats for doing absolutely nothing to aid in the writing process whatsoever, and for sitting on my manuscript, meowing through my writing sprints, and spilling water on my laptop; you were all very helpful.

Thanks as ever to my amazing agent, Barbara Poelle; here's to the next ten amazing years on this journey together. I can't wait to see what the next ten will bring.

Thank you to my editor, Kristin Rens, for continuing to believe in this story and for putting so much heart and care into making it shine. Thank you to the entire team at Balzer + Bray for their hard work, creative genius, patience, love, generosity of time and spirit, and for giving this story a place in the world.

Last but never least, thank you to my readers for following my stories for all these years, or for just now cracking open one of their spines. I wouldn't be here without all of your support and love.